FURIOUS BATTLE, TENDER CONQUEST

Jeremy swiftly kicked the door in. "I will not have doors in my own house locked against me," he growled, moving menacingly toward Ariana.

She backed away from the pirate until she came up short against the edge of the bed. "Please, Jeremy, I'm betrothed. . . ."

"You're dead to him, English. Your home is with me now. Let me love you. . . ."

"When he comes for me, he will kill you!" the terrified beauty spat.

Her words drove the gentleness from him. "The hell with your betrothed." He crushed her to him, forcing her lips apart, plundering and searching her mouth while he caressed her flesh. . . .

BELOVED PIRATE
CASEY STUART

ZEBRA BOOKS
KENSINGTON PUBLISHING CORP.

ZEBRA BOOKS

are published by

Kensington Publishing Corp.
475 Park Avenue South
New York, NY 10016

First printing: May, 1988

Printed in the United States of America

This book is dedicated to my husband, Bill, for keeping me on the right track and for always giving me encouragement. And as always, for the rest of my family, including Brandy, the golden retriever who has filled the void that Rebel left.

The evil that men do lives after them,
The good is oft interred with their bones.

Shakespeare

Prologue

The Caribbean Sea

1685

In the early summer of 1685, the British ship *Goodwill* was heading back to England after a spice expedition to the West Indies. She was a small ship of sixteen guns with a crew of thirty commanded by Captain Donald Davis. Also aboard were Lord Charles Leighton and his young son Jeremy.

It had been a good trip and had accomplished what Lord Leighton had hoped: it had taken his son's mind off the death of his mother. Leighton watched the dark-haired boy struggle with the knot one of the seamen was teaching him. The boy's gray eyes were intense with the task, then his bright laughter floated across the wind as he accomplished the difficult knot.

"Did you see, Father? I did it in two tries."

"I saw, Jeremy," his father smiled proudly. Though the boy was only five, he showed a great intelligence for learning quickly.

"I want to be a seaman when I grow up," Jeremy Leighton said with boyish enthusiasm.

"And who will take care of our holdings in England?" Lord Leighton asked, a smile in his eyes.

"You will have to, Father, I'm going to sea," he answered in a determined voice.

Lord Leighton laughed and ruffled his son's black hair lovingly. "We'll see what we can do about that."

"Ship away!" the lookout shouted.

Captain Davis stood at the helm with his spyglass trained on the fast-approaching ship.

"What flag does she fly?" Lord Leighton asked.

"She flies no flag," Captain Davis answered, "but she looks to be a Spanish design. She has at least thirty guns."

"Shouldn't you order your men to arms before they get any closer?" Leighton suggested.

"It would be suicide to try to fight them," the captain answered.

Lord Leighton stared at him in disbelief. "My God, man, you can't mean to surrender!"

"We'll ask for quarter, Lord Leighton. They'll take what they want and leave us alone."

"I never thought you'd be a coward, Captain Davis," Leighton said in disgust. "The King shall hear about this, if we live to tell the story."

"I've waited too many years to captain a ship, sir, and I'm not going to let those Spanish pirates blow it out of the water. I'm sure if we just do as they ask, there'll be no problem."

"You're a fool, Captain Davis."

A white flag of surrender was hoisted as Captain Davis ordered the sails lowered. Lord Leighton had an ominious feeling as he watched the ship approach. He quickly hid his young son in a coil of rope, instructing him not to move or make a sound under any condition.

An ugly black-haired pirate with a patch over one eye was the first to board the *Goodwill*. As Captain Davis stepped forward to hand over his sword he was slashed down in his tracks.

Jeremy watched in horror from his hiding place as the seamen who had been his friends were murdered. He could see his father dueling with the pirates, killing one after another, but then he saw the one-eyed pirate come up behind

11

his father and raise his cutlass.

"Father!" Jeremy screamed as Lord Leighton fell to the deck. The boy ran from his hiding place. "Murderer! Murderer!" he cried. The pirate raised his fist and slammed it into Jeremy's face, knocking him unconscious.

"Captain, there's a ship approaching," one of the pirates shouted.

The one-eyed pirate wiped the blood off Captain Davis' spyglass and studied the ship. "Hurry up and get everything aboard."

"Why don't we just stand and fight?" the pirate asked.

"Because we have a hold full of riches, you stupid fool. Do you want to take a chance on losing everything we have?"

"What do you make of it, captain?" the helmsman on the *Folly* asked as they watched the Spanish ship sail away.

"I'd say the stinking Spaniards have been plundering in our territory again."

"Murdering is more like it," the helmsman said in disgust. "It looks like the bastard has set the ship on fire."

"Get as close as you can, Smythe," Avery Corbett ordered. "Kennedy, you and I will board and see if anyone or anything has been left behind."

Avery Corbett leaped aboard the burning

12

ship and his first mate followed. "Look below
. . . see if there is a log in the captain's cabin.

At first glance Corbett thought everyone was
dead, but then movement on the quarterdeck
caught his eyes. He was amazed to find a small
child crying over one of the bodies. Blood and
soot covered the young boy's face and clothes.

"Please, Father, don't die," the child cried
pitifully. *Please don't die!*

Avery knelt beside the man. He had numer-
ous wounds and was lying in a puddle of his
own blood. His pulse was faint and a death
rattle came from his chest.

"There is nothing you can do for him, boy,"
Avery said gently.

To Avery's amazement the man opened his
eyes. "Jeremy . . . take care of Jeremy," he
whispered with his last breath.

"I'll get him, Father," the boy cried. "I'll kill
him, I promise . . . ."

The ship lurched to port as it began to sink.
"Come on, boy, we've got to get off the ship."
Avery picked up the child and made his way
through the flames. Suddenly one of the masts
came crashing down on the deck where they
had just knelt, consuming the boy's father in a
fiery pyre.

"Father!" the child screamed, beating against
Avery Corbett's back.

"He was already dead, son. Nothing more
can hurt him."

A rope was flung to him from the *Folly*. With the boy under his arm, Avery Corbett swung out over the sea and landed on the deck of his ship.

He was alarmed when he saw the look on the boy's face: his complexion had turned ashen and his eyes looked dead. Corbett had seen the look before, on his own mother's face when she'd gone mad after seeing her husband butchered by Spaniards. He wasn't going to let that happen to this child.

"Smythe, take us home," Avery ordered as he carried the child to his cabin.

And then it started like a guilty thing,
Upon a fearful summons.

Shakespeare

Chapter One

New Providence, the Bahamas

1712

Mary Corbett watched her son directing the work on his ship as she sat on the quay mending sails. Jeremy's bronze skin glistened with perspiration in the bright sunlight as he leaned his muscular body into lifting one of the kegs of rum to the deck. She had to smile to herself as another of the island women interrupted his work to offer him a cool drink. At one time or another during the past few hours, half the women on the island had come by to offer him refreshment, or just to gawk at him.

Tears of pride came to her eyes as she

17

watched her son wrestle playfully with his father, then put his arm around Avery's shoulder affectionately. It was hard to believe this was the same child Avery had brought home so many years ago. Jeremy had been silent and rebellious for almost a year after arriving at New Providence. It had been terrible to watch such a young child being eaten up with hatred, but as time went by he came out of his shell and finally turned into a loving son—the son she and Avery had always wanted, but could never have.

They had never been able to get the boy to speak of what had happened on the *Goodwill* nor to talk about his background in England. Mary didn't know if he had blanked it out of his mind or just couldn't bring himself to talk about it. He had been known as Jeremy Corbett since the terrible day when he'd witnessed his father's death at the hands of Spanish pirates. If he remembered his real last name, he never mentioned it. Avery was the only one who knew anything about the boy's background—he knew what his last name was from the logbook they'd taken from the ship—but he'd never told Mary or Jeremy what it disclosed, firmly holding to his decision to do as the boy's father had asked in his dying breath: to take care of his son.

Mary's only regret had been that they'd had to raise the boy in a terrible environment. She'd fought hard to educate Jeremy and to try to get him to do something besides pirating, but it had been a losing battle. Avery had allowed her to educate him, but when Jeremy was old enough to choose what he wanted to do, he decided to go to sea with his father. At least his education had made him a leader, she thought. He could read, write, do numbers, and speak four languages. There weren't many pirates who could claim such accomplishments, unless they were like her Avery, who'd been loyal to King Charles until a so-called friend schemed to have him exiled from England by accusing him of treason.

Mary shuddered, digging her needle into the canvas sail with such sudden force that it broke. She wouldn't think about those days of running and nearly starving. They'd made a good life for themselves on New Providence. The Brotherhood of Pirates had a strange sense of loyalty and respect for one another, and this made life for her on the island at least bearable. The pirates considered Jeremy and Avery their leaders, so Mary was treated with the utmost respect — better than she'd been treated in England after the fiasco with the King, she thought bitterly. It was a shame things were changing so drastically on the island. Even Avery had finally agreed it was time to look for someplace else to settle. At one time there were only a few pirates who called New Providence home, but then when England finally defeated Spain, many former privateersmen turned pirate. On a given day there were five hundred ships in the harbor, bringing every description of pirate looking for ways to spend his money and vent his cruelty. They had always had an appointed governor who at least kept some law and order, but lately there were so many pirates that they had begun to name their own to govern the island.

Mary looked up in time to see Tia Bouché, the female pirate known as "Sea Witch," board her son's ship. Gritting her teeth, she forced her attention back to her mending as she saw them embrace in a long, passionate kiss. Of all the women on the island, why did Jeremy choose to be intimate with that tramp, Mary wondered bitterly. She was the bastard daughter of Spanish señorita and the bloodthirsty French pirate called Remy Bouché. Fortunately for everyone, including Tia's mother, Elena, Remy was killed in a duel when Tia was just a babe. Elena took the pirate's name, thus establishing claim to his ship and his sparse belongings, and had built a small empire from that—and from being whore to half the pirates on the island. In Mary's opinion, the daughter had followed in her footsteps. Tia couldn't be more than twenty, yet she already had a boy-child who was nearly four, a child some said was Jeremy's—but Mary didn't believe it. She knew in her heart that Jeremy would have claimed the boy if it had been his.

When Mary looked up again she saw her tall blond husband coming toward her. He could easily compete with Jeremy for the women, she thought proudly, but he'd better not if he valued his life, she smiled to herself.

"Mary, love, you don't have to do that," Avery said, taking the heavy sail from his wife's lap.

"I know, but I don't mind. It keeps me busy until it's time to give lessons to the children."

Avery took a seat on the rock wall next to his wife and stared out over the ships that anchored in the harbor. "Jeremy will be sailing in the morning."

"Yes, I know. He said he'd come to the house this evening, but I see Tia has other plans for him," she said bitterly.

"He'll be there," Avery said, hugging his wife. "Jeremy would never disappoint you."

"I just wish he didn't have such a fascination with that tramp," Mary said, tears coming to her eyes. "If only he had a chance to meet some decent woman . . . ."

"Mary, Jeremy is a young man just feeling his oats. Marriage is the last thing he's thinking about when he has every woman who sees him falling all over him. Stop worrying about Tia. She's just one of many to him, and that's the way it should be at his age."

"I hope you're right. I'd hate to see him fall under her spell."

Avery laughed. "Like I fell under your spell?"

Mary pushed playfully at him. "Of course you did. If I remember correctly, I had to pursue you for months before I could even get you to look at me. I believe you were 'sowing your oats' at the time," she laughed.

"Ah yes, but look what I settled down with: a beautiful woman with so many talents," he said as he kissed her nose and eyes. "Let's go back to the house," he said, nuzzling her neck. "I've a terrible hunger for you."

Tia Bouché watched Jeremy lift the last of the oak barrels and place it on the deck. A glance at his well-chiseled, deeply tanned features sent shivers down her spine. Everything about him was so well put together with painstaking care and precision. She smiled, licking her lips as she thought about him lying naked beside her. Everything from his dark curly hair and steel-gray eyes to his . . . .

"I'm going to be a while before I can leave, Tia," Jeremy interrupted her thoughts. "Do you want to go on with Jean Paul?"

"No, I like watching you work," she answered, her gold eyes sparkling mischievously. "Perhaps I should sail with you this trip, caro."

"You know I don't allow women on my ship when we're sailing," he said, patting her on the derrière.

"I didn't realize you were superstitious."

"I'm not, but I know you'd be a distraction to me and my men," he laughed. "It's bad enough having you around *Devil's Reach* when my men are around. Besides, I have to concentrate on capturing some rich Spanish vessel."

"What is this vendetta against the Spanish?" Tia asked. "I realize very few of the pirates at New Providence care for them, but you seem to hate them more than anyone. You've robbed four of their ships this past month, and the word is they're out to get you."

"Let them try," Jeremy answered. There was no fear in his voice, only careless arrogance.

"Does it have something to do with this one-eyed pirate you've been searching for since you started sailing?"

"It has everything to do with him. Come, I've done all I can do here for now. Let's go to the Tiger's Den. I suddenly have a terrible thirst."

"No," Tia said, rubbing her body against his. "Let us go down to your cabin. You can drink there."

Jeremy stared down into her seductive, cat-like eyes. "Is there ever a time when you're not ready to jump in bed, Tia?"

"Not when you're around, my love," she smiled up at him. "I'd give up Jean Paul and everyone else if you'd stay with me."

Jeremy threw back his head and laughed. "I know you better, sea witch. One man couldn't

23

keep you satisfied."

"You could, Jeremy," she said, her eyes holding his as she rubbed up against him.

Jeremy smacked her on the derrière and pushed her ahead of him toward the hatch. "It would probably kill a better man than me," he laughed.

"Ah yes, but what a way to go," she teased as she danced ahead of him."

"Barlow, see that we're not disturbed," Jeremy said with a wink to his first mate.

The sunlight glistened off the water and reflected on the large windows that spanned the stern of Jeremy's ship. A large bed was built in under the windows, and dark mahogany furniture fastened to the floor decorated the room. It was a beautiful cabin and Tia envied Jeremy for having the *Black Moriah*. She knew how much he prized it. It had been a gift to him from Avery, a prize taken from a Spanish lord when Jeremy was sailing with him.

"I still think you should let me sail with you," Tia said as she ran her tapered fingers over Jeremy's bronzed skin. "We could have sun-drenched days and moonlit nights for making love on that large bed."

"We've already discussed that," he said, pushing her blouse down off her shoulders. He captured a dark nipple between his teeth and nibbled.

"Harder," she ordered, raking her nails down

the hard muscles of his back. "Oh, God, but I am obsessed with you!" she panted as she pulled at his tight-fitting breeches. "Damn you, Jeremy, get out of those things!"

Jeremy picked her up and tossed her on the bed, then sat down and slowly removed his boots. He watched Tia slither on the bed, touching her breasts, then moving her hand to touch between her thighs.

"Hurry, my stud. I can't wait much longer."

Jeremy moved to lie on top of her, imprisoning her squirming body. She moaned as his weight crushed her flat against the bed. "Do it to me, Jeremy," she begged in a ragged whisper.

"You're a bitch in heat, Tia," he whispered as he nibbled her bottom lip. "Be still and let me seduce you."

"No," she moaned, "ride me, Jeremy."

Ignoring her pleading, Jeremy pinned her arms above her head while he teased one nipple.

"Bastard . . . diablo," she hissed, wrapping her legs around his body. "Stop torturing me. Enter me now or I'll carve your heart out!"

Jeremy plunged into her, driven on by her passionate moans and pleadings. She bucked beneath him, meeting each thrust with her own. Animal lust took over until they were both soaked with perspiration and lay exhausted.

"You are magnificent, my 'Black Moriah,' "

Tia said, leaning up on one elbow to look down into Jeremy's gray eyes. "The others care only for themselves," she said as she ran a long fingernail across his chest and down his firm stomach. "You give me much pleasure."

"The feeling is mutual, Tia," he said, his energy spent.

"Tell me," she coaxed, "have you ever had anyone as good as me?"

"You are one of a kind," he laughed. "Now get dressed. I have to be at my mother's in half an hour."

"No, stay with me," she pouted. "We can make love all evening."

"I'm sorry, Tia," Jeremy said, pulling away from her. "I leave in the morning and I need my strength."

"Jean Paul has asked me to marry him," she said as she watched Jeremy dress. She enjoyed the sight of his rippling muscles and sunbronzed skin. Just looking at him made her pulse race.

"I think you should accept his offer. Jean Paul is a good man."

"Why don't you ask me to marry you?" she pouted, still lying naked on the bed.

"I'm not the marrying kind," he laughed.

"Perhaps if Mary Corbett approved of me you'd consider it."

"My mother has nothing to do with it."

"I can tell she doesn't like me. She thinks her

26

son is too good for the bastard daughter of Elena Romera and Remy Bouché."

"You are imagining things," he said, pulling his boots on. He stood up and checked his image in the silver plate hanging on the wall. "Are you staying here by yourself?" he asked, a tinge of impatience in his voice.

"I was hoping you would change your mind and stay with me," she pouted.

"I won't disappoint Mary and Avery," he said as he tucked a thin-bladed knife in a sheath in his boot. "I won't see them for a month or more."

"What about me?" she asked, sitting up. "You won't see me either."

Jeremy leaned over and fondled her breasts. "Why don't you find Jean Paul? He was feeling a bit neglected when he left here."

"Oh, men!" she said in exasperation. "How can you make love to me one minute and then send me to your friend the next?"

"You forget, it is Jean Paul who shares you with me. You were his woman before I met you."

"But I prefer you."

"Tia, I've got to go," Jeremy said as he headed for the door.

"Wait, Jeremy," Tia persisted. "Please come here. I have something for you."

Jeremy slowly walked back to the bed. "What is it now, Tia?"

"Sit down and close your eyes."

"Oh hell, Tia, I don't have time to play games. . . ."

"Jeremy, humor me for just a moment, please."

Jeremy sat on the side of the bed and closed his eyes. He kept them closed as Tia lifted his hand and laid it across her lap.

"Keep them closed, now," she murmured as she removed the knife from his boot.

"Jesus Christ!" Jeremy's eyes flew open as Tia slashed his wrist with his own knife. He stared down at the blood pulsing from the cut. "What the hell do you think you're doing?" he asked, twisting her wrist until she dropped the knife.

"I wanted to give you something to remember me by," she said, wiping his blood across her breast. "You will always carry that scar and be reminded of me now."

"Damn it, woman, this time you've gone too far," he said, angrily shoving her away from him. He stood up and wrapped a scarf around his wrist. "You're damned lucky I don't use that knife on you."

"You don't mean that," she purred, moving seductively on the bed. "Stay with me, guerido. I will let you put your mark on me."

Jeremy turned and headed for the door. "If I get blood poisoning from this cute little trick of yours, I'll glady slit your lovely throat. Now get dressed and get the hell out of here."

On the way to his parents' cottage he decided that he'd enjoy being away from New Providence for a while; Tia had become too possessive. He had to admit that most of the time he enjoyed her, but he'd always known nothing would ever come of the relationship. The woman was stupid if she didn't think seriously about Jean Paul's offer to wed her and be a father to Luis. If she kept up her self-destructive ways, no one would want her.

Thou art slave to fate, chance, kings, and
desperate men

John Donne

Chapter Two

The Governor's Mansion, Bermuda

Lady Ariana Wellsley rushed down the curved staircase in a rustle of silk and taffeta. The bun in her thick, chestnut-brown hair, which Mattie had worked so hard to control, nearly came loose as she came to an abrupt stop before her father.

"I don't know why I have to return to England at this time, Father. Surely my marriage to Brett could wait a little longer. Your duties here will be over in a few months and we could all return to England at the same time."

William Wellsley laughed at his daughter. "If I remember correctly, two years ago you didn't want to leave England to join me here."

Ariana's green eyes sparkled with tears. "I

know, Father; but I have come to love it here. Besides, you yourself said I was an asset to your career."

"And that's true, my dear, but Brett is tired of waiting for his bride, and I can't say that I blame him. You are almost twenty years old and I should have insisted on this marriage taking place several years ago. If Brett hadn't agreed to wait, you would probably have a flock of children around you by now."

"It just goes to show you that Brett isn't any more eager for this wedding than I am. Ever since we were children we've been told that one day we would marry, but I don't believe either of us ever thought that time would actually come."

"Well it has, my dear, and now you must return to London and take up the social activities already planned for you."

Ariana nervously ran her hand over the smooth, satiny finish of the banister. "Do you really think Brett and I are suited for each other, Father? I mean . . . we enjoy different things. . . ."

"You mean you're a high-spirited, stubborn female without a care in the world, and Brett is consumed with his title and inheriting his aunt's fortune," her father laughed.

"Something like that," she smiled. "You know, Father, Brett does indulge in gambling."

Her father laughed and hugged her. "Most of

us enjoy a game or two, my dear. Once you and Brett are married, he'll settle down, and I'd almost be willing to wager he won't think about gambling when he has such a beautiful wife at home waiting for him."

Ariana wasn't as sure as her father. She'd heard the rumors about her future husband and his excesses before they'd left London. "All I want is to be as happy as you and Mother are."

"Ah, but it hasn't always been the case, my dear. Your mother's French blood caused us considerable problems in the beginning. That's why I feel so strongly that you must marry someone of your own background, and your mother would be the first to agree. This marriage was arranged before you were even born; we knew Leighton blood and Wellsley blood would be an excellent match."

"But you and Mother were in love . . . ."

William put his arm around his daughter's shoulders. "You will come to love Brett in time. He's a fine young man and will one day be a very rich one as well."

"That doesn't matter to me," Ariana retorted. "I don't care anything about money."

"I know you say it doesn't matter," her father laughed. "That's because you've never had to do without anything."

Denise Wellsley appeared at the top of the stairs giving last-minute instructions to the staff. "Come along, Lanie," she said to

Ariana's younger sister. "The *Heron* is due to leave at noon, and we don't want to keep Captain Grayson waiting."

Lanie threw an exasperated look at Ariana and shook her head. The girls were two years apart but were often mistaken for twins. Both had beautiful chestnut hair like their mother's, but while Ariana's eyes were the green of the sea, Lanie's were a soft velvet brown. "We're the only passengers Captain Grayson is carrying, Mother. I don't think he'll leave without us," she remarked impishly.

"Mattie, is my hatbox in the carriage?" Denise asked her busy maid, ignoring her daughter's reasoning.

"It was sent ahead with the other luggage," Mattie answered. "If you take another thing there won't be room for any of us," she mumbled, having been with Lady Wellsley long enough to know that her mistress invariably traveled with too many things.

"I'll wager mother has forgotten how dreary the weather can be in London," Ariana commented.

"Your mother adapts very well," her father smiled as he watched his lovely wife descend the stairs. "I'm hoping you'll take after her in that way."

"I'm just hoping we don't see this 'Black Moriah' person," Mattie mumbled, having heard rumors that the infamous pirate was in the area. "It just isn't right, people getting on little ships and sailing across the ocean. I tell you, if God meant us to travel on water, he'd have given us fins."

"Now, Mattie, I don't want to hear any more of that," William scolded, seeing the panic in his wife's lovely eyes. "I thought you knew better than to listen to the island girls."

"Is this 'Black Moriah' a man from Africa?" Denise asked.

"No," her father laughed. "He's known by the name of his ship, and I can assure you, he won't bother you. He only preys on Spanish ships," William assured the frightened ladies.

"I hope you're right, sir," Mattie replied, "All I can say is if I ever put these old feet on English soil again, I'm never going to leave it."

"Oh, I think it would be exciting to see pirates," Lanie exclaimed. At the horrified look on her mother's face, she shrugged her shoulders. "Of course, I'd only want to meet friendly, handsome pirates. . . ."

The *Heron* was a large ship equipped with large, comfortable passenger cabins. Denise shared a cabin with her maid while Ariana and Lanie enjoyed an adjoining cabin packed with all their belongings.

The first few days at sea were clear and beautiful, and the ladies fell into a daily routine of walking on deck each morning and afternoon. Lanie immediately fell in love with a young seaman who hadn't even spoken to her. As a matter of fact, he hadn't even looked at her, nor had any of the other crew members. Ariana was always uneasy when they were on deck. The crew seemed scared to death, and she couldn't imagine why. There was no way for her to know that Captain Grayson ruled his men with an iron hand and had warned his crew that anyone who dared even to glance at the family of Governor Wellsley would forfeit his life. His crew knew only too well that the captain's threats should be taken seriously. On the trip from England, one of their mates had been keelhauled for stealing a keg of rum from the hold.

Their meals were taken each evening with the captain and his first lieutenant, Mason Taylor. Ariana and Lanie both looked forward to this hour, when they enjoyed interesting and witty conversations over an excellently prepared meal.

The third day at sea dawned cloudy and the seas were rough. Denise and Lanie and their maid spent the day in the cabin seasick, but Ariana found the high seas exhilarating and enjoyed watching the crew handling the sails in the heavy winds.

By evening the expert preparation of food did little to entice her family to leave their cabin to join the captain for dinner, but Ariana prepared to go, claiming a hearty appetite.

"How can you even think about food?" her mother asked as she sipped a cup of tea.

"The fresh air makes me hungry, Mother. Besides, the cook is preparing fish that were caught this morning, and I'm told he is expert in doing so."

"Please," Lanie moaned, turning a pale shade of green. "Go, and promise you won't come back here discussing what you ate."

Ariana leaned over and kissed her mother on the forehead. "I'm sorry, Mother. Get some sleep and perhaps you'll feel like having something later."

"It seems you have a strong constitution, Lady Wellsley," the First Lieutenant said with admiration in his voice.

"I've been sailing since I was a child, Lieutenant Taylor. If I were a man I'd have my own ship. Instead, I have to return to England to marry and become a respectable young matron," she said with bitterness in her voice.

The Lieutenant laughed. "You could always be a pirate. I'm told there are several women who captain ships in the Caribbean."

"I've heard about them also," Ariana shuddered. "They are cruel, heartless women who could match any seaman at drinking or brawling."

"Not all of them," Lieutenant Taylor assured her. "There is one called the *Sea Witch* who is a real beauty. I believe she's Spanish," he said, pouring Ariana another glass of wine. "She wore her black hair in a long braid hanging down her back, and her eyes were gold, almost topaz. . . ."

Ariana had a feeling the young lieutenant had forgotten she was in the room. "I take it you've met her?" she asked, breaking into his thoughts.

"Yes, and lived to tell about it," he laughed. "I was on a ship she captured. After plundering the ship, she asked if any of us wanted to join her. Several of the seamen did, and even a few officers, but when the rest of us voiced our desire to return to England, she wished us fair weather."

"That's remarkable," Ariana exclaimed. "I had heard stories about her, but none that were flattering."

"Aye, I've heard she can be cruel also. I suppose we were just lucky. I've heard since that she uses New Providence in the Bahamas as her headquarters."

"What do you know of this pirate they call 'Black Moriah?' " Ariana asked.

"Only that he's known as the 'gentleman pirate' and prefers Spanish prizes to English. And we are all thankful for that," he said emphatically. "If the Spanish ever capture him, he's in for a long, painful death, I'm afraid."

"I wonder why he only preys on Spanish ships?" Ariana mused.

Suddenly the ship lurched to starboard, sending even the lodestone dishes and goblets sliding across the table.

"The storm seems to be getting worse," Ariana commented.

"Yes, I'm afraid we're in for a bad one. Otherwise I'm sure the captain would have joined us by now."

"I think I'll look in on my family. When I left the cabin they were felling terrible."

The lieutenant stood up and pulled back Ariana's chair. "They aren't the only ones . . . Half the crew are sick."

"I wouldn't think seamen would have trouble with rough seas," Ariana said, amused.

"We had to take on many new crewmen in Bermuda, and you never know how much real sea experience they've had," Mason commented.

"Why would you have to take on a new crew?" Ariana asked. "Didn't you have a full crew when you sailed from England?"

"Aye, but our captain is a hard man and we always loose a lot of our crew when we make our first port."

"That's terrible. I'm sure the owners of the ship can't be too pleased about it."

"He makes money for them, Lady Wellsley, and that's all they care about."

"What about you, lieutenant? How do you put up with it?"

"I hope to captain my own ship in a few years, and I don't want to do anything to jeopardize that."

"And well you should remember that, Lieutenant," the Captain said from the doorway. "You're needed on deck. Lady Wellsley, I suggest you get back to your cabin and stay there. The next twenty-four hours are not going to be pleasant."

During the night the intensity of the storm grew. The ship fought mountains of water that burst over the bow as they dropped into the troughs between the waves. The timbers in the cabin creaked and groaned and Ariana wondered fearfully if the ship would hold together. She slipped into her mother's cabin to find her with a deathlike grip on the bunk, her eyes wide with fear. Mattie was chanting prayers on the other side of the room.

"We are going to drown," Denise cried. "Oh God, why didn't I listen to you and wait for your father?"

Ariana wondered if her mother could be right. How could this small ship hope to hold together against such seas? "We are not going

42

to drown," she assured her, laying a cool, damp cloth on her mother's brow. "I'm sure Captain Grayson and his ship have ridden out many a storm." She shivered as she remembered her conversation with Lieutenant Mason, and the fact that most of the crew had just signed on.

"What can I do to help, Ariana?" Lanie asked from the doorway that joined the cabins.

Ariana glanced at her sister swaying in the doorway, her complexion still a very sickly green. "Why don't you come get in this bunk with mother?" Ariana suggested, thinking she could take care of both of them more easily that way. "I'll sleep with Mattie as soon as Mother's feeling better."

No one on the ship slept during the night. Ariana had to tie her mother and Mattie into their bunks so they wouldn't be thrown about the cabin, and then she and Lanie braced themselves and held on for dear life. Ariana silently praying that they would make it. By morning she was battered and bruised from being tossed around the cabin. Even more alarming was the fact that she was soaked to the skin from water swirling around the cabin floor.

She tried to tend to her mother and Lanie by holding onto their bunks, but it was nearly impossible. As the screaming wind became louder, Lady Wellsley joined Mattie in prayer.

"Do you really think we're going to be all right?" Lanie asked, her large brown eyes filled with tears.

"I'm sure of it, sweet," Ariana assured.

"This is not the kind of excitement I was hoping for," she said, her voice trembling with fear. "How can you be so brave, Ariana?"

"I'm not brave, Lanie," she confessed, patting her sister's tear-streaked face. "I'm just the only one who isn't seasick."

"Do you know what worries me, Ariana?"

"Now, tell me," Ariana smiled.

"I'd hate never to have had a chance to be with a man," Lanie said sadly.

"Oh, silly," Ariana laughed. "What a thing to be worried about!"

"You can say that, Ariana. You will be married when we get home—*if* we get home."

"Come now, stop worrying. We're going to be just fine, and someday you will have your Prince Charming."

"I hope so," Lanie sniffed.

But things didn't get better; they got worse by the minute. "We'll be all right, we'll be all right," Ariana said over and over. "The storm will be over soon."

Tears filled her mother's eyes and she embraced Ariana. "If we don't make it, I want you girls to know how much I love you. You've been good daughters."

"Don't talk like that, Mother," Ariana

scolded. "Of course we're going to make it. Someday we'll sit in the drawing room of Wellsley Manor sipping tea and laughing about our adventures on the *Heron*."

The ship rolled on its side, throwing Ariana against the hard edge of the bunk, where she cracked her head. For a moment she thought she was going to pass out.

"Ariana, are you all right?" Lanie cried in panic.

Ariana took a deep breath, forcing the blackness away, but her head hurt terribly. "I think so," she answered in a raspy voice.

The door of the cabin suddenly flew open and Lieutenant Taylor stood in the doorway, his hair plastered to his skull and his eyes wide with fear. "Ladies, we've got to get you up on deck. The ship is breaking up," he shouted over the roar of the wind.

Ariana untied her mother while Lanie helped Mattie to her feet.

"Hold onto one another," Lieutenant Taylor ordered. "When you get to the hatch, there will be lifelines to help you. In this wind, you'll have to use every ounce of strength you have to hold on. The boats are being put over the side now, but I don't know if there is room for everyone."

Ariana glanced at the lieutenant. What did that mean, she wondered in fear. As they reached the hatch, the wind hit her so hard that

45

it knocked her back down the stairs. She struggled again, doubting that there was any way her mother and Mattie would be able to hold on. She breathed a sigh of relief when Captain Grayson suddenly appeared to help.

Grabbing ahold of the ropes, they fought against the wind, moving as if in slow motion. Ariana was shocked by the scene on deck. Fallen masts with tattered sails were strewn everywhere. It was an obstacle course just getting to the rail of the ship. When Ariana looked down into the foaming sea she could see one boat had already been lowered over the side, and the men were holding onto a rope ladder tied to the rail.

"Hurry, ladies," Captain Grayson ordered. "Hang onto the rope, Lady Wellsley," he said to her mother. "The men below will help you."

"I don't know if I can. . . ." Denise Wellsley cried.

"You have to!" the Captain said, pushing her toward the rope ladder.

Ariana thought her mother was going to refuse for a moment, but with a look of pure horror on her face she took hold of the rope ladder and began to descend. Halfway down she dropped into the boat and was caught by one of the seamen. Mattie reluctantly followed the same procedure, then Lanie was quickly lowered into waiting arms.

Ariana screamed out in pure terror as a wave

46

washed over the boat, pulling it away from the *Heron*. "Mother!" she screamed, searching the foaming sea for the boat.

"It's all right, Lady Wellsley, there's the boat," Lieutenant Taylor pointed out. "It's still afloat. . . ."

The ship pitched to port, throwing men and cargo into the sea. Lieutenant Taylor clung to one of the fallen masts with one arm and kept Ariana from being thrown overboard with the other. All around them the seamen were in a state of panic. The one remaining boat was lowered, and before the lieutenant could get Ariana to it, it was overfilled with seamen to the point of sinking.

"What are we going to do?" she cried.

There was a terrible rumbling sound as the ship began to sink. "Jump!" the lieutenant shouted.

You were a stranger to sorrow: therefore Fate
has cursed you.

Euripides

Chapter Three

The *Black Moriah* was on course for the Bahama Islands after successfully capturing two Spanish galleons loaded with gold and after riding out a hurricane with only minor damage. To celebrate, Captain Jeremy Corbett, also known as the Black Moriah, ordered a barrel of rum tapped.

Even though the trip had been financially successful, Jeremy was disappointed that he hadn't been able to learn anything about the one-eyed Spanish pirate who'd killed his father. It had been almost twenty years, but he knew the man was still active because he'd been involved in the capture of a British ship a year earlier. One of the British seamen who'd survived and was now sailing with the Sea Witch had told him the grisly story, down to describing exactly what this pirate, know as Salizar, looked like. The only thing Jeremy hadn't known was that the pirate claimed some Moroccan ancestry as well as Spanish. That could allow for the difficulty in finding him.

"Aren't you going to have some rum, captain?" Tom Fairfax, his quartermaster, asked.

"Maybe later, Tom. You go on and celebrate with the men . . . you deserve it."

"All the credit goes to you, captain. You're the best, and every man on board knows it. You've made us all rich."

Jeremy laughed. "Rich until you get back to port . . . then you'll spend it all on drink and women."

"There's more where this came from, right, captain?" Fairfax laughed.

"They might not all be as rich as these two prizes, Tom, but they are out there," Jeremy agreed.

"And maybe next time we'll find your one-eyed pirate. You know all the men are always on the alert for any word of him."

"I know, Tom, and I appreciate it."

"Something dead ahead in the water, captain," the lookout shouted.

"Take the wheel, Tom," Jeremy ordered. Focusing on the object with his spyglass, Jeremy tried to make out what it was. "It looks like debris from a ship . . . no, wait, I think there might be someone on it. "McNally, lower a boat and take a look," Jeremy shouted to one of the seamen.

Everyone waited in anticipation as McNally and another seaman reached the floating object. Jeremy, watching through the spyglass, could tell that his men had lifted two people into the boat.

"What do you make of it, captain?" Tom Fairfax asked.

"I suppose they could have been casualties of the storm," Jeremy answered as the men returned to the ship.

"They're more dead than alive, captain," McNally reported.

"Have Doc see if he can do anything for them," Jeremy instructed before turning back to the wheel.

"Yes sir, captain," McNally said. Damnedest thing I've ever seen, though," he mumbled as he turned away.

Jeremy turned back to his seaman. "What are you talking about?"

"One of them is a woman, sir. A young woman with very little clothing on."

His men parted to let Jeremy through. He was stunned when he saw the young girl.

"Sweet Jesus," he swore as he knelt beside her. Her skin was red and dry, and her dark hair was streaked with gold from the sun and salt water. The few undergarments she had on were tattered and left little to the imagination. Jeremy ran his finger gently across the tender skin on her lips that had cracked from lack of water in the heat. How in God's name had she survived at all, he wondered.

"Will they make it, Doc?" Jeremy asked the ship's surgeon.

"I don't know, captain. Both of them are dehydrated and have sun poisoning. No telling how long they've been exposed to the elements. That storm we ran into was four days ago. My guess would be that they were caught in it."

Jeremy studied the girl's fine features and long lashes. He would bet that she'd been a real beauty. Damn it, she was too young to die, he thought angrily.

"Take both of them below," Jeremy ordered. "Put the man in with Tom, and the girl can have my cabin. Do everything you can for them, Doc. There's an extra twenty pieces of gold if you can pull them through."

The girl's arm fell lifelessly away from her body as McNally picked her up and carried her toward the hatch. "Easy with her," Jeremy shouted.

Jeremy sat on the side of the bed and lifted the girl's head so he could give her water. She had been on the ship five hours now, and neither she nor the young man had regained consciousness. "Come on, just a little more," he urged, as she choked on the water.

Jeremy's breath caught in his throat as the cover fell away. Doc had removed what was left of her ragged undergarments, and the skin that had been covered was in stark contrast to the skin burned by the sun. She must have been out there quite a while for her skin to have burned to that degree, Jeremy thought silently.

After bathing her face with a damp cloth, Jeremy settled in a chair and propped his feet on the edge of the bed. He sipped his drink as he studied the girl, wondering if the man could be her husband. McNally had said they were found floating on a hatch cover, so they must have been together on a ship that had gone down in the storm. It was strange, though, that they hadn't found any other survivors. He supposed he'd just have to wait for her to regain consciousness before he knew the whole story.

Jeremy sat his glass down and closed his eyes. He dozed lightly until there was movement on the bed. The girl moaned and clutched her stomach in pain. Recognizing the symptoms, Jeremy placed the wash basin at the side of the bed.

"Lean over here, little one. You'll feel better

if you get that salt water off your stomach."

She was sick only once, but he was certain that she would start getting better. Gently he smoothed her hair away from her face, then laid a cool cloth on her forehead. "I bet you'd be a pretty little thing if you were cleaned up."

The girl opened her eyes and stared at him for a brief moment, then fell into a deep sleep for the next eighteen hours.

"That's probably the best thing that could have happened," Doc announced when Jeremy told him what had happened. "The young fellow is still having a time of it, but then maybe I'm not giving him as much tender care as the lass is getting," he said with a twinkle in his eye.

"Come on, Doc, she's just a scrawny kid," Jeremy laughed, "not my type at all."

"Ha," Doc snorted as he turned away. "You couldn't be that blind."

That afternoon when Jeremy went to his cabin to look in on the girl, he found Dobson, one of his seamen, leaning over her, his grimy hand on her bare skin.

Jeremy grabbed him by the collar and threw him against the wall. "What the hell are you doing here?" he asked angrily.

"I just was checking to see if she needed anything," the dirty seaman grunted. "Ain't likely she's going to live anyway."

"Get the hell out of here, and when we reach port, collect what's coming to you and don't come back. I've turned my back on your drinking and gambling, but I will not have you sneaking around my cabin."

"Sure, captain, I understand. You want her all to yourself." He grinned a toothless grin.

"I'll break your worthless neck." Jeremy started toward him, but the seaman was smart enough to break for the door and run from the cabin.

When he was alone again, Jeremy stripped and bathed, using a small barrel of fresh water.

Ariana opened her eyes and was shocked to see a man with only a towel wrapped around his lean hips. His skin was tanned a dark bronze, and his chest was wide and muscular. Where was she, she wondered. Suddenly gray eyes met hers, and he smiled.

"Hello." She was still staring at him, but he wasn't sure she was really seeing him. Her green eyes seemed to stare right through him.

"My name is Corbett, Jeremy Corbett," he said, sitting down on the side of the bed. "We picked you up a few days ago."

"Mason . . . is he alive?" she asked in a raspy British accent.

"Aye, he's alive," Jeremy answered as he poured her a glass of water "Is he your husband?" There was no answer, and when Jeremy

57

looked up, the girl was unconscious again.

"We'll have to talk again," he said, gently touching the side of her face.

It was dark when the *Black Moriah* dropped anchor in the harbor of New Providence. Jeremy preferred it that way, unwilling to let the riffraff and busybodies on the island know about the young girl he was taking to Devil's Reach.

While Tom Fairfax left to borrow the governor's carriage, one of the few on the island, Jeremy gave orders for Doc to see that the young man was cared for.

"Are you sure you don't want to take both of them to Devil's Reach?" Doc asked, a knowing glint in his old eyes.

"I'd just as soon not," Jeremy answered. "As you said, the girl seems to be improving more rapidly than the young man, so she won't need your constant attention. I would appreciate it, though, if you'd come out and check her each day."

"You still don't know if he's her husband," Doc reminded him.

"I don't plan to marry her, Doc," Jeremy answered irritably. "I only want to see that she gets well. If I left her in town, there's no telling what would happen to her with the cutthroats who call New Providence home. I've already had to throw Dobson off the ship because of the woman. If the man is her husband, he'll thank me for protecting her."

"I'm not sure he'll see it that way," Doc mumbled as Jeremy headed toward his cabin to get the girl.

It had been three days since he'd brought her to Devil's Reach and still she hadn't regained full consciousness. Doc had been there each day, but all he could do was shake his head and tell Jeremy that only time would tell.

"Come on, little one, it's time you woke up. You're safe now," a deep voice gently commanded.

Someone was trying to pull her from the safe, warm cocoon that surrounded her. His hands were so gentle, his voice so kind. . . .

"I promise that nothing will harm you," he said, stroking her hair. "All I want is to see you well so you can laugh and enjoy the things I enjoy. Devil's Reach is a beautiful place. It overlooks the sea and has flowers everywhere."

There was a silence for a minute and Ariana longed to hear his voice again.

"Please, English, pull out of this deep sleep. If you don't do it soon, it may be too late. You need food and fresh fruit. . . ."

English? Who was this "English" he was talking to? She felt a kiss on her forehead, then heard footsteps fading away. She wanted to wake up and tell him to stay, but she was so tired. She could feel the heat of the sun on her face. Was she still floating on the sea . . . her mother . . . oh God, what had happened to her mother? She had to wake up . . . she had to know if they were all right. . . .

Ariana forced her eyes open, shielding them from the bright sunlight shining in the open window. It was a minute before she could focus on her surroundings. She was in a large bed draped with white mosquito netting. This was her cocoon, she thought. She tried to lean up on one elbow but found she was too weak. Lying back on the pillow, she looked up to see a richly carved chest with a beautiful picture of a bird hanging over it. She remembered being on a ship, and a dark bearded man, but where was she now? How long had she been unconscious?

Ariana gasped as the door opened and she stared into piercing gray eyes.

"Welcome back," the man said with a smile on his handsome face. "I was beginning to think I'd lost you."

Lost me? What is he talking about? she wondered silently.

He sat on the side of the bed, a glass of fresh-squeezed juice in his hand. Her eyes were greener than he'd remembered, he thought. "Do you think you can drink this?"

Ariana shook her head yes and tried to sit up, then fell back, this time realizing she didn't have a stitch of clothes on. Her eyes darted to Jeremy's face.

"You needn't be modest in front of me, English. You and I have been through quite a lot together."

Ariana blushed deeply. Oh God, what had happened while she was unconscious? "My mother . . . where are my mother and sister?" she asked in a raspy voice.

Jeremy feared she was still delirious. "I don't know where they are, little one. Only the young man was with you when we found you."

Tears ran down Ariana's cheeks as she lay back on the pillow. "I must send a message."

"There will be time for that later. Right now we have to get you well."

"Who are you?" she asked after taking a sip of the juice he offered.

"Don't you remember being on my ship?"

Ariana was silent for a moment, racking her brain to remember. She remembered the handsome man wrapped in a towel. . . . "I remember a bearded man. . . ."

His deep laughter surprised her. "That was me. I always grow a beard when I'm at sea."

"Where are we now?"

"You're at my home in the islands," he answered.

"Oh, thank God!" she exclaimed. "Then

we're not far from Bermuda."

"We're a hell of a long way from Bermuda," he answered, surprised at his own irritability with the girl's questions. "What's in Bermuda, anyway?"

"My father is Lord Wellsley, governor of the island."

Jeremy's eyes widened. He was so surprised by the identity of his guest that for a moment he was speechless. He stood up and placed the glass on the table. "What is your name, and how did you end up floating on a piece of wood in the sea?"

"I'm Lady Ariana Wellsley," she informed him. "I was aboard the ship *Heron* with my mother, my sister and a friend, heading for England to be married."

So she was going to marry the young man, he thought bitterly.

"We had been at sea only a few days when a storm came up." She closed her eyes and took a deep breath. "It was terrible. The ship began to break up and everyone was ordered to the boats." She hesitated again. "I watched my mother, my sister and Mattie get into the last boat, but before I could get in, a wave hit it and washed it away from the ship. Then the ship started to roll and Mason screamed for me to jump." She was silent for a long moment. "After that, all I can remember is being hot one moment and freezing cold the next . . . and wanting water so badly." Tears ran down her cheeks. "I was so thirsty."

"You are safe now," he assured her, patting her hand. "Doc says you will be fine, but you need complete rest and lots of good food. I can provide both here at Devil's Reach."

"Who is Doc, and what is Devil's Reach?" she asked, fighting to keep her eyes open. It was amazing to her that just a few minutes of conversation could have exhausted her so completely.

"Doc is the ship's surgeon on *Black Moriah*. Now finish this," he said, handing her the glass of juice. We'll talk again later after you rest for a while. Henri said I should feed you broth and juice for a few days before you have solid food."

Black Moriah rang a bell, but she couldn't remember where she'd heard it before. "I'm starved," she murmured as she drifted off to sleep.

Jeremy stood for a long moment looking down on her. So she was a lady, he thought silently. If his crew knew that, they'd expect him to ransom her to her father. He'd done it before . . . why did the idea sicken him now?

A tap at the door interrupted his thoughts. Helga, his housekeeper, stuck her head in the door. "Sir, your mother and father are here," she said in Dutch.

Thanking her, Jeremy followed her out the

door, warmly greeting his parents. "Let's sit out on the veranda," he said, placing his arms around their shoulders. "Kennedy has prepared a rum punch that is excellent."

"How is the girl?" Mary Corbett asked.

"She was conscious for a few minutes this afternoon, Jeremy answered as he accepted a drink from the seaman who acted as his butler on land. "Doc says her recovery will be slow, but she should recover fully."

"Perhaps you should let me take her home," Mary suggested. "It would be better if—"

"No! She can't be moved," Jeremy answered abruptly. "Besides, I thought you were sailing with Avery in the morning."

Mary glanced at her husband, then back at her son. Why was he acting so strangely? she wondered. "I had planned to go with him, but if you need me I'll be glad to stay."

"Thank you, Mother," he said, hugging her, "but I have everything under control."

"Can I at least look in on her? I'm sure she'd feel better having a woman to talk to."

"You can look in on her now if you like," Jeremy suggested, certain that the girl was still asleep.

"Have you learned her identity yet?" Avery Corbett asked as his wife left the veranda.

"No, she hasn't been conscious long enough to say much." He hated to lie to his family, but he didn't want his father to think he'd gone

64

soft. God, he didn't understand why he was protecting this girl himself. How could he expect them to understand?

"How long will you be gone?" Jeremy asked, hoping to change the subject.

"A few months."

"Are you still planning to look into the Carolina coastal area I told you about?"

"Aye, things are getting out of hand here, son. I'm afraid this whole place is going to go up like a powder keg, and I don't want Mary here when it does. I've made enough money to buy us some land and build a big house for her where she can have friends. If what you told us about this land is true, it may be exactly what we're looking for."

"I envy you, Avery," Jeremy said, sipping his drink.

"Why do you say that, son?"

"You have someone to make a fresh start with. I've gotten so the only time I'm happy is when I'm at sea. How is it I can't stand my own kind lately?"

"Perhaps that's because they're not your kind, son. You may be a pirate, but you're not like the lawless, murdering breed that has taken over the island."

Jeremy angrily threw his cheroot out into the sand. "I'm not so different, Avery. That's what frightens me. When I started, it was exciting; but now it sickens me to watch the poor frightened souls we rob."

"Perhaps it's time for you to move on too."

"What do I move to? You and Mary are the only people I care anything about."

"Come to the Carolinas with us. There is nothing that would make your mother or me happier, and you were the one who found this paradise."

"That's all you need," Jeremy laughed. "A wayward son living with you."

"Think about it, son."

Jeremy put his arm around his father's shoulder. "Thanks, I will. And I want you to promise to be careful," Jeremy warned.

Avery laughed. "Listen to who's telling who to be careful now."

"Well, I mean it. Putting into port can be dangerous if anyone discovers who you are."

"I'm aware of that, son," Avery said, hugging him. "We'll be careful."

"She wasn't awake," Mary said, rejoining them. "My, but she must have had a bad time of it. Poor little thing is so sunburned and dirty, and she doesn't look like she's eaten in weeks."

"There's no telling how long she was drifting out there on the sea," Jeremy commented. "It's a miracle that she's alive."

"She could certainly use a woman's touch getting cleaned up," Mary suggested, watching her son's face. Just what was his involvment with this girl? She certainly didn't look like the type he would be interested in, She thought.

"I'm going to talk to Helga about it," Jeremy answered.

"I thought Helga only came to Devil's Reach to cook your meals," Mary questioned.

"She does, but she's agreed to help with the girl if I need it."

"She's liable to frighten the girl to death," Avery laughed. "I know she scares me to death."

"It's her language," Jeremy suggested. "She always seems abrupt."

"Isn't it time she learned English?" Avery asked.

"Mother taught me to speak Dutch, so we get along just fine. Besides, she's an excellent cook, as you shall see now," he said as Helga signaled him from the doorway.

Mary was silent as she and Avery walked home. She had watched her son excuse himself three times during dinner to check on the girl. He had tried to be a charming host, but it was easy to see his mind was someplace else.

"Is something wrong, Mary?" Avery asked.

She wrapped her arm in her husband's as they walked. "I was just thinking about Jeremy's strange behavior tonight. I don't know how it's possible when the girl hasn't been conscious, but I'd swear he has strong feelings for her. God only knows why," she exclaimed. "The poor thing was a mess. Her hair was dirty and stringy from salt water, and her skin has begun to peel in places, and she's as skinny as a rail. Now you tell me that's the type of woman our son usually likes."

"I suppose he's feeling protective," Avery mused. "Besides, I thought you wanted him to get his mind off of Tia Bouché."

"I do, but something about his behavior tonight concerns me." Mary stopped and hugged her husband. "Listen to me sounding like a mother hen," she laughed. "I suppose by the time we return, the girl will be gone and Jeremy will be visiting every woman on the island again."

"Aye, poor Jeremy," Avery laughed. "He lives such a hard life."

After everyone had gone, Jeremy carried a bowl of broth and a glass of red wine into Ariana's room. She opened her eyes and stared at him as he set the tray on the side table.

"How long have I been asleep?" she asked, noticing the lighted lamp.

"Four or five hours," he answered as he sat on the side of the bed. He tucked a napkin under her chin, then picked up the bowl and a spoon. "Helga made this broth for you. She claims it will have you up in no time."

"Ugh!" Ariana turned up her nose. "I'm starving. Can't I have some solid food?"

Jeremy rolled his eyes heavenward. "You must be getting better," he sighed, forcing a spoon of broth to her mouth.

"I can feed myself," she protested, reaching for the bowl.

"Perhaps tomorrow." He moved the bowl out of her reach. "Now open up."

"Captain Corbett, I'm very grateful to you for saving my life, but I'm not going to get better until I start taking care of myself."

"Jeremy," he corrected, pushing another spoon of broth into her mouth. "If your stomach accepts broth this evening, then perhaps tomorrow you can have solids."

"You are too kind," she grumbled as she continued to accept the broth.

"If you're a good girl, English, I'll let you have a glass of wine."

"Stop treating me like a child," she snapped, "and stop calling me 'English'. My name is Ariana."

"I've been calling you 'English' since I picked you up in the middle of the sea," he smiled as he patiently lifted another spoon of broth into her mouth. "It suits you better."

"How dare you . . . !" Jeremy cut off her protests as he dabbed her mouth with the napkin.

"I think it's time you had a bath. You're beginning to reek."

Her eyes widened in disbelief. "You certainly are no gentleman," she declared heatedly.

"I never claimed to be one, m'lady," he retorted, handing her the glass of wine.

She took a sip, then looked up at him. "A bath would be wonderful, and very much appreciated."

"If it takes a bath to tame you, then so be it," he laughed.

"Captain Corbett, where is Mason?" she asked as he reached the door.

His gray eyes hardened as he turned and stared at her. "All I know is that he's alive," he answered, "and I told you to call me 'Jeremy'."

"That doesn't answer my questions. Where is he? Is he on the island?" she persisted.

"How the hell should I know where your boyfriend is? He's a grown man and should be able to take care of himself."

Ariana stared at Jeremy, a puzzled look on her face. "You forget, he was in the same condition I was."

"I told you, he's alive. That's all I know," he said now storming from the room.

What in the world is wrong with him, she wondered. One minute he seemed so pleasant, the next he was a growling bear. And what did he mean by boyfriend? How dare he!

Jeremy leaned against the door, wondering

70

what the hell was wrong with him. Why did he blow up every time the girl mentioned her fiancé? It was only natural she should be concerned about him. The young man had probably been instrumental in helping her survive while they were at sea. Tomorrow he'd get a report from Doc and relay it to her, he decided. He supposed it was the only decent thing to do.

A little later Jeremy kicked the door of her room open and entered with two large pails of hot water. "Cover up, English. I have someone following with more water." Ariana quickly disappeared beneath the covers. "You needn't be so modest. Jean Paul isn't going to molest you," he laughed as he poured the steaming water into the copper tub.

"These damn things are heavy," the other man said, struggling through the door with two large copper kettles.

"Jean Paul, meet English," Jeremy said, adding to Ariana's embarrassment.

"How do you do, mademoiselle," Jean Paul said in a strong French accent. He glanced at the heap beneath the covers. "Is she very ugly?" he asked.

Ariana had to laugh. She peeked out from under the covers and saw a handsome young man. She guessed he was probably in his late twenties. All she could see from beneath the covers were wide shoulders and light brown hair. "Will the two of you please leave me alone so I can bathe?"

"Thank you for your help, Jean Paul. I can handle it from here."

"I'd wager you can," Jean Paul laughed as he left the room.

"You can also leave now, Jeremy," Ariana said, peeking from beneath the covers.

"Thank you, English," he said with an exaggerated bow. "You are too kind, but I'm not leaving you alone so you can fall and break your neck after everything you've been through already. Whether you realize or not, you are as weak as a kitten and the exertion is going to exhaust you."

"That may be true, Captain . . . Jeremy," she corrected, "but if you think for one moment I'm going to take a bath with you in the room—"

"Listen to me, English," he cut off her protests. "Either you get into the tub on your own, or I'll pick you up and put you in it. Either way, I'm going to be right here while you bathe!"

"You wouldn't dare!" Ariana hissed, her eyes wide with shock.

"Of course I would," he laughed. "You forget, I've been taking care of you all this time, and I might add," he grinned, his eyes bright with mischief, "you haven't had a stitch of clothes on since we fished you out of the sea."

"Oh . . . oh, you are terrible!" she sputtered with rage. "What kind of man are you?"

"One who is losing patience, English. Now into the tub," he ordered, moving menacingly toward her.

"All right, all right, but please turn around," she begged.

"You're going to be too weak to do this on your own," he persisted. "I'll tell you what, I'll close my eyes."

"Turn down the lamp first," Ariana insisted.

He was right, she realized as soon as she tried to stand up on her own. "Just give me your arm," she reluctantly suggested, "and be sure you keep your eyes closed!"

He led her to the tub, and when she refused to let the covering go until he turned away, he announced she was on her own and left her to pour himself a glass of wine.

She slowly lowered her painfully thin body into the steaming water. "Oh, this is heavenly," she sighed.

"There is soap next to the towels on the chair beside you," he said as he eased his tall frame into a chair in the shadows.

"Where are you?" she asked, trying to see him.

"I'm right over here if you need me. Just relax and enjoy your bath."

Ariana was sure he was watching her, but as he had reminded her, he had been the one taking care of her for over a week. Besides, what could he see from the other side of a darkened room? If she were honest with herself, she'd have to admit that she was glad he was there. She really was too weak to be alone. Suddenly she giggled.

"What's so funny?" he asked.

"I was just thinking, it would be terrible to have survived those days floating on a hatch cover to drown in a copper tub."

Jeremy laughed with her. "That is precisely why I am here, m'lady."

"This soap smells wonderful," she said, inhaling deeply. "Does it belong to your wife?"

"I have no wife," he answered curtly, then fell silent as he watched her. Her breasts were small compared to Tia's, and her nipples were coral instead of brown. He ran his tongue over his lip, thinking silently how lovely she was, even though she was much too thin. He felt his loins tighten, imagining her responding to his lovemaking. Downing the remainder of his wine, he stood up and poured another glass.

"Are you still there?" she asked.

"Aye, I'm here."

"Jeremy, I'm going to need something to wear," she said as she soaped a long, slender leg.

"I've already taken care of that. The armoire

74

and chest are filled with clothes for you."

Ariana turned and tried to see him. "But how . . . when?"

"While you were unconscious."

"But why would you do that?

"I'd take care of anyone who was a guest in my house." He stifled a laugh as he watched her clumsily try to wash her own hair. It was apparent this wasn't a task she performed by herself.

"Since there isn't a maid to help you, I shall offer my services," he said, kneeling behind her.

"No! You promised!" She dipped down into the water up to her chin.

"For God's sake, English, it's apparent that you can't properly wash your hair without help. I assure you, I have no intention of forcing myself on you while you're bathing."

While I'm bathing? she thought horrified. *Does that mean that he may try something later?*

"You've beautiful hair," he said as he vigorously lathered it. "I didn't realize it was so thick."

Ariana was silent, trying to keep herself covered in as much water as possible.

"All right, now dip under," he instructed, giving her a gentle push. After he was convinced that her hair was clean, he began to scrub her back.

"No! Absolutely not," she protested, grabbing the bar of soap from his hand. "I have no further need of your services."

Jeremy laughed. "Very good, m'lady. I shall slither back to my corner.

"I'm sorry," she said after a few moments' silence. "I appreciate what you've done for me, but I have never had a man take care of me."

"I understand," he smiled in the darkness.

Again there was silence as she splashed around in the water. "Jeremy, what do you do?"

"What do you mean?"

"Are you in the shipping business, or what? You seem to live very well."

"Yes, I suppose I do," was all he said.

They were both silent for a few more minutes. "You know, Jeremy," she said, breaking the silence, "I must leave here as soon as possible, or my reputation will be ruined.

Jeremy laughed. "No one on New Providence worries about reputation, English."

"Well, I can tell you they do in London, and also Bermuda," she replied indignantly.

"That's why I said Bermuda was a long way away. New Providence is filled with pirates and cutthroats. You're not safe on the street here, even in daylight."

"Why do you live in such a place?"

"All right, English," he said from behind her, "it's time for you to get out before you catch cold," he ordered, ignoring her questions.

"I can get out alone," she insisted. "Please,

just turn around."

"You haven't the strength to fight me, so just stand up and let me wrap this towel around you."

"Please, Jeremy, this is most embarrassing. . . ."

"There isn't any reason for it to be," he said as he lifted her by the elbows. When he began to rub her briskly she yanked away, nearly falling.

"Stop being foolish, English. If you'll just be still, I'll have you back in bed in no time."

"This isn't right," she protested, tears rolling down her face. "Why do you insist on embarrassing me this way?"

"Embarrasing you is not my intention," he said softly.

She didn't fight him when he picked her up and carried her to the bed. What was the use, she thought bitterly. He'd do what he wanted anyway.

"Now sit right there," he ordered, placing her on the side of the bed while he went to the chest at the foot of it. He removed a sheer white gown and handed it to her.

Her eyes widened in disbelief at the transparency of the gossamer nightdress. "It's beautiful," she said in awe, "but I can't wear something like this. This is what a woman would wear on her wedding night. Isn't there something a little . . . I mean a material you can't see through. Maybe some undergarments would be better. . . ." she stammered.

"I'm sorry, English, you'll have to wear this. Undergarments were one thing that I couldn't have made. When a ship comes to port from England or Ireland, I'll see what I can get for you."

She shook her head in disbelief. "You don't mean . . . surely someone could make something . . . I can't just go without . . . ."

Jeremy leaned over and kissed her forehead. "Sleep well, little one. I'll see you in the morning."

Joining Jean Paul on the veranda, Jeremy poured himself a glass of brandy, then settled his tall frame in a chair across from his friend.

"What are you going to do with the girl?" Jean Paul asked.

"When she is well I'll decide."

"What about Tia?"

"What about her?" Jeremy snapped. "She's your woman."

"Ha, tell her that. I'm not stupid, mon ami. I know she prefers you."

"There has never been anything between Tia and me except sex," Jeremy explained, "and you were the one that insisted we share so no one else moved in on her while you were at sea."

78

"Aye, I remember," Jean Paul said, "but now you no longer wish to share." Jeremy didn't say anything. "What is there between you and this English wench?"

Jeremy ran his hand through his hair. "Damned if I know. I'm drawn to her, but I'm not sure why. From the first moment I saw her I felt a strange attraction. . . ."

Jean Paul laughed. "You devil, and here I thought you were just being a good samaritan. What about this man who was with her? Didn't you say he was her fiancé?"

"Aye, she said they were on their way to England to be married."

"You've got yourself a problem, mon ami."

"Not at all. The young man should make a good hand for one of the ships leaving New Providence in a week or so."

"Ah, what a soft-hearted bloke you are. You're going to let him recuperate before you have him shanghaied."

"Just shut up, Moreau. I'm not in the mood for your sarcasm this evening."

"Pardon," he laughed. "I think I'll go to the Tiger's Den and find myself a woman. It's been lonely around here without Tia. Do you want to come along?"

"No, I don't think so."

Jeremy sat alone studying the amber liquid in his glass. What was he going to do with the girl? Should he let her contact her family before it was too late — before he was lost to those green eyes the color of the sea, and the curve of her slender neck?

"Christ," he swore, slamming his glass down on the table. It was already too late. He wanted the girl!

There's no such thing as chance;
And what to us seems merest accident
Springs from the deepest source of destiny.

Schiller

Chapter Four

Ariana tried to talk with Helga the next morning, but it was useless. The woman only spoke Dutch, and that was one of the few languages Ariana didn't speak.

After enjoying melon and fresh-baked bread for breakfast, she decided to test her strength by walking around the large room a few times. She cautiously made her way to the window, where she had a beautiful view of the sea. Again she wondered what her host did to enable him to live in such luxury. Returning her attention to the room, she admired the beautiful Persian rugs that covered the gleaming wood floors. Her bed was enormous, with a beautiful yellow coverlet and drapes of sheer netting. The walls were decorated with beautiful paintings and silver candle sconces.

Opening the armoire, Ariana glanced at the dresses her host had procured for her. They were made of lightweight cotton in lovely soft colors. Some were tight at the waist with full skirts coming only to the ankles, and several were made to be worn off the shoulders. These are fine for recuperating here, she thought, but what will I do when I'm ready to leave? She dug through the dresses, still hoping to find some undergarments, but all she found was a beautiful emerald-green silk dressing gown. Making her way carefully back to the bed, Ariana sat on the side and slipped on the silk robe. It felt wonderful against her skin.

She stood up again and admired the robe in the large gilt mirror. Suddenly dizziness washed over her and she turned to grasp the bed, knocking over the water decanter in the process.

The door suddenly flew open and Jeremy rushed in. "My God, are you all right, English?" he exclaimed, placing an arm around her shoulders.

"I'm fine, really. I just got a little lightheaded," she explained.

"What were you doing out of bed?"

"I can't stay in bed all the time," she answered. "You can't imagine how bored I am. Besides, it's a beautiful day and I just wanted to look out."

Jeremy smiled down at her. "Since you're already in your dressing gown, would you like to sit on the veranda for a while?"

"Oh, yes, I'd love to."

Jeremy easily picked her up and carried her toward the door. "Is this really necessary?" she asked as they went down a long white corridor.

"Absolutely. I'll not have you stumbling around and hurting yourself."

Ariana giggled. "I don't stumble around."

"Well, this way I'll be sure of it."

They went through an arched doorway into the bright sunshine. "Oh, Jeremy, this is beautiful," she exclaimed, taking in the spectacular view of the sea and the profusion of flowers and palm trees.

"I'm glad you approve. Now sit right here while I have Helga bring us some juice."

Ariana raised her face to the sun and stretched. It was so beautiful here! The veranda was surrounded by a wall made of stones and shells, and was covered with hibicus and bougainvillea. It painfully reminded her of their home in Bermuda, and of the fact that she still hadn't been able to send a message to her father.

As soon as Jeremy reappeared she started on him. "I must send a message to my father,

Jeremy."

"I told you, in time," he answered. "Just relax and enjoy the view."

"But I don't even know if my mother and sister survived. My God, can't you imagine what my family must be going through?"

Jeremy set his glass of juice down and took her hands. "I'll make some inquiries." He softened at the sight of tears in her eyes. "I know a ship that will be leaving for Bermuda in the next few days. When the time comes, we'll talk about a message."

Ariana threw her arms around his neck. "Thank you, Jeremy." When she moved back he continued to hold her waist. His eyes turned a silver gray as he stared at her. Taking a deep breath, he looked away, then back into her face, and shook his head, forcing his desire down. He suddenly kissed her on the nose before standing up and staring out to sea.

"Jeremy, is something wrong?"

"Wrong?" he laughed. "What could be wrong?" A moment later he took the chair across from her. "I need to get you a hat to shade your face."

"I'm afraid I've already ruined my complexion. Mother would have a fit if she saw my freckles and tanned skin."

"I think you look absolutely beautiful. The green of your robe matches your eyes."

"Thank you," she whispered, blushing at the

way his eyes took in every inch of her.

"Do you live here alone?" she asked.

"Aye. I have family who live a few miles down the beach, but they are away right now. When I'm at Devil's Reach, Helga comes each day to prepare meals, and Kennedy acts as my valet, and, I might add, does everything else that needs to be done. When we're at sea he's the best first lieutenant you'd ever find."

"You said Devil's Reach? What is that?"

"That's what I call this place. It looks like Paradise, but I needed to remind myself that I'm still within the Devil's Reach."

"How odd," Ariana said, studying the man opposite her. Silence fell between them, and again Jeremy stood up and looked out over the water. "It looks like a storm is brewing at sea."

Ariana shivered. "Maybe we should go back inside."

Jeremy laughed as he sat back down. "There's no need to go just yet. It may even go around us."

"I hope so," she said, then fell silent, studying the juice in her glass.

"Are you thinking about the shipwreck?" he asked, taking her small hand in his large one.

"I was just thinking about my mother and sister, and all the other people. I hope they all made it to safety."

"They stood a far better chance then you did, English, and look how it turned out for you."

Ariana turned a dazzling smile on him. "That's true. Mason and I were very lucky. I'm eager to see him again. Do you know any more about his condition?"

Still assuming that Mason was her fiancé, a dark look came over Jeremy's face. "I'm told he is up and about and talking about getting passage on one of the ships leaving soon," he lied.

"Surely he wouldn't do that without seeing me first," Ariana exclaimed.

"He knows where you are," he lied again, having instructed everyone that he didn't want the man to know where Ariana was.

"I don't understand it," she said, rubbing her temples. "If he is up and about, why hasn't he come to see me?"

"Don't tire yourself thinking about it. The only thing you need to think about is getting well."

"Yes, I suppose you're right," she agreed, watching him light up a cheroot. Again she thought what an extremely handsome and virile man he was. His wide shoulders stretched against the fabric of his white shirt, and his dark breeches hugged muscular thighs. She imagined he was very popular with the ladies. Brett was tall and slim, with sandy brown hair and blue eyes. He didn't exude masculinity as Jeremy did, but she had noticed women looked at him in a particular way. Ariana had to smile, thinking of Brett wearing his shirt open, or sailing a ship and ordering fierce pirates around.

"Is that a smile I see, English?"

Ariana's face turned pink. "I was just thinking about my home and family."

"Is your sister younger or older than you?" he asked.

"She's almost two years younger, but a lot of people mistake us for twins. We have the same coloring, except for our eyes. Lanie has beautiful brown eyes."

"And you have beautiful green ones, the color of the sea," he said softly.

"Thank you," she said, looking away.

"How long have you been away from England?" he asked.

"Almost two years. I loved living in Bermuda. Life was so slow and carefree. I imagine it is the same here."

Jeremy laughed. "Hardly. The Bahama Islands have become the base of operations for pirates. When they're not out looking for prizes, they're debauching themselves in New Providence."

"But it is so beautiful here!" Ariana said, looking out over the wide expanse of white sand.

"On this side of the island it is. In town the only permanent buildings are the taverns and brothels. The rest is virtually a tent town of pirates and smugglers."

"Why did you ever settle here?"

Jeremy threw his cheroot across the wall, then turned and faced Ariana. "I was raised here, English. For years my father was the leader of the pirates. Now I'm their leader."

Ariana's eyes widened in shock. "You're a pirate?"

"Aye," he said calmly. "I'm better known as the 'Black Moriah.' "

"But you couldn't be. . . ."

Jeremy laughed at her confusion. "Why not? Haven't you wondered how I live so well?"

"Yes, but you have the manners and speech of a gentleman."

"There are many of us here who are gentlemen, English. We just happen to make a living stealing from others."

Ariana fell silent. She was in the hands of the Black Moriah, the notorious pirate she'd heard so much about. Until this moment she hadn't felt threatened, but now. . . .

"Have you heard of me, English?" he asked, wondering why the sudden silence.

"Yes," she answered.

"You have nothing to fear as long as you're under my protection," he assured, hoping to ease her mind.

"I am very tired," she said, quickly standing up. "I think I'll lie down for awhile."

Jeremy took hold of her arm before she could move away. "Are you suddenly afraid of me, English?"

Ariana's green eyes met his. "I don't know. This is all such a revelation. Should I be afraid of you?"

Jeremy studied her for a long moment. If she knew how much he desired her, she'd run like a scared rabbit.

"Should I be afraid?" she repeated.

"Very definitely, English," he laughed, wrapping her arm in his. "Will you join me for dinner on the veranda this evening?" he asked as they walked back to her room.

She didn't know what to make of the man. One minute he informed her he was a notorious pirate, and the next he was inviting her to have dinner with him. How could she possibly be afraid of him when he'd saved her life and nursed her back to health? "Yes, I should like that very much, if you promise I can have solid food."

"I promise," he said kissing her on the forehead. "Rest well."

That evening she selected one of the soft pastel dresses folded in the armoire. When Jeremy came for her he was pleasantly surprised at how charming she looked. He escorted her to the candlelit veranda and poured her a glass of wine.

"Helga has prepared something special for

you this evening."

"I hope I can remember my manners and not wolf my food down," she laughed, "but I seem to be starved all the time."

"That's normal, after being without food for some time," he answered.

Helga served chicken that had been soaked in fruit juices and roasted on a spit. To Ariana it was the most delicious thing she'd ever eaten. "She is amazing," she said between bites. "Do you realize what a wonderful cook Helga is?"

"Of course I do," he laughed, "but I'm glad you agree. May I pour you more wine?" he asked.

"Just a little," she agreed, already feeling quite giddy. "Do you always eat like this?"

"Like what?" he laughed.

"Such excellent food, and on the veranda surrounded by flowers, beneath the stars."

"Ah, you are a romantic at heart," he smiled. "I believe you're enjoying yourself, little one."

Ariana sipped her wine. "I must admit I am. How could I not? The food is excellent, the atmosphere is perfect, and the company is charming."

"Thank you," he bowed over her hand. "I shall cherish those words for the rest of my life."

"Oh come," she laughed, "you're teasing me now."

Suddenly she looked into his eyes, and she

knew he wasn't teasing her. There was something there . . . something she didn't understand, or wasn't even sure she wanted to understand.

"Please, I'd like a little more wine." She held out her glass to break the spell. "The wine is also excellent."

"It came off a Spanish galleon I captured just before finding you."

"Oh," was all she said, having forgotten for the moment that he was a pirate.

"If it makes any difference, I only capture Spanish ships, and an occasional mogul's ship.

"Do you kill people?"

"If it's necessary." Seeing the look of horror in her eyes, Jeremy explained. "I learned at a very early age that it's a cruel world we live in. Unfortunately, on the high seas one doesn't think twice about killing."

"That's in your world, Jeremy, not mine."

"What about the duels, the palace executions, the starving women and children on the streets of London? You don't consider all that cruel?"

"Of course it's cruel," she said defensively, "but it certainly isn't the same thing."

"It's all in the way you look at it, English."

"I suppose it is," she said quietly. "You said you learned at a very early age. What di   n mean by that?"

Jeremy swirled the liquid around in his glass

93

as if lost in thought. She thought he had chosen not to answer her.

"I'll make it short and to the point, English. Avery and Mary Corbett aren't my real parents. My mother died when I was very small, so my father took me with him on a spice expedition to the islands. On the return trip we were boarded by Spanish pirates. They killed everyone on board, including my father, and left me for dead, setting fire to the ship before leaving. That's when Avery Corbett found me. Mary and Avery raised me as their own son from that time, and I'm very grateful to them."

"Oh, Jeremy, I'm so sorry," she said in a choked voice. "What a terrible thing to happen to a child!"

"Enough about the past, English," he said as he stood up. "Do you think you're up to a walk on the beach?"

She smiled up at him, the candlelight making her eyes shine like emeralds. "I'd like to try."

They walked silently for awhile, Ariana thinking about what Jeremy had told her. "Why haven't you ever tried to find your real family?

"I have no roots except here with Mary and Avery. They've been my parents, my teachers, my friends."

"Why did you take their name?"

"I don't even remember what my real name was. Mary said it's a period of my life that I've tried to block out. Look up there, English,"

Jeremy said pointing to the stars. "That's Orion, the Great Hunter. He was placed among the stars after his death."

"It's beautiful," she said, understanding that he didn't want to dwell on his past.

As they were looking up, a shooting star dropped from the sky into the ocean. Jeremy took her hand and moved toward the surf.

"They say if you make a wish on a shooting star it will come true," Ariana said.

"Then I shall make a wish, English," Jeremy said, pulling her into his arms. "I wish that you will accept your fate."

Before she could guess his intentions, he put his hand under her chin and lifted her mouth to his. "No, Jeremy." She tried to pull away, but he held her firm. His mouth closed over hers, gentle at first, yet demanding; then against every measure of her will, her arms slipped around him and he pulled her closer. Her pulse was throbbing in an unsteady beat, and she was sure her knees weren't going to hold her up. When the kiss ended, he stared down at her and smiled.

"I suppose that was taking unfair advantage of you."

"Yes, it was," she said breathlessly.

"Did you enjoy it, English?"

"That's not fair," she said, moving away toward the water.

"I didn't think you'd be a coward."

Ariana walked barefoot into the water up to her ankles. "I'm not a coward," she said, splashing the water. "I've given my word to marry someone, Jeremy. I cannot take that lightly."

"And you think I should respect that?" he said, taking her hand again.

"Yes, I hope you will."

Jeremy stared into her eyes. "I'm sorry, little one, but I'm afraid I can't make you that promise. I've never been known for my willpower. . . ."

It was a long time before Ariana drifted off to sleep that night. Her mind reeled with all she had learned that day. The revelation that shocked her the most was that Jeremy Corbett was the Black Moriah. He could have taken advantage of her these past days, but he hadn't. He'd been a perfect gentleman, even when she'd bathed in front of him. She closed her eyes and pictured him sitting across from her with his shirt open and his dark hair tousled by the wind. She would have to keep her guard up, she told herself. This feeling she had in the pit of her stomach every time he touched her, or when she'd even think about the way he kissed her, just wasn't natural.

The next morning Kennedy informed her that Captain Corbett had to go into town to take care of some business and that he would return shortly. Ariana was enjoying a breakfast of fruit and sweet rolls on the veranda when Kennedy appeared again, a worried look on his weathered face.

"Pardon me, m'lady, but Miss Bouché is here for the captain, and when I told her he wasn't here, she insisted on seeing you."

"Who is she, Kennedy?"

"Ah, I guess you could say. . . ."

"I'm Tia Bouché, the Sea Witch," the woman announced from the doorway.

"The Sea Witch," Ariana said, taking in the costume of tight-fitting pants and a low-cut red blouse. "Yes, I've heard of you. Won't you sit down, Miss Bouché? Perhaps you'd care for a cup of tea?"

"No, but I'd like a drink, Kennedy," she said, sitting across the table from Ariana. "So you're the poor waif Jeremy fished out of the sea."

Ariana was surprised at the woman's unbridled hostility. "Jeremy did save me, but I could hardly be called a poor waif, Miss Bouché. I'm Lady Ariana Wellsley."

Tia's amber eyes widened. "A real high-and-mighty lady. What do you think about that, Kennedy?" she asked as he set her glass on the table.

"I have no thoughts on the matter," he said,

quickly disappearing back into the house.

"*My* Jeremy is always thinking," she smiled before downing the drink in one gulp. "I'm sure you'll bring a handsome price."

Ariana didn't hear Tia mention the handsome price. She was still on *"my Jeremy."*

"*Your* Jeremy?" she asked, an eyebrow raised.

"You're damned right he is," Tia said, leaning across the table, "and you'll do well not to forget it. I'd just as soon cut your throat as look at you."

Ariana suppressed an involuntary shudder. "I'm not about to get into a spitting match with you, Miss Bouché. Perhaps it would be best if you left and came back when Jeremy was home."

"What are you doing here, Tia?" Jeremy asked from the doorway.

"Hello, darling!" She ran to him, wrapping her arms around his neck and kissing him soundly. Ariana felt as if her blood was boiling with anger, and she wasn't even sure why. When he finally came up for air, he turned to Ariana.

"I imagine you two have met."

"We have," Ariana snapped.

"You're coming up in the world, my love," Tia said snidely. "I understand you've got yourself a real lady. She may be a blueblood, but I doubt she can hold a candle to me when it comes to satisfying you in bed."

Ariana's eyes widened in shock. "How dare

98

you!"

"Shut up, Tia. If you've only come to insult my guest, then I suggest you leave."

Tia wrapped her arms around Jeremy's waist, smiling seductively at him. "Is that any way to talk to your woman, caro?"

Jeremy removed her arms and took a step backward. "Shall I see you to the door?"

"Of course, darling. In private you can tell me how much you've missed me."

As Jeremy led Tia back into the house, she turned to Ariana. "I'm planning a party next week. You're invited, Lady whatever your name was. Perhaps it will give my party a little class," she laughed.

Ariana was nowhere in sight when Jeremy returned to the veranda minutes later. He was beginning to worry when he didn't find her after searching the house, but then he spied her from the bedroom window as she walked on the beach.

"English, wait," he shouted as he jogged toward her. "I'm sorry about Tia," he said, grabbing her arm. "She is a bit impulsive."

"It's time for me to leave, Jeremy."

"No! You're not well enough yet."

"All you do is lie to me. You promised days ago that I could send a message, but you haven't done anything about it. I feel completely isolated here. Until today, Tia Bouché was the only woman I've seen, except for Helga. I cannot stand this any longer, Jeremy."

"Who do you want to see? I told you the island is swarming with pirates and smugglers. You certainly don't want to associate with them."

Tears filled Ariana's eyes. "I want to go home, Jeremy . . . I want to know if my mother and sister are alive . . . I want to see Mason . . . to know that he is well," she cried.

"Damn it, I've told you that he is well."

"Why, Jeremy? Why are you keeping me a prisoner?"

"Don't you know, English?" he asked, taking hold of her arms. Ariana stared into his smoldering gray eyes.

"No, I don't know." She tried to pull from his grip.

"I've tried to be patient so I wouldn't frighten you, but my patience is wearing thin. I want you, English. I want you like I've never wanted any other woman."

Ariana swallowed with difficulty, her throat suddenly parched. She shook her head, but could not force out any words.

"I have everything you could want here, English. You'll live in luxury. I'll get you an English-speaking maid, whatever you want," he pleaded.

"I want to go home," she cried, breaking

from his grasp and running toward the house.

Jeremy followed her, angry that things hadn't gone as planned. "Damn Tia!" he cursed. He had planned to woo English, patiently waiting for her to come round to his way of thinking.

He followed her to the house, but when he reached the bedroom door he found it locked. "Damn it, English, open this door!"

"Leave me alone, Jeremy."

Jeremy swiftly kicked in the door. "I will not have doors in my own house locked against me," he growled, moving menacing toward her.

"I want to see Mason," she shouted, unable to think of anyone else who might help her.

His eyes glistened like shards of glass. "Your boyfriend can't help you here, English."

She backed away from him until she came up short against the edge of the bed. "Please, Jeremy, I'm betrothed. . . ."

"You are dead to him, English. Your home is with me now. Let me love you."

"When he comes for me, he will kill you!" she cried.

Her words drove the gentleness from him. "The hell with your betrothed!" He crushed her to him, forcing her lips apart, plundering and searching her mouth while he caressed her breasts.

Ariana went limp against him, shocked by the urgency of his kiss and the feel of his warm hand on her skin. *No, no, no,* her mind screamed. *Fight him, fight him!* She drew up her knee and tried to shove it where it would hurt most, but instead she connected with a hard, muscled thigh.

Jeremy cursed and shoved her away. She thought her efforts had changed his intent, but instead he grasped the loose neck of her dress and in one quick movement tore it from her body.

Ariana stood naked before him, her slender body trembling with fear. This couldn't be the same man who had been so gentle, who had nursed her back to health. . . .

As he gazed at her slim beauty, Jeremy felt his breath catch in his throat, and his desire erupted like a volcano. Swinging her up into his arms he laid her on the bed, then sat beside her, holding her hands above her head. "Please don't fight me, English. You'll only be hurt."

His mouth closed over hers and again she began to struggle, arching her back and kicking out at him. "No!" she screamed, twisting her face away from his warm lips.

He stood up and began to remove his clothes. She watched in curious fascination as he removed the white shirt, baring his dark, muscular chest. Her eyes fell to his flat stomach above the waist of his breeches. Suddenly a spasm of terror shook her body as he removed his boots and then the tight black breeches, exposing his manhood, full and large with desire. "I will not let you do this," she shrieked, leaping from the bed.

He stood naked before her, a beautiful bronze god, representing everything she'd ever been curious about, but had never known.

"Come to me, English," he gently coaxed.

Ariana backed against the writing desk. "Stay away from me. I will not let you ruin me."

"I have no intention of ruining you," he said as he closed the distance between them. "What is going to take place between us will be beautiful and pleasurable."

"I will hate you," she warned.

"No you won't, English," he said, holding out his hand to her.

As he moved closer, Ariana turned and grabbed for the nearest thing on the desk. It was a beautiful crystal bud vase. She bought it down on the edge of the desk, breaking it into sharp jagged pieces. "Stay away from me," she warned, holding a piece of the glass as her weapon.

Jeremy stared at her as she stood frozen, like a trapped animal, her eyes darkening with turmoil. Her sun-streaked hair tumbled over her shoulders, giving her the look of a wild creature. His eyes lingered on her full mouth, then moved down to the gentle swelling of her breasts.

"Put it down, English. There is nothing in the world that is going to stop me from loving you."

"No! Stay away from me! I swear, if you come any closer I'll cut your manhood off!"

Even though he was sure she meant every word, he had to laugh. "I love a challenge, little one, but this is absurd."

He lunged toward her, and as he did she instinctively brought the sharp glass up, slashing a ragged gash across his chest.

"Oh God," she gasped in horror as she realized what she had done. "Why couldn't you just leave me alone!" she cried.

Jeremy stared down at the thin line of blood, then grabbed her and pulled her against him. "I would kill a man for less than this, English." He felt her shudder of fear. "But I have other plans for you." He swung her up in his arms, then laid her on the bed. He climbed on her, pinning her body beneath him. His manhood throbbed against her, and with a low moan, he captured one coral-tipped nipple.

She struggled against him, but instead of deterring him, she succeeded only in exhausting herself.

"I won't hurt you, English. Just lie still and let me love you. Open your eyes and look at me."

When she opened her eyes, she was shocked at the sight of blood on his chest. "You must do something about that," she gasped in horror.

"Later," he whispered as he gently nibbled on her bottom lip. "You are so beautiful," he whispered, his lips moving from her mouth to leave a moist trail over her breast and stomach.

"No, oh no," she cried as her body began to betray her. "Please don't do this to me," she pleaded as his kisses moved lower.

Reminding himself that she was still a virgin, Jeremy reluctantly came back to her warm mouth. "Everything about you is beautiful, English. I want to devour you."

Ariana continued to protest, but she clung to him like a drowning person. Jeremy gently spread her thighs, then knelt between her legs. He lifted her hips to meet him, and quickly guided himself to enter her. Her cry of pain died in her throat as he covered her mouth in a consuming kiss. His large hands were clasping her hips, drawing her to meet each thrust. The pain was subsiding and an intense awareness of her body's urges took over. She felt possessed, as if he had taken control of her body. His hands explored everywhere, touching her gently as they rocked in an animal rhythm.

Jeremy willed himself to hold back, aware that the soft body beneath him had surrendered and was caught up in the same web of desire he felt. Kissing her, he whispered, "Tell me you want me, English. Let me hear you say the words."

Ariana shook her head no. "I hate you . . . I hate you," she cried, yet still she clung to him.

Driven by something he didn't understand, Jeremy took her in a wild intensity, determined to brand her as his. No other man would ever have her: she belonged to him.

In a rush of exquisite pleasure, Ariana clasped him to her, feeling his warm blood mingle with the perspiration on her body. She heard him moan and felt his seed flood her.

When at last the incredible feeling had passed and reality had returned, she turned her face into the pillow and began to sob until she felt the touch of a cool cloth against the back of her neck. She turned over and met Jeremy's soft, concerned gaze. He had already dressed, except for his shirt, where the ugly red gash still oozed blood. How could she have done such a thing, she wondered.

"Oh God, what have I become?" she cried. "I hate you for making me like this."

"A minute ago you didn't hate me."

"I did, and I hate myself too," she said, hiding her face.

"Because you enjoyed it?" he laughed softly. "Why can't you admit it was beautiful, English?"

"No, it was wrong and immoral, and you've ruined me."

Jeremy gently touched the cloth to her tear-streaked cheeks. "I haven't ruined you, my love. It was only right that I be the one to take your virginity. Fate brought you to me, and nothing is going to take you away."

"Oh God, then I am your prisoner?" she sobbed.

"A very pampered one," he smiled, undaunted. "I'll give you anything you want, English."

"I want my freedom," she demanded.

"Anything but that," he said coldly. "Why do you insist on staying betrothed to this other man? I've talked to him, and I can't understand what the attraction is."

"What are you talking about?" Ariana asked, totally confused.

"This Taylor fellow. He fells me he is without funds and has no means of getting any. Your fiancé doesn't even want to return to England, so where does that leave you?"

"My fiancé . . . Taylor?" Ariana laughed. "You thought Mason Taylor was my fiancé?"

Jeremy's eyes narrowed dangerously. "Do you mean he's not?"

"No, of course not. My fiancé is Lord Brett Leighton of London."

Jeremy stood up and instinctively pressed the wet cloth to his wound. "Do you mind telling me what Mason Taylor is to you? By God, you've certainly asked for him often enough."

107

Ariana smiled, feeling she finally had the upper hand. "I don't think the relationship between Mason and me is any of your business."

"Well, I'm making it my business, English," he answered in a dangerous tone. "I know he isn't your lover. You proved that a few minutes ago."

"You're a man of the world. You should know there are other ways of making love," she said, remembering her girlfriends giving her that fact among a fit of giggles.

Jeremy threw his shirt over his shoulder and headed for the door. "Thank you for giving me reason to kill the bastard. I'd hate to kill an innocent man."

"Jeremy, no!" she screamed, leaping from the bed. "Please, you can't mean that."

He opened the door, ignoring her pleading.

"Wait — I lied, Jeremy. Mason is just a friend. He saved my life on the ship. That's all." Her green eyes filled with tears as she held his arm, pleading for her friend's life. He jerked his arm away and walked away from her down the whitewashed corridor. "Please, Jeremy, tell me you won't kill him. I couldn't live with that on my conscience."

Jeremy kept walking. "What kind of man are you?" she screamed as he still ignored her. When he had disappeared through the door, she leaned her head against the cool wall, trying to calm herself.

What a stupid question. She knew what kind of man he was: he was a pirate who took what he wanted, no matter the consequences, and he was the leader of every bloodthirsty cutthroat on the island.

The dictates of the heart are the voice of fate.

Schiller

Chapter Five

Jeremy stormed into the Tiger's Den ready to take on anyone who even looked at him the wrong way. The girl was driving him crazy. Here he had already made plans to have young Taylor shanghaied and the pour soul wasn't even her fiancé. Well, at least that solved one problem. Her fiancé was far away and by now probably assumed she was dead. Spotting Jean Paul at a table in the corner, he joined him.

"Ah, the great Black Moriah honors us with his company," he said, pulling back a chair. "I'm surprised to see you here, mon ami. I thought you'd be busy with your English lady."

"Shut up," Jeremy warned, pouring himself a stiff drink. "I'm not in the mood for any of your sarcasm."

Seeing the red fading through Jeremy's shirt, Jean Paul leaned forward and pulled it aside. "Having trouble handling the young lady?" he asked, an eyebrow raised.

"I'm warning you, Jean Paul, mind your own business."

"Or perhaps you were enjoying the same ritual Tia subjected you to."

Jeremy's eyes darted to his friend's face. "How the hell did you know about that?"

"Tia told me."

"Well, this wasn't quite the same thing. This lady threatened to cut off my manhood and did a commendable job trying."

As Jean Paul laughed, Jeremy's ill mood faded and he joined his friend. "God, but she was worth it."

"Ah, so you have bedded the wench."

"Aye, I bedded her," Jeremy smiled. "She was like no other woman I've ever had."

"Better than our Tia?" Jean Paul asked in mock surprise.

"Our Tia has a sadistic streak that I've grown tired of," Jeremy said, studying his drink.

"Her passion for a little pain suits me just fine, but of course, that has never appealed to you, has it?"

114

Jeremy shot his friend a dark look, then poured himself another drink. "I've gotten where I have by being fair, but there isn't a man under me who doesn't know what would happen if he crossed me."

"Yes, I suppose that's true. I do remember that time you ran Fuller through for kidnaping that Spanish wench." Jean Paul raised an eyebrow. "Does that not sound familiar?"

"The girl was still a child, and after Fuller was through with her she bled to death. What would you have done in my place?" Jeremy asked irritably.

"I would probably have done the same thing. I never liked that bastard anyway."

"My men always have orders that no one is to be harmed unless he challenges us. That's the way I want it, and if any of my crew doesn't like it, then they can find someone else to sail with."

Jeremy suddenly slammed his drink down on the table. "Why the hell am I explaining this to you?"

"It took your mind off your *lady*," Jean Paul laughed.

"So it did," Jeremy admitted, pouring another drink. "Tell me, how is the young man I rescued?"

"Young Taylor? He's doing fine. He's taken a liking to Doc's daughter Gideon. I'm afraid he's going to be an unhappy man when he wakes up in the hold of a ship."

"Forget that," Jeremy said, taking a bag of gold out from his pocket. "See that he gets this. I want him to enjoy our little island paradise for a while."

Jean Paul stared at the bag of gold. "But I thought you wanted him to disappear."

"I've changed my mind."

"In other words, you now find it advantageous to keep him around."

"You could say that," Jeremy said, downing his drink. "Will you take care of it?'

"Of course, mon ami. Now tell me, what do you plan to do with the lady? Are you going to ransom her?"

Jeremy studied his empty glass for a moment. "No, not now, anyway."

"Not until you tire of her, eh, mon ami? Ah, perhaps there is hope for you yet. Tell me, what is this I hear about Dorsey giving you trouble?"

"The man is a lecher. I told him when we anchored I wanted him off the ship and out of my sight. He was a damned troublemaker anyway."

"So I've heard. He's not telling a very pretty story about the circumstances of his departure, mon ami. Keep a close eye on that one."

"Thank you for the warning," Jeremy said, flipping a coin on the table. "I'm going to head back to Devil's Reach."

"Will you be coming to Tia's party?"

"I doubt it."

"That's a shame. She's outdone herself this year for your benefit. Or perhaps I should say for Ariana's benefit. She's invited all the officers of the ships in the harbor, and even the governor is attending."

Jeremy laughed. "I must admit, it sounds interesting. Perhaps I will consider it. I'm afraid isolation doesn't not seem to agree with English."

Tired of drinking, Jeremy began to walk back toward Devil's Reach. Instead of going to the house, he found himself at the ocean's edge. The sun was setting, turning the water to a golden glow. He pulled his boots off, then the rest of his clothes, and plunged into the crystal water, swimming until his head was clear. He had been doing this since he was a boy. Mary had always said the water cleansed his soul; maybe she was right, he thought as he cut through the water.

He seemed troubled, Ariana mused as she watched him from her bedroom window. As well he should be. Maybe his conscience was bothering him, she hoped bitterly.

Ariana turned away, then a few minutes later looked back. He was but a speck in the water now. What is he doing? she wondered, alarmed at the distance he had swam from shore. My God, what would become of her if he should drown? She'd probably be up for grabs among his crew.

She breathed a sigh of relief when he turned and took powerful strokes back to the beach. She felt a warmth flood her body as she watched him emerge naked from the water like a bronze god. "My God, Ariana Wellsley, but you've the soul of a harlot," she admonished herself. How could she have such feelings for the man who had taken her virginity?

She pressed her fingers to her temples and paced the room, still upset about the strange feelings she had toward this man. What frightened her the most was that after she'd heard stories about how terrible the act of copulating was, her mother had comforted her and told her that it was wonderful if you were with the right man—a man who would take the time to give you pleasure. "Damn him," she swore, throwing a glass ashtray across the room. Why, why had she let herself enjoy it? she moaned. How could her body have betrayed her so?

Tears came to Ariana's eyes. "Oh Mother, I pray God I see you soon. I am so confused. Perhaps you can tell me how I could have such feelings for this strange man."

That evening Jeremy had Helga prepare a cold meal to be served on the veranda. When he went to get Ariana, he found her sound asleep. Sitting on the edge of the bed, he touched her tear-streaked face. What was it about this girl that gave her the power to undo him? All he could think about was pleasing her, making her his possession. He'd never felt this way before. Woman were to be used for one thing; a man was always a better companion — until now.

Ariana opened her eyes and stared at Jeremy. The tender look on his face took her by surprise. He leaned forward and kissed her parted lips. When he drew back, surprised at her response, she broke the spell.

"Is Mason . . . I mean, you didn't."

"I have decided to leave Taylor's fate in your hands, English. As long as you are my charming companion, you need not fear for his safety."

Ariana's eyes widened in disbelief. "What do you mean?"

"We will sleep together from now on, and you will come willingly to me. And at all other times you will curb your acerbic tongue."

"That's blackmail!"

"Aye, so it is; but at least I'm giving you the option of keeping your friend alive. Besides, I will have you no matter what you choose to do."

She choked back a defeated cry. "You are despicable, loathsome, foul . . . oh God, how I hate you!" she cried.

"I know, love, you've told me that often enough today. Now I'm starved and Helga has prepared us a meal on the veranda."

She picked at her food, forcing herself to examine her situation calmly. She could have been plucked from the sea by a cruel, bloodthirsty pirate who turned her over to his crew to be raped and killed by them, and then thrown into the sea never to be heard of again. She had heard of such things before.

Looking up from her plate, she studied Jeremy's face as he picked at his food. She could also have been saved by someone who was ugly, repulsive, and foul-tempered. Taking a bite of fruit, she thought that perhaps that would have been better. Then she wouldn't have to continually chastise herself for admiring his good looks. But God, he was beautiful. His black wavy hair glistened as the setting sun highlighted it, and she had the strangest urge to run her fingers through the dark waves.

She slammed her fork on the table. She was a harlot! There was no other word for it. How could a decent woman long to touch a man who had assaulted her?

"Are you all right, English?"

Sternly she commanded herself not to dwell on the feelings he evoked. "No! I am not all right! How could I be, when I'm being held prisoner and blackmailed?"

Jeremy laughed. "Come, English, you're being overly dramatic. Stop and think about how lucky you are to have been picked up by me, and not some blackhearted, bloodthirsty pirate."

He was reading her mind again, she thought angrily. "I will withhold judgment on that until I sail from this place."

"Perhaps you won't want to go back to England."

"That's ridiculous."

"We'll see," he said, taking a bite of lobster.

"Why won't you let me go before you get into any more trouble? My father is a very important man, and he will make things extremely difficult for you if I tell him to."

"There is that possibility," he agreed thoughtfully, and she realized he was mocking her.

"You're a fool!" she snapped. "You may be an important man on this little island, but you can't get away with kidnaping English nobility and not pay the price."

Jeremy calmly took another bite. "First, my love, I did not kidnap you. If you recall, I saved your life. Second, you better pray no one from England comes here to rescue you, because it will mean their death."

"Damn you!" she said furiously. "Why do you insist on keeping me here?"

He smiled, showing even white teeth. "I was tired of not having stimulating company to converse with and beautiful company to look at."

"How selfish you are to keep me away from my family and fiancé."

"Aye, it is selfish, but then I never claimed to be considerate, like your London dandies. When I see something I want, I take it—and I want you."

She swept him a look of disgust, then fell silent, again pushing around the food on her plate.

He heaved a mock sigh. "I have upset you again."

"You are infuriating."

"Infuriating, selfish, and foolish. You're going to turn my head, English. Now let's start fresh and try to have a pleasant evening." When Ariana didn't say anything, he picked up her fork and stabbed a piece of lobster meat, "You must try the lobster. Helga would be hurt if she thought you didn't like it."

Glaring at him, Ariana reluctantly took the bite offered, then her eyes widened. "It's wonderful."

Jeremy laughed. "I thought you'd enjoy it once you stopped shoving it all over your plate."

"I must find out how she prepared it. I had lobster in Bermuda, but it never tasted like this."

"It has something to do with lemon, but that's all I know. Did you enjoy Bermuda?" he asked casually.

"Oh yes, very much . . . I hated to leave there. I could ride, swim, or just kick my shoes off and walk in the sand whenever I wanted to."

"I've always enjoyed putting into port there," Jeremy commented. "As a matter of fact, I was in St. George's harbor just a few months ago."

"I'm surprised they'd let you visit there."

"Now, English, we're having a pleasant conversation," he reminded her.

Ariana sipped her wine. "You must do very well at this . . . this pirating."

"Aye, very well." He smiled at her effort to be pleasant.

"Your ship . . . is it a good one?"

"The *Black Moriah?* She is the best. My father captured her from the Spanish while I was sailing with him. When I was eighteen he gave her to me."

"The name is strange, as is the name of your home."

"I suppose I have a penchant for strange names," he smiled. "Moriah means wind, so its name is *Black Wind* in English. I used a Spanish name so they would not forget it."

"I'm sure your dastardly deeds against them keep you fresh in their minds."

"I hope so," he answered in a cold voice. "May I pour you some more wine?"

"Yes, please. How did you come to be known as the 'Black Moriah?'"

"It just happened. Everyone knew the name of the ship, and before I knew it they were calling me by the same name."

"It's well that your ship had a decent name," she said, leaning back in her chair to stare up at the stars. "You could be known as the pelican or whale."

Jeremy laughed. "That's very true."

"It is such a beautiful evening," she sighed.

"I ordered it just for you."

"Then I thank you," she smiled, feeling heady from the wine. "Have you ever been to the colonies?"

"I've been to the Carolina coast. Why do you ask?"

"I met a couple in Bermuda who were on their way to Virginia to claim a land grant. They had such glowing stories and such high hopes."

Jeremy propped his feet up on a chair and leaned back with his hands behind his head. "I can understand why. I anchored in an inlet off the coast one time. The only sound was the marsh grasses whispering in the wind, and an occasional sea gull's laugh. The sand was white and fine, and sea oats stood tall and silent like sentinels on the shifting dunes. In the distance there were pine trees as far as the eye could see."

"It sounds beautiful," Ariana sighed, caught up in the picture he was painting.

"It was. When I was standing on the deck of my ship looking out over the virgin forests, I made myself a promise that one day I would return."

"To settle?" she asked.

"Aye. As soon as I have taken care of some old business," he murmured to himself.

"I've often thought how exciting it would be to settle in the New World."

"It's not an impossible dream."

"Oh, I could never imagine Brett there. He's from an old established family in London." She laughed. "He even likes the crowded conditions and the terrible London weather."

"And this is who you want to marry? My God, you will surely die of boredom before you're twenty."

She suddenly realized she was telling this man things she had never admitted to anyone. "Brett is a wonderful man, and he will make me very happy."

"How can you want to spend the rest of your life with a man you don't love?"

Ariana stared at him in disbelief. "I never said I didn't love Brett. . . ."

"Do you love him?" Jeremy asked.

Ariana continued to stare at him. Did she love Brett? It was a simple question, but there was no simple answer. She didn't know what her feelings were. "That's really none of your business," she snapped.

"That answers my question, doesn't it, English?"

"It does nothing of the sort," she contradicted angrily. "Brett is handsome, and . . . and a fine person."

Jeremy laughed. "Drink your wine, love."

Silence fell between them for a few long minutes. "So you enjoy riding?" he finally said.

"Yes, very much, but not sidesaddle," she emphasized with a shake of her head. "In Bermuda I borrowed a pair of breeches from the stableboy and rode like a man."

Jeremy laughed. "I can see you now. I shall have to see what I can do about getting you some riding clothes."

"Do you have horses?"

"Aye, unfortunately they're not ridden often enough. I'm afraid they are all quite wild."

"Oh, Jeremy, let me exercise them," she begged, excited at the prospect of having something to do.

"We'll exercise them together, but first the clothes. Kennedy!" he shouted. A moment later the leather-faced seaman appeared.

"I have an assignment for you, my friend.

The lady needs a pair of breeches, a shirt, and riding boots. Do you think you can manage it?"

Kennedy studied Ariana's long-legged figure as he rubbed his chin in thought. "Aye, I'll look into it right away, sir."

"Do you really think he can come up with all that?" Ariana laughed.

"I've no doubt of it, English," he answered assuredly. "Kennedy is a wonder, as you will find out. There is very little he can't do."

Ariana smiled, her eyes bright with wine and the prospect of riding. "I had a horse named Gray Lady in England," she sighed. "She was a gift from Brett's aunt. She could beat any horse who dared challenge us."

"What a little hellion you must be," he laughed. "I imagine you've been a handful ever since the day you were born."

The relaxed charm of his smile made Ariana's insides quiver. Why did he have to be so damned handsome? She cleared her throat and forced her attention on the wine in her glass. "My parents believed that I should become accomplished in whatever interested me. Granted, they did give me quite a bit of freedom."

"You are very fortunate to have such wise parents."

"Then you understand why I wish to rejoin them?"

"You are also quite devious, my love," he laughed. "Somehow you always manage to turn the conversation back to your leaving here."

"That is uppermost in my mind. How can you expect me not to dwell on it?"

"I suppose I can't," he admitted. "Not yet, anyway."

"You must let me go, sooner or later."

"Must I?" he asked, his gaze holding hers.

"Am I to be held a prisoner for the rest of my life? If so, never turn your back on me," she warned, "because I will always be looking for a way to escape."

"Then I suppose I shall never be able to let you out of my sight," he said, unconcerned. "Particularly at Tia's party."

"We are going to a party?" she asked, forgetting her dislike of the sea witch as she considered the prospect of seeing people.

"I suppose if I keep you isolated much longer, rumor will have it that I have a madwoman locked up here."

"And well you might, if I don't get out and see people," she exclaimed.

"And here I thought you were enjoying my company. Some acquaintances have said I am a brilliant conversationalist, charming, and handsome to boot."

"Is that what they say?" she laughed. Suddenly she stilled. "Jeremy, I have nothing to wear to a party."

"I've already taken care of that. You'll find a dress for the occasion in the armoire."

"And undergarments?" she tentatively asked.

"No," he stated flatly.

"Damn it, you can't expect me to go out in public without undergarments."

"Yes, I can, English," he answered with a mischievous glint in his gray eyes. "I will enjoy knowing that you wear nothing beneath your silk dress."

"You can just go to hell!" she swore as she stood up, knocking her chair over backward. "I will not be humiliated in this way!"

Jeremy grabbed her by the wrist and pulled her into his lap. "Stop fighting me, English. It's only going to make your life miserable, not to mention young Taylor's."

"How can you be so heartless?" she spat, trying to twist away from him.

"I'm not heartless, little one. Perhaps my obsession with you makes me seem so, but all you have to do is submit to my lovemaking and my company. Is that so bad? Just think about how it felt when my hands moved over your body. Do you remember what it felt like when my teeth nibbled your taut nipples?" he asked, his voice deep and sensual. "Don't you realize how beautiful and desirable you are? Can't you feel what you do to me, English?"

She was well aware of the hardness of him against her leg and she tried to twist away as his hand moved upward on her thigh.

"No, damn you!" She struggled to get away. "So *that* is why I have no undergarments. You think it will make it easier for you to *seduce* me."

Jeremy chuckled, pulling her back against his body. His mouth closed over hers as his hand resumed its trail up her inner thigh until he entwined his fingers in the nest of her dark hair. She felt a sudden burst of heat flood her body.

No, no, she pleaded silently with her body. I don't want to feel . . . I don't want to need. . . .

He had pulled the loose neckline off her shoulders, exposing her breasts to the warm night air and to his warm mouth.

"Please," she whispered brokenly. "Please, I don't want to feel this way." Even as she pleaded, she pressed her body against his.

"You feel this way because you want me as much as I want you," he whispered against her neck.

"It isn't right," she breathed as she placed kisses along his chin and jawline. "It isn't right. . . ."

"Do you remember what it felt like when I was deep inside you, English?" he asked, his voice slurred with desire. "When I think of the way you tightened around me, I can hardly keep my hands off you."

She stared at him, her eyes dark with desire. "Yes," she whispered, the word wrenched from her throat. "Yes, I remember."

Jeremy laughed deep in his throat. "We are finally making progress," he said triumphantly as he stood up with her in his arms and headed for the bedroom.

I must be cruel, only to be kind.

Shakespeare

Chapter Six

Jeremy bathed and dressed in his own quarters, leaving Helga to assist Ariana in getting ready for the party. When he was finished he headed for the bedroom that they now both shared and met Helga in the hallway. "Is she ready?" he asked in Dutch.

"I'm sorry, sir, but she says she has changed her mind," Helga answered in her language.

Jeremy laughed. "Why should I have expected anything different? Go on home, Helga. I'll take over from here," he instructed.

Silently he opened the door and found

Ariana sitting in her chemise before the cheval glass. She was brushing her hair absentmindedly, as if she were a million miles away. For several minutes he went unnoticed and took advantage of the time to appreciate her beauty. He had finally given in to letting her wear undergarments to the party, and after seeing her in the soft, delicate chemise he wondered why he had objected to such clothing. She looked more appealing than ever.

"Like everything about you, your hair is exquisite."

Ariana jumped at the sound of his voice. She stared at him, taken aback by his fine clothes. He was wearing black breeches, shiny black boots, and a dark wine-colored waistcoat. A white ruffled collar at his throat set off his dark good looks. "I didn't hear you come in." She forced her eyes back to the mirror.

"You did seem lost in thought," he said as he pulled her hair up off her neck and placed a kiss on her warm skin. "Were you thinking how you would charm every man at the party?" he teased.

Jeremy didn't know it, but he had said the wrong thing. As the evening approached, she had become more nervous about attending a party at Tia Bouché's, and his comment only served to spur her anxiety. "Tell me what is expected. Do I play the whore for your friends?"

Jeremy's fingers dug into the pale skin of her shoulders. "You will whore for no one, English. You belong to me, and you'll do well to remember it."

"Well, I've changed my mind. I don't wish to go."

"What the hell is the matter with you? I thought you wanted to attend this affair."

"I've had time to think about it, and I don't think it would be wise."

"Let me be the judge of that, English," he said, removing the gold satin dress from the armoire. "You will look beautiful in this gown I had made for you."

"Shouldn't a whore wear red?" she asked sarcastically.

Jeremy looked at her, one dark eyebrow raised. "If you are trying to make my angry, English, be warned: I will take out my anger in bed."

Ariana grabbed the dress from him and stepped into it, then turned her back for him to fasten it. When he had finished, he opened a drawer in the chest and took out a black velvet box. Her eyes widened as he removed a beautiful diamond-and-topaz necklace.

"Have you robbed the crown jewels?"

"The crown jewels of Spain, perhaps," he

laughed.

Ariana wasn't certain if he was serious or not, but she stood very still as he fastened the clasp. Each pear-shaped topaz was surrounded by diamonds, and one teardrop jewel hung in the cleavage of her breasts.

"It is breathtaking," she gasped, unable to take her eyes off the necklace.

"It pales in comparison to your beauty," he replied, running a finger along the exposed skin of her breasts.

Ariana quickly turned away. "I shouldn't wear them. I don't want anyone to think I accept gifts from you."

"You will wear them, English. I want tonight to be special."

"Special?" she laughed bitterly. "A pirate and his whore. Well, you can dress up and pretend to be a gentleman, but you and I both know better," she spat.

Jeremy's patience was wearing thin. "And you can talk and act like a lady, English, but you and I both know better."

Ariana drew a ragged breath and without thought to the consequences, slapped him soundly. His gray eyes narrowed as he held her wrist in a vise-like grip. She trembled, anticipating his reaction, but she wasn't prepared for him to release her wrist and smile at her.

"You must learn when to pull in your claws,

English. That little act will cost you, but I will let you dwell all evening on what your punishment will be," he said lazily. "But rest assured, I shall have my revenge."

"You can't hurt me," she said childishly. "You've already taken my virginity."

"You're such an innocent," he smiled. "Come, my dear, Jean Paul is waiting with a carriage.

As they walked down the hallway, Ariana glanced again at his fine attire. "Where did you steal those clothes?" she asked petulantly.

"I hate to disappoint you, vixen, but I have a tailor in the village. Do you approve?"

"Pirate clothes suit you better," she hissed.

"I have to agree," he laughed amicably.

The party was the strangest affair Ariana had ever seen. Tia's house wasn't as large as Jeremy's, but it was surrounded by walled gardens and patios. Most of the guests mingled outside, while inside were tables of food and a group of musicians who played continually. The men outnumbered the women five to one, and Ariana was certain that most of the women there were prostitutes. The variety of dress was a sight to behold, with rough-looking pirates displaying their finery like peacocks. They wore silk, satin, and even velvet suits trimmed in jewels and fur. Ariana was glad Jeremy chose not to wear gaudy clothing.

Jeremy was greeted warmly by the governor and his wife. "My dear friend, it has been a long time since we were honored with your company," the governor greeted Jeremy, "but now I see what has been occupying your time."

"May I introduce my guest, Lady Ariana Wellsley?"

"It is my pleasure, Lady Wellsley," the governor said. "I had heard our handsome friend here had a beautiful houseguest."

"I am angry with you, Jeremy," the governor's wife exclaimed. "Why haven't you brought this charming young lady to visit us?"

"She has been a trifle under the weather, m'lady."

"I'm sorry to hear that, my dear." The governor's wife patted Ariana's hand. "I hope you are better now."

Ariana couldn't help but like the couple. Their concern and genuine warmth were welcome after Tia Bouché's cold welcome—cold to her, but certainly warm to Jeremy. It was a full minute before he had been able to extricate himself from her clinging embrace.

"How long has it been since you were in England, m'lord?" Ariana asked, hoping to learn something of her family.

"Oh my, it's been years," he laughed. "I'm afraid our welcome there would be anything but pleasant."

"But you are an appointed official. . . ."

"My dear child, I am no longer here at the appointment of the British Crown, but at the appointment of the pirates. If it were not for the likes of Avery and Jeremy Corbett, and a few others like him, New Providence would be more of a hellhole than it is. Those of us who are wise know we will all prosper only if we can keep our lovely island from becoming another Sodom."

"We are much safer being appointed by the pirates," the governor's wife explained. "The last appointed Governor of the Crown ended up being killed by the pirates."

"I have explained to Ariana that there is no law in New Providence except that of fist and cutlass," Jeremy said, surprising her when he used her real name for the first time.

"Ah yes, but the Corbetts continue their efforts to bring education and civilization to our small community," the governor added. "That is one reason for affairs such as this. It reminds these barbarians what civilized behavior is."

"Yes, but unfortunately they forget by morning," Jeremy commented dryly.

"Have you met Mary and Avery yet?" the

141

governor asked.

"No, they have been away since I arrived, but I look forward to meeting them," she answered honestly. She was more than a little curious to see what kind of people could live among the pirates, yet still raise an educated son with the values that Jeremy seemed to possess.

"You are in for a rare treat," the governor's wife smiled. "Mary Corbett is an angel."

At that moment Jean Paul and Tia joined them. Tia gave Ariana a scathing look. "Isn't that one of the dresses you took from that Spanish woman aboard the *Dolita?*"

Jeremy glared at her, but Tia remained undaunted, having gotten the reaction she wanted from Ariana. "Don't worry, my dear," she said, patting Ariana's hand. "The poor woman whom it belonged to can't wear it at the bottom of the sea."

Ariana's hand went to her throat. "The dress was made for you, English. It was not stolen," Jeremy assured her.

"But of course," Tia said in mock apology. "Forgive me, I have spoken without thinking. My memory sometimes plays tricks on me."

Turning her back to Ariana, she smiled at Jeremy. "There will be dancing before long, Jeremy. I shall expect you to dance the first dance with me, as always," she said snidely, glancing at Ariana.

"I'm afraid you will have to carry on without us," the governor apologized. "Catherine's sister and family are visiting, and we promised to join them for a late supper."

While Tia left to walk them to the door, Jeremy turned to Ariana. "Rather than cause a scene, I will dance the first dance with her, and then we will be together the rest of the evening."

"Don't concern yourself with me. I shall find someone to occupy myself with."

"English, don't push me. I wouldn't want your punishment to be too severe later this evening," he warned.

"Introduce me, Captain Corbett," a tall, handsome man said, slapping Jeremy on the back. "I had heard you were keeping a wench all to yourself, and now I see why."

Ariana watched the muscle tighten in Jeremy's jaw as he introduced them. "This is Francois Saint-Gilles, better known as the Frenchman," Jeremy said with ice in his voice.

Deciding that here was a way to have her own revenge, Ariana smiled warmly and held her hand out to the Frenchman. He was almost as tall as Jeremy, with sandy blond hair and brown eyes, and a charming smile that seemed to go along with his accent. He looked enough like Jean Paul to pass for his brother, and when she mentioned it, she was told that they were distant cousins.

"My escort tells me he will be dancing the first dance with Miss Bouché. May I be so bold as to ask if you would be my companion?"

She thought for a moment that Jeremy was going to break all her fingers as he squeezed her hand, but then Tia returned and whisked him away before he could say anything. He gave her a black look as he glanced back over his shoulder, and when she smiled at him she delighted to see the muscle in his jaw clench in anger.

Ariana and the Frenchman stood side by side watching as the dancing started. It was like nothing she had ever seen, a mixture of Irish, English, and the primitive dances she had seen the black islanders perform.

"If you would rather not," the Frenchman said, noticing her hesitancy. "Perhaps you would rather have a glass of champagne."

"That would be wonderful," she answered in French.

"Ah, you speak my language. What a delight it is to hear." François took her arm and led her toward the refreshments. "I understand Captain Corbett saved your life," he continued in French.

"Yes, he did." She smiled up into his soft

brown eyes. "I was on a ship bound for London when a storm hit us. Lieutenant Taylor and myself drifted for days at sea until Captain Corbett rescued us."

"You are very lucky to have been saved. The sea can be so treacherous. I must admit, I envy Captain Corbett. He was a very lucky man to have come across you."

"If that is a compliment, then I thank you," she smiled, thinking what a charming man this François Saint-Gilles was. She accepted the glass of champagne, pretending she didn't notice how he touched her hand as he handed it to her. Again they watched the dancers. She felt a slow burn as she watched Tia perform a pagan dance with Jeremy. The music was wild and pulsing with a primitive beat. As Tia moved in front of Jeremy, she lifted her hair up off her neck, teasing him and brushing suggestively against him. Ariana couldn't believe the look of pure, raw passion on the woman's face. She was inviting Jeremy to take her right there on the dance floor. When the music ended, Tia threw her arms around Jeremy's neck and kissed him long and hard. Everyone cheered at the display.

"You're going to have your hands full competing with that one," François said good-naturedly. "Tia is a she-devil."

"I don't intend to compete with her," Ariana

answered tersely. "My stay on this island is only temporary until I can find passage to England."

"Perhaps I could be of assistance."

As she noticed Jeremy coming towards them, she slipped her arm into the Frenchman's. "If you are willing to be my teacher, I would like to try the next dance."

"It would be my pleasure," he smiled.

As they passed Jeremy, she was delighted at the look of anger on his face. Two can play at this game, she thought smugly.

The music wasn't as wild, but Ariana managed to give her own version of a seductive dance. As François swung her off her feet, she caught sight of the black look on Jeremy's face. Jean Paul stood next to him, a restraining hold on his arm.

"What do you think of your *lady* now?" Tia spat. "Let François have her. I am more woman than she'll ever be."

Jeremy didn't answer. He knew if he didn't get out of there and cool off he would kill the Frenchman with his bare hands.

When Ariana and François left the dance floor, Tia was waiting. "You are very good, Lady Wellsley, A few more lessons from François and you'll be as good as I am."

"She needs no lessons from me," François laughed.

"Leave us, François. I wish to talk with the lady."

François bowed over Ariana's hand and reluctantly left. "What do you want, Tia?"

"I've tried to tell you that Jeremy is my man. Now I think you have seen with your own eyes how he feels about me."

"I saw you dancing, if that's what you're talking about."

"Look at my wrist," she ordered, holding out her arm. "Does this look familiar to you? Jeremy has the same scar on his wrist. He did this to me one night when we were making mad, passionate love. He said it was to always be a reminder that I belonged to him, no matter what happened. We are married by blood, Lady Wellsley. Do you understand that? I have a son by him."

Ariana had trouble finding words. She stared at the wicked-looking scar on Tia's wrist. "I shall be returning to England as soon as I can find a ship to take me," she spat. "You and Jeremy Corbett deserve each other!"

She turned and headed for the door, blinded by tears of anger. Suddenly a hand snaked out and grabbed her.

"Where do you think you're going?" Jeremy asked.

"I'm leaving here," she said between gritted teeth.

"With the Frenchman?" he asked, putting a painful pressure on her arm.

"It's none of your damned business what I do. Go back in there with your whore. I can take care of myself."

Tia moved from behind Jeremy, a smile of satisfaction on her face. "Don't tell me there is already trouble in Paradise?"

"We'll be leaving now, Tia. Ariana and I thank you for the invitation."

Ariana kicked out at his shin as he twisted her arm. "Isn't that right, my love?"

"Speak for yourself, you bastard. Personally, I'd rather attend a hanging."

"You should take the poor child home, Jeremy," Tia purred. "She seems distraught. And please don't forget you promised to take Luis sailing tomorrow."

"I am well aware of my promise, Tia," Jeremy growled, still wresting to control English.

Tia smiled sweetly at Ariana. "Luis is my son. He idolizes Jeremy, but then why shouldn't he?"

"Why shouldn't he indeed?" Ariana said in disgust as Jeremy pulled her out the door.

"That foolish display has left you wide open to the advances of every low-life on the island," he growled, shoving her toward the carriage where Jean Paul waited. "I'll probably

148

end up having to kill half the men who attended."

"Not on my account, Captain Corbett. I don't plan to be here long enough to cause you any more trouble," she retorted.

"Jeremy, trouble," Jean Paul warned as he held the carriage door open."

Jeremy turned around and stopped François Saint-Gilles in his tracks. "I'm warning you, stay away from the lady, Saint-Gilles. She belongs to me."

Saint-Gilles placed his hand on the hilt of his sword. "She doesn't look like she wants to go with you, Corbett."

"She doesn't have any say in the matter. You should know about things like that," Jeremy said with a warning in his dark eyes.

Saint-Gilles smiled and backed a few steps away. "Until we meet again, mademoiselle," he said.

"Please help me locate a ship going to England?" she pleaded in French. *"My father will reward you handsomely."*

Without warning Jeremy picked her up and set her firmly in the carriage, then climbed in next to her. She scurried as far away as possible and stared angrily out the window.

They were no further than the dirt road when he pulled her roughly against him. "What did you say to Saint-Gilles?" he asked, infuriated.

"We were discussing the weather," she answered caustically.

"You're a beautiful liar," he said in perfect French, *"but you're lucky I don't wring your pretty neck for that bit of deception."*

Ariana's eyes flew to his face. "Damn you, Jeremy Corbett!"

He smiled arrogantly. "I promise you, those words will be on your lips often tonight, my love."

Ariana moved back to her side of the carriage again and fell silent. She was grateful Jeremy made no effort to converse with her again. She thought about his threat and wondered what he could possibly do to her that he hadn't already done. She supposed he could beat her, but he hadn't resorted to violence so far. Then the thought of the scar on Tia's wrist made her shiver. Perhaps he was capable of it.

"Are you cold?" he asked.

"No, damn you," she answered.

Jeremy's deep laughter filled the carriage. "Ah, the things I have planned for you, English. . . ."

When they were alone at Devil's Reach she turned on him. "What kind of man are you to father a son and then not claim him?"

"It's quite possible I've fathered sons, but none that I know of," he answered uncon-

150

cerned as he pushed her toward the bedroom.

"Are you going to stand there and tell me that Tia's son is not your own?"

"Luis is not my son," he answered as he pushed her into the bedroom.

"I don't believe you," she spat. "The woman told me he was your son."

"Just take my word for it, English; the boy is not mine."

"Why should I believe you?" she persisted. "She is your mistress, isn't she?"

"Jeremy removed his jacket, then his boots. "Tia and I were lovers at one time. There is no longer anything between us."

"Ha. It seems you have a lot to learn about women, Jeremy Corbett. She practically seduced you while you were dancing. And I didn't notice you objecting."

Jeremy removed his shirt. "English, if you think picking a fight with me will make me forget that you have punishment coming to you, you are mistaken. Now get undressed."

Ariana glared at him, her hands on her hips. "I am not a child to be punished at your whim."

"Oh, I'm well aware of that," he smiled, "and the punishment I have in mind is not what I would deal out to a child. No, my love, what I have in mind is definitely for a woman. . . ."

151

"I will not submit to you again. I'm tired of this cat-and-mouse game. You promised to send a message to my family," she said, backing away. "And I don't believe you will hurt Mason. . . ."

Jeremy's gray eyes darkened. "Believe it, precious," he warned. "Now undress or I shall have to tear that lovely gown from your body."

"Damn you, Jeremy!" she screamed in frustration. "Why do you insist on treating me this way?"

"Why do you continually fight me?" he returned. "We have something very special. Why can't you accept that?"

"How can I when I am being forced against my will to submit to you? How would you feel if the situation were reversed?

"Damn it, English, I'm in no mood to debate this tonight. I want you now!"

"You're nothing but a rutting animal," she screamed, throwing her hairbrush at him.

Jeremy calmly removed his breeches and stood before her in his glory. "Come here, English!" he ordered.

"No! I won't enjoy it, Jeremy. I'll lie like a corpse beneath you."

"Do you want me to tie you to the bed, English?"

Ariana's eyes widened and her pulse quickened. "You wouldn't dare. Just stay away from me, Jeremy. I mean it."

"What a sin to ruin that lovely gown," he said, moving menacingly toward her. "The way it fits you has nearly driven me insane all evening. But then I can always have another made just like it."

Ariana picked up a vase of flowers. "Stay away from me," she screamed, throwing it at him. Jeremy fended it off and it crashed to the floor. "Damn you, damn you to hell!" she cried, looking for something else to throw.

Jeremy grabbed her and tossed her on the bed, then straddled her. He lifted her skirt and began to remove her stockings. Ariana kicked and fought, determined to deny him. When one stocking was removed, he tied it around her wrist, then tied the other end to the bedpost. She fought even harder as he removed the other stocking, but her efforts were useless.

"I will never forgive you," she screamed as he tied the other wrist.

"Yes you will, love. I guarantee in just a few minutes you will be purring like a kitten."

Suddenly she remembered what Tia had said about Jeremy cutting her wrist. "Go play these sick games with your whore. The two of you deserve each other."

He leaned over her, his face only inches away. "Do I detect a hint of jealousy?"

"Jealous of *you?*" she cried indignantly.

153

"How could I be when I hate you?"

"There is a very fine line between love and hate, English. Sometimes we cross it and aren't even aware of it."

Jeremy was jolted by his own words as he realized how true they were. For a long moment they silently stared into each other's eyes.

"Untie me this instant," Ariana ordered, breaking the spell.

Jeremy laughed deep in his throat and reached for his boot. Ariana watched in horror as he removed a knife. She shrank back into the mattress, thinking he meant to use it on her. She had seen a gentle side, but the side Tia described was a side she didn't want to know.

"Don't look so frightened, love. I wouldn't do anything to scar that lovely body."

He ran the knife from the neckline to the hem of her satin dress, then across each sleeve, quickly and efficiently freeing her. The undergarments followed in like fashion.

"You are so beautiful," he whispered. "I should keep you like this."

"I won't submit to you . . . I won't!" she repeated breathlessly.

She tried to still the heaving of her breasts as he moved his hands gently over her body, caressing and teasing. She lay rigid, willing herself not to react to his caresses, but when his mouth closed over one nipple and gently nibbled at it, a moan escaped and she knew she was lost.

His eyes blazed down at her, a triumphant smile on his mouth. "Tonight, my love, you are going to learn what it is to be loved completely." As he spoke his hand ran down her stomach to her thigh, lingering there with feathery caresses.

"Anticipation is part of the pleasure, English. Did you know that? You wonder when and how I'm going to ease the torment that is building inside of you."

"I hate you," she whispered, fighting her own demons as her body treacherously responded to his touch.

Jeremy's warm mouth left a trail of kisses across her breasts and down her stomach. She bucked beneath him, struggling against her binding. "Lie still, little one, and accept your punishment," he ordered huskily. "I promise you will find it a most pleasurable means of torture."

She waited with tensed muscles, unable to imagine what he intended. He hovered over her, his mouth leaving a trail of warm wet kisses across her stomach and up the inside of her thighs. Her nerves were drawn taut, shrieking for this torture to come to an end. Suddenly he was between her legs, gently spreading them apart, and she waited for him to enter—but he didn't. Instead, his warm mouth closed over her velvet warmness.

She heard her own voice crying out, a mixture of desire and humiliation as his tongue drove deeply into her softness. "No, no! Damn you, damn you!" she cried out hoarsely, hardly recognizing her own voice.

His mouth seemed to sear her, branding her as his possession, as she cried out wildly for release of the devils inside her who were making her respond. Suddenly, with a force that left her breathless, a wave of pleasure washed over her, leaving her unsure of what was happening to her. Shaken and near fainting, she made no protest as he moved to enter her. A jagged moan escaped from his throat as she felt the fires mounting inside again. She matched his rhythm, urging him on.

"Please, please," she cried, until another incredible spasm of pleasure rushed through her. His mouth closed over hers and a tremendous shudder passed from him to her. It surged over them, then ebbed, leaving them spent and exhausted.

Jeremy untied her hands and briskly rubbed the circulation back into her wrists. She silently watched him, her eyes glistening with tears. "Are you all right, love?" he asked, concern in his voice.

Ariana turned her head away, staring at the hangings over the bed. No, she wasn't all right. The realization that this man who held her captive also possessed her body and soul was too much to bear. He had used her, humiliated her, and she had let him, even urged him on in the end. Up until now she had hoped for her release, but now she seriously doubted it would ever happen. And if it did, would she ever be able to face her family and friends?

"Talk to me, English," Jeremy said, turning her face to meet his.

"Why, Jeremy? Why do you hold me here against my will?"

"Isn't it obvious, little one?" he answered softly, seeing the pain in her eyes.

"No, nothing is obvious," she cried. At that moment she thought she hated him, yet still she wrapped her arms around his neck and cried, clinging to him like a hurt child.

"Oh God, English, don't do this to me. I never meant to hurt you. I thought it would pleasure you. . . ."

"It did, Jeremy," she sobbed. "That's what is wrong."

Jeremy kissed the tears on her face and laughed softly. "You are precious to me," he whispered, his voice like a gentle caress. I need you with me, English, don't you understand that?"

His words floated vaguely through her mind as she drifted off to sleep enveloped in the warmth and safety of his arms.

Doubt that the stars are fire;
Doubt that the sun doth move;
Doubt truth to be a liar;
But never doubt that I love.

Shakespeare

Chapter Seven

Jeremy lay studying the woman at his side, a mixture of confusing thoughts going through his head. His lifelong quest to find the man who had killed his father was still in the recesses of his mind, but there was no denying that Lady Ariana Wellsley had become his predominant quest. He had come close to admitting something to her tonight that he hadn't even admitted to himself: he loved her.

Unable to sleep because of his thoughts, Jeremy slipped Ariana out of his arms and left the bed. He pulled his breeches on, then poured himself a snifter of brandy and went to the veranda.

Even before knowing the girl, he had begun to realize he wasn't cut out for the life of a pirate. What had started out as an adventure had turned into a constant battle to keep his men from killing the people that they robbed. There was a time when you could be a "gentleman" pirate like his father, but that time seemed to be gone. Even Avery had seen the change coming and was looking for a place to start a new life, a new beginning. If he had a woman at his side, he could start a new life, but could he convince English to share that life with him? He wouldn't be asking her to live in poverty. He had enough gold for them to live in luxury for the rest of their lives. He could become a respectable planter so their children would grow up never knowing what their father had been. My God, listen to me, he smiled. I have our whole future planned.

He stared out over the black sea and decided he needed a swim. If ever he needed to cleanse his mind it was now.

It was almost dawn when Jeremy slipped back into bed beside Ariana. She moved into his arms, fitting her slender body next to his. He tried to will himself to sleep, but the soft body against his groin was too much to bear. He kissed her parted lips and to his surprise, she answered his hunger. Feeling her melt against him, he looked into her face and met her eyes, now bright with passion.

"Where were you?" she whispered.

"Walking and swimming," he answered. "Did you miss me?"

"The bed seemed very empty without you," she admitted.

"I couldn't sleep so I decided just to get up for a while."

"Do you have something on your mind, Jeremy?" she whispered.

"Aye, but it will keep," he said, placing his fingers to her lips to silence her words. "Right now all I want to do is make love to you again."

Ariana wrapped her arms around his neck and moved closer. What followed was like nothing they'd ever experienced together. For the first time Jeremy realized what it was like to make love, instead of just satisfying lust. And afterward there were no spoken words between them—only a new understanding.

Several miles away another conversation was being held in bed. "You said you would help me," Tia said angrily. "Why now do you change your mind?"

"You failed to tell me the whole story," François answered. "I'm not a fool. Jeremy Corbett made it very clear that the lady belonged to him.

"Bah, she is but an infatuation. Once she is out of his life he will be mine again."

"My, but you are insatiable. Are you not satisfied with half the men on the island?"

"More than half," she smiled wickedly as she ran a long sharp nail down the Frenchman's chest. "Would you give me up for that English milquetoast?"

"Never," François lied, remembering the feel of Ariana Wellsley in his arms as they danced. In truth, he'd give his right arm to possess a woman like her.

"I didn't think so," Tia smiled triumphantly. "We must do something to get rid of the woman."

"We?" François raised one dark eyebrow. "What is in this for me, cherie?"

"You admired the English ship I captured, the *Bristol*. It is yours if you get rid of the woman."

The Frenchman whistled. "If you want Corbett so badly, why don't you just kill the Englishwoman?"

"Believe me, I've considered it often, but if Jeremy ever found out, I would lose him for sure."

"Ah, what a tangled web we weave . . . so, the *Bristol* would be mine if I got rid of Lady Wellsley," he mused. "It seems to me that there should be a way we could do this and collect some of the lady's gold in the process."

"Ransom?" Tia asked. "But how could we do that without Jeremy knowing?"

"The lady is most anxious to return home, so when Corbett is not around, I shall offer her my assistance. Then I will just hold her prisoner on my ship until the ransom is paid."

"You are brilliant," Tia exclaimed excitedly. "Jeremy will think that she found a way to get back to England, and he will come to me for comfort. Oh, this is wonderful!" Tia clapped her hands in glee.

"All I have to do is find a way to talk to the lady alone," François said.

"That should be simple. Jeremy is taking Luis sailing in the morning. Lady Ariana Wellsley will be alone at Devil's Reach."

"If we move swiftly, perhaps I can get her away from there while Corbett is gone. In the meantime, you need to send a message to her family."

"Ah, yes," Tia said, rubbing her hands together. "And I'm sure our Lady Wellsley must be worth a fortune."

While they were having breakfast beneath clear blue skies, Luis, Tia's seven-year-old son, arrived. He was a handsome child, with a dark complexion. The only resemblance she could see to Jeremy was the wavy black hair, but the boy was definitely Tia's son with his catlike gold eyes.

"We'd like you to come with us," Jeremy interrupted her thoughts.

"No, you two go on. I'll be fine."

"Tell her, Luis. We need someone to bait our hooks."

The boy smiled at Ariana, laughter in his eyes. "Aye, we need someone who isn't afraid to do that."

"Go on with you," Ariana laughed. "The two of you don't need me trailing along."

Ariana finally agreed just to put an end to their badgering. She had to admit, Luis was a delightful child. It was obvious that he and Jeremy were use to going on outings together. The repartee between the two kept her laughing.

"Duck," Jeremy warned as the boom swung starboard.

The wind caught the wide-brimmed hat Jeremy had brought her from town, and he grabbed it just before it hit the water. "Keep that thing on, English. If you get any more freckles you'll be able to pass for an Indian."

"Thank you," she answered haughtily, stuffing the hat down on her head.

Luis took her hand and told her not to worry, that he would take care of her. She hadn't bothered to tell either one of them that she loved sailing and was really quite good at it.

"Can you swim, Lady . . . Lady," the boy looked to Jeremy for help.

"Why don't you just call me Ariana," she laughed, "and yes, I can swim."

"Ari . . . Arian," the boy stuttered over her name.

"Why don't you just call her 'English,' like I do?" Jeremy laughed, tousling the boy's hair.

"Would that be all right?" he asked Ariana.

She sent Jeremy a look of feigned disgust, then gave Luis a charming smile. "Yes, that will be fine.

"I always knew you liked it," Jeremy chuckled, pleased with himself.

"It's fine for Luis, but not for you," she

167

said curtly.

Jeremy wasn't fooled. He could see the merriment in her eyes. He leaned back, relaxing his grip on the tiller, content to watch English as she raised her face to the sun and breathed deeply of the sea air.

"I had thought you might be afraid of sailing after your experience."

"No," she smiled, "I suppose I have loved the sea too long to let one bad experience change my feelings."

"Good, I'm glad to hear that. I can't stand women who are weak and faint-hearted."

Suddenly the sail luffed because of Jeremy's inattention, and he had to quickly tack until it caught the wind again.

"I could do better than that," she challenged.

"Is that right?" he laughed. "Well come here and let's see what you can do."

Ariana carefully changed places with Jeremy, taking over the tiller with confidence. She leaned back against the stern, contently smiling at the surprised look on his face.

"Your talents never cease to amaze me, English."

Even though he made no reference to anything other than her sailing skills, she felt a warm flush rise to her face when he winked at her.

"You're lovely when you blush," he teased.

"Why don't you just be quiet?" she warned, nodding toward the boy. Jeremy just laughed at her embarrassment.

"Are you going to stay at Devil's Reach forever?" Luis asked.

Ariana's eyes met Jeremy's. "You'll have to ask him," she answered, trying to keep her voice steady.

Jeremy smiled at the boy. "She'll stay there forever if I have my way."

"Good, because I like her," the boy said cheerfully.

"So do I," Jeremy whispered loudly enough for her to hear. "I don't know too many woman who can handle a boat like she can."

"Don't forget Tia," the boy reminded him innocently.

Again his eyes met Ariana's. "Yes, that's true," he agreed. "Your mother is a fine sailor."

"I'm going to have a ship like *Black Moriah* one day," Luis said proudly. "She's the finest ship in New Providence."

"I agree with you," Jeremy laughed, "but don't let your mother hear you say that."

"I'm afraid I don't remember much about your ship," Ariana said.

"Then I shall have to take you aboard. She was refloated just a few days ago."

"Refloated?" Ariana asked.

"Yes," Jeremy laughed. "She's been careened so she could be scraped of barnacles and sea worms. Haven't you ever seen a ship beached and rolled on its side?"

"Yes, but I didn't know that was what it was called."

"Ah, so you don't know everything," he teased.

"Will you let English captain the *Black Moriah?*" Luis asked.

Jeremy leaned back against the bow. "What do you think, Luis? Is she good enough?"

"Oh yes, I think so," Luis answered with boyish enthusiasm.

Ariana laughed. "You'd better be careful, Captain Corbett; I have always dreamed of having my own ship and sailing all over the world."

"Have you, now?" Jeremy asked, his eyes twinkling. "Perhaps you shall have your wish, Captain English," he teased. "Stranger things have happened."

They fished and crabbed off a small island most of the afternoon, stopping only to have a meal of cheese, bread, and some fruit that Luis picked from one of the many fruit trees on the island.

After eating, Jeremy and Luis went back to fishing, but Ariana chose to lie on the beach under a palm. She had dozed there for nearly an hour when Jeremy's voice woke her.

His body cast a shadow over her face. "How do you expect me to keep my mind on fishing when I can see you lying here on the sand looking so desirable?"

Ariana smiled but didn't open her eyes. "I found it very difficult to keep my mind on my nap seeing you half-naked and all shiny and bronzed in the sunlight."

"So you like my body?" he drawled lazily as he dropped down beside her.

"I suppose now I'll never hear the end of it," Ariana said, opening her eyes to look into Jeremy's smiling face.

"I've been telling you since the day I picked you out of the sea that I thought you were the most beautiful, desirable woman I've ever seen, and I haven't noticed it going to your head."

"I'm not sure about that," she mused. "I'm definitely not the same person who left Bermuda."

"No, love, you're a woman now. A very

171

desirable and beautiful woman."

Ariana stared into Jeremy's eyes, contemplating telling him that she loved him, but she couldn't make herself say it — at least not until she was sure he felt the same way.

"What's on your mind, little one?" Jeremy asked, lifting her chin to kiss her soft mouth.

"I was just thinking. . . ."

"English, English, come see what I caught!" Luis shouted from the water's edge.

Ariana looked at Jeremy, who still waited to hear what she had on her mind, but she couldn't make herself say it. Perhaps it had something to do with Brett waiting in London for word of her. "Go and see what he caught," Jeremy laughed. "I'll join you in a few minutes."

Jeremy watched her run toward Luis and excitedly exclaim over his fish. He smiled to himself, thinking what a wonderful mother she would make for his children: he'd want them all to have her emerald-green eyes.

Suddenly he noticed that she and Luis had given up fishing for a swim and he decided to join them. "Is there room for one more?" he shouted as he ran past them and dived into deeper water.

"Jeremy, Jeremy, wait for me," Luis shouted, taking off after his hero.

172

Ariana watched them disappear under water, then both came up laughing. He put the boy on his shoulders and dived again, this time grabbing her ankles and pulling her down with them. All three came up sputtering and laughing.

"Stop it, you fool. You'll drown all of us," she laughed before the two of them pulled her under again. Ariana finally broke loose and swam swiftly away from them.

"Would you look at that?" Jeremy said. "By God, woman, is there anything you can't do?"

"Nothing!" she laughed. "So be warned."

They sailed back to Devil's Reach as the sun was setting. Luis slept with his head in Ariana's lap, at peace with the world.

"I cannot imagine you on the filthy streets of London," Jeremy commented, unable to take his eyes off her flushed face and wind-blown hair. "You belong in this environment."

Ariana didn't answer. She smoothed the hair away from her face, and stared out over the sea. He was right — she hated London with its filth and poverty. That had been the reason she hadn't wanted to leave Bermuda. The men in London were such pompous fools — including Brett, who thought a woman's place was at home while he enjoyed himself at the gaming houses with ladies of the evening. Well, he had a rude awakening coming if he thought their life was going to follow such a pattern.

Ariana almost laughed out loud. She really didn't have to worry about that any longer. If she ever returned to London, Brett would probably be married to someone else. It was strange; that thought didn't bother her.

She stared at Jeremy and thought about what life would be like with him. She had never known what it was to desire someone, yet just looking at him made her heart skip a beat. And he did things to make her happy. God, she couldn't remember ever doing anything with Brett that wasn't just what *he* had wanted to do. She shivered as she remembered a time they had gone to a dog fight. It had been a terrible experience. She would never forget the horror of watching two dogs try to kill each other while grown men cheered them on. She had been sick on the way home, and Brett had laughed at her as he counted his winnings and ignored her delicate state. Jeremy was a pirate with a reputation that frightened half the country, yet she could never imagine him enjoying such a thing.

"Are you all right, English?"

"Yes, I'm fine," she answered.

"You let your nose burn again." He smiled.

Ariana touched her nose. "You'd think I'd learn, wouldn't you?"

"Freckles and sunburn become you."

"That's because you've never seen me any other way," she laughed.

"Damn!" Jeremy suddenly swore.

"What's wrong?" Ariana asked, looking in the direction of his angry stare.

"I can see Tia on the veranda. I had hoped to end this beautiful day without having to deal with her."

"Why does Luis call his mother Tia?" she asked, stroking the boy's head.

"She prefers it that way," Jeremy answered as he dropped the sails. "As you've probably noticed, Tia isn't a particularly motherly figure. The boy lives with his grandmother most of the time, but even that isn't the best environment."

"Why not?" Ariana asked.

"It just isn't the way a boy should be raised," Jeremy said as he beached the boat. "Jean Paul has tried to talk Tia into marrying him so the boy would at least have a father, but she refused to do so."

Jeremy picked up the boy, then offered Ariana his hand. "Brace yourself," he said as Tia came rushing towards them.

175

"You didn't tell me she was going with you!" she screamed, furious that her plan to have Saint-Gilles get to Ariana had been foiled.

"What I do is none of your damned business," Jeremy said, walking past her.

"The hell it isn't," she said, grabbing his arm. "When *our* son is involved, it's my business."

Jeremy froze in his tracks. By now Luis was awake and stared in puzzlement at Jeremy and his mother. "I will deal with you later, Tia," he said between gritted teeth. "It's time you took Luis back to his grandmother."

"Do I have to go, Jeremy?" the boy pleaded.

"It's best for now, Luis. We'll do this again soon."

"Do you promise?" He turned trusting eyes up to Jeremy. "And can English come, too?"

"You stay away from my son!" Tia screamed at Ariana.

"No, Tia, please," the boy cried, "she's a very nice lady."

"Luis, I promise we'll go out again soon, and English will go with us. Now go on to the house," Jeremy ordered. "I need to talk to Tia for a minute."

As the boy ran toward the house, Tia

turned on Ariana. "You are playing games with the wrong person, you English tramp. Maybe you don't know who you're dealing with."

"Oh, I know *what* I'm dealing with," Ariana spat. "A woman who cares nothing for her son. How can you lie to that boy and let him think his own father doesn't want him?"

Tia shoved Ariana, but she stood stood her ground, while Jeremy stepped aside and waited. "I'm the Sea Witch," she snarled. "No one crosses me."

Ariana shoved her back. "Sea Bitch is more like it!"

"I'll cut your heart out," Tia warned.

"Enough!" Jeremy ordered, stepping between the two women. "Tia, if you ever lie about me being Luis' father again, they'll find you floating in the channel. I love that boy, and I wish to God he had a decent mother and father. Now take him home before he sees me break your damned neck."

Ariana shivered at the coldness of Jeremy's threat, but Tia didn't seem fazed.

"I'll make you pay," she warned as she backed away, her gold eyes blazing. "You'll regret crossing me." She pointed at finger at Ariana.

They stood silently and watched Tia until

she reached the house. "I'm sorry, English," Jeremy said, putting his arm around her trembling shoulder.

"I can't stay here, Jeremy," she began to cry. "I could never fit into your life with all the violence and hatred in it." She turned and began to run toward the house.

"English, wait!" he shouted after her, but she didn't stop. "Woman," he hissed. "She stood up to Tia as if she'd been doing it all her life, and then she says she can't live with violence . . . how the hell can you figure them out?

Somehow Ariana made it known to Helga that she didn't want to be disturbed, so Jeremy decided to leave her alone. Still dressed in his cutoff pants, he sat on the veranda drinking and watching an approaching storm. He could see jagged lightning bolts shooting from the sky into the sea. This would be the first storm to hit the island since he'd brought English here, and it looked like it was going to be a severe one.

Suddenly Kennedy appeared in the doorway. "I sent Jones to the ship to be sure all was secure, sir."

"Thank you, Kennedy. Why don't you go on

home to your family now?"

"Are you sure, sir?"

"Aye. Since everything is secure here, I'm going to walk down to Avery's house. I know he left everything shuttered, but I'd feel better if I checked it."

"Right, sir. Captain Corbett wouldn't like to find his house blown away," Kennedy laughed.

After securing his father and mother's house, Jeremy started back to Devil's Reach. The sky was already black and the surf pounded against the shore. The wind began to whip the sand, and then the rains came down in torrents. By the time Jeremy arrived at Devil's Reach he was drenched.

He was surprised to find everything in darkness when he reached the house. As he opened the door of the bedroom, there was an incredible flash of lightning and an explosive crack of thunder. English's silhouette was outlined in the silver light and she let out a bloodcurdling scream.

"English, it's me," he said, shaking her.

"Oh God, where were you?" she sobbed. "I couldn't find anyone, and all the lamps blew out in the wind."

Jeremy thought that was strange. The lamps

were protected by glass chimneys and had never blown out before. "It's all right, love. I'm here now." He stroked her hair. "Take my hand while I light a lamp."

After he lit the lamp Jeremy glanced around the room. How could every lamp in the house blow out at the same time, he wondered silently.

"I was so afraid, Jeremy," she admitted, clinging to him. "I thought I heard someone in here, but no one would answer."

"Perhaps you heard Helga as she was leaving," he reasoned.

"No—Helga told me good night," she shivered. "Jeremy, you're soaked!" she exclaimed, suddenly realizing her dressing gown had become wet.

"I thought I'd be back from my parents' house before the storm broke, but I didn't make it."

"I suggest we both get into dry clothes."

"I'd rather just get out of these wet ones," he said, pulling her into his arms. "I've been thinking about you all evening, English."

"I'm sorry about the way I acted today, Jeremy, but the way you live is so different from the way I was raised."

"I know, English, and perhaps I can change that." As Jeremy stared at her, he noticed movement on her shoulder. Quickly, trying not to alarm her, he brushed a large spider off her robe and stomped it.

"What was it?" she asked.

"Just a bug," he answered, picking her up and carrying her to the bedroom.

It was amazing to her that all he had to do was touch her and she was already aware of a tightness in her stomach and a sudden shortage of breath. She rubbed her hands over the corded muscles of his upper arms, then laid her head against his bare chest.

Suddenly the wind tore a shutter loose and it began a steady beat against the house—a beat that equaled the pounding of her heart.

"Jeremy, the storm," she whispered. "It's going to be bad."

"It's nothing compared to the storm brewing in this room," he whispered against her mouth.

She clung to him, savoring the sweet taste of brandy on his breath. His lips moved down to her throat, searing her satiny skin as he touched where her pulse beat erratically.

"I ache with desire for you," he whispered against her ear. "I can't seem to get enough of you." He sat her lightly on her feet, then slowly removed the dressing gown. His hands caressed her shoulders, then her slender waist and flat stomach.

Of their own volition her hands pulled at the brief clothing he wore. He moaned as she pushed the fabric down, exposing his skin. She caught her breath as she felt his swollen manhood against her bare skin. She felt a shiver of abandon and moved to touch him.

Jeremy was lost in his own world, enjoying the exquisite feeling of having her willing and hungry for him. A flash of lightning lit the room for a long moment, and he stared into her wild, green eyes. He claimed her mouth as he backed her against the bed, gently pushing her on it, and following to lie on top. He moved lazily, playing with her body.

Ariana pulled him closer, running her hands down the length of his back and hips. His mouth trailed kisses over her breasts, teasing each nipple until she thought she'd go crazy. His hand moved between her legs, touching and teasing her until she was in a breathless frenzy.

"You didn't tell me I was to be tormented," she said in a hoarse whisper.

"Aye, but what sweet torment," he replied.

"Jeremy, I must tell you. . . ." she raised his face to look at her. "I love you. . . ."

"I know," he smiled. "I've been waiting all week for you to tell me. I could see it in your

My only love sprung from my only hate!
Too early seen unknown, and known
too late!

Shakespeare

Chapter Eight

The next evening Jean Paul joined them for dinner on the veranda. Ariana liked him and always enjoyed the stories he told about his experiences as a pirate. Like Jeremy he was different from most pirates, having been born a gentleman in Paris.

"I went by the beach this afternoon and noticed they had already refloated the *Black Moriah*," Jean Paul said. "I suppose you'll be thinking about sailing soon."

"Aye, I'm afraid my crew is beginning to get restless."

187

"You should do what I do, mon ami—let one of your officers captain your ship when you don't feel like going out. It has worked very well for me."

"And one of these days you're liable to find yourself without a ship," Jeremy warned.

"There is always that chance, but I'm not too concerned. To be honest with you, I'm beginning to find the life of piracy quite boring."

"Aye, I must agree with you," Jeremy answered, staring into his drink. "It just isn't the same."

Ariana looked up from her plate, surprise in her eyes, but she didn't say anything.

"What we should do is sail together," Jean Paul laughed. "That way when things are slow we can drink and gamble together, and talk about all the adventures we've had."

"And all the women you've enjoyed," Ariana quipped.

"That sounds fine, Jean Paul, but I think I'd rather take English along for entertainment," Jeremy laughed.

"Suit yourself," Jean Paul said, pretending to be insulted.

"Would you really take me along?" Ariana asked.

"Perhaps one of these days. You did say you wanted to be a pirate, didn't you?"

188

eyes every time you looked at me. You don't know how happy this makes me, English. I've known from that first day we fished you out of the sea that I loved you."

"Oh, Jeremy, what are we going to do?"

Jeremy laughed deep in his throat. "We're going to make love."

"No, I said I always wanted to have my own ship," she corrected, "but even a pirate ship is better than none. I could be of help. I'm an expert with a pistol."

Jeremy and Jean Paul laughed. "I'd say she has the makings of a pirate," Jean Paul said.

"Do you mean to tell me you can load a flintlock pistol?"

"Of course. I told you my father wanted me to be good at whatever I attempted."

"You never cease to amaze me, English. You're an excellent horsewoman, a fair sailor, and now you tell me you're an expert with a pistol."

"A fair sailor?" Ariana exclaimed.

"I didn't think I'd get away with that," he laughed. "She really was quite good on the sloop, Jean Paul, but of course, a ship is a different matter."

"Tell me," Jean Paul asked, "Have you any beautiful sisters?"

"As a matter of fact, I do," Ariana said, amused. "My sister Lanie is very much like me."

"But is she as beautiful?" he queried.

"She's more beautiful," she said modestly, "but I'm the smarter."

"I believe that," Jeremy laughed. "How many women do you know who can wrap a man around their little finger in just a few days?"

"Oh, is that what I've done?" she asked, hiding a smile.

"I think it's time I said good night," Jean Paul said. He leaned over and kissed Ariana on the cheek, then laughed at Jeremy's expression. "Why should you have all the enjoyment? I've become fond of your *English* myself."

"Just don't get any ideas," Jeremy warned good-naturedly. "I won't share her with anyone."

"I didn't think you would," Jean Paul said, slapping his friend on the back. "Perhaps I will have to sail to England and find her sister," he laughed.

"English, if you'll excuse us for a moment, I'm going to walk Jean Paul to the door."

"Of course," she smiled.

"It really isn't necessary," Jean Paul said. "I know my way out."

"I know, but there is a matter I wish to discuss with you," Jeremy said, leading the way into the house.

Once out of earshot, Jeremy turned to Jean Paul. "I'm afraid Tia is up to her old tricks."

"What do you mean?"

"Yesterday she warned English that she had crossed the wrong person and she would have her revenge. Well, last night during the storm, someone was in the house when I wasn't there

190

and left this. I killed it as it crawled up English's shoulder." Jeremy unfolded a piece of paper and produced the remains of the deadly spider.

Jean Paul whistled. "I knew she was upset, but I didn't think she'd go this far."

"Will you see what you can find out?"

"Of course, but I'm not staying at her house right now. Our friend François Saint-Gilles has the lady's attentions at the moment."

"I don't trust that bastard, either," Jeremy swore.

"Not too many people do. But don't worry, I'll ask around and see what I can find out."

The next few days passed pleasantly for Ariana. While Jeremy worked over his charts and ledgers, she decided to explore the gardens and the beach. It wasn't until the third day that she realized Kennedy was never far from her. At first she thought it was just a coincidence that he was always working in the garden when she was there, or that he was always fishing while she was on the beach, but then when she found a beautiful flowered path to explore, she noticed Kennedy was right behind her. She quickened her pace and he quickened his.

She whipped around and walked swiftly

191

back toward him so fast that he didn't have a chance to disappear or pretend to be occupied with something. "Why are you following me?" she snapped.

"I'm sorry, m'lady . . . I was following orders. New Providence can be a very dangerous place."

"For God's sake, I'm not a hundred yards from Devil's Reach. Am I still considered a prisoner here?"

"The captain only wants to protect you," Kennedy explained.

Ariana instantly felt sorry for her rudeness to Jeremy's friend, and hastened to add, "I'm not blaming you, Kennedy, and I'm sorry if I sounded so harsh, but I will take this up with your captain."

Ariana headed back to the house, getting angrier by the minute. "How dare you try to keep me a prisoner here!" she shouted as she entered the library.

Jeremy and Jean Paul both looked up startled. "I'm sorry, I didn't know you were occupied," she apologized, "but I wish to talk with you now."

"What's the problem, English?" Jeremy asked.

"Why is Kennedy following me like a mother hen?"

"Only to protect you when I'm not there to

192

do it."

"Why do I need protection here at Devil's Reach?" Ariana asked, frustrated.

"It's just a precaution, love. Please, just humor me."

When she really thought about it, it didn't seem so unreasonable, and she felt foolish. "Has he always been so overbearing, Jean Paul?" she asked, noticing that he still pretended to be interested in something on the desk.

Jean Paul looked up and smiled. "I think it is only where you're concerned, Ariana, but then I fear I would be the same way if you were my lady."

"Well, let me give you both some advice. A woman doesn't like to feel as if she's being held prisoner."

"We will take your advice under consideration," Jeremy laughed.

"Forgive my intrusion. I'll let you get back to your business. Helga will be serving lunch on the veranda in an hour."

"We were just finishing up, English. Jean Paul and I were discussing going into town after lunch to check out the last of the supplies to go aboard *Black Moriah*. Would you like to join us?"

"Would I like to go?" she laughed. "Of course I would. I've been dying to see what

New Providence is like."

"I'm afraid you're in for a disappointment, English."

"I suggest we forget the whole damned thing. Tia Corbett isn't letting anyone near the lady," Saint-Gilles said.

"We can't forget it. I've already sent a message to her parents telling them she was being held for ransom. In a few days they should receive it, and then in a matter of weeks we should hear from them."

"Then you'd better find a way to get to Lady Wellsley. I don't intend to hang around New Providence much longer."

"Just think of the easy money, François. Jeremy is the one keeping her prisoner, but we'll be the ones to get the ransom, and also to get rid of the woman."

"And of course, that is what this is really all about, isn't it, cherie? You hope to have Corbett back in your bed."

Tia smiled and wrapped her arms around the Frenchman's neck. "That too, but it won't change anything between you and me."

"You're a conniving bitch, Tia Bouché. I don't know why any of us puts up with you."

"Don't you?" she asked, rubbing against him. "Shall I show you why?"

Saint-Gilles unwrapped her arms from around his neck. "First, let's finish our business. Tell me what you plan to do if Lady Wellsley is still with Corbett when the party arrives with the ransom money."

"She won't still be with him. As soon as you can get near her, tell her in French that you want to help her. Then, when we can arrange a meeting, she will be captured and held on your ship—and you can do with her as you like."

"If Corbett ever finds out what we're up to, he'll kill both of us," Saint-Gilles warned.

"He won't find out. This is just between you and me, and I don't think either of us will say anything.

As Jeremy had predicted, she was disappointed with New Providence. It was dirty, and it smelled of garbage and overripe fruit. It was also overrun with an assortment of drunken riffraff who called themselves pirates and buccaneers, and with women who sold their bodies to the highest bidder.

Dressed in an ankle-length white cotton dress, sandals, and a wide-brimmed straw hat, Ariana made quite a stir as they mingled with the crowds. There was almost a carnival atmosphere, with jugglers, dancers, and musicians everywhere. They moved between piles of lemons, limes, and bananas, where hawkers sang out their wares. Everyone greeted Jeremy warmly, congratulating him on his success, all the while smiling at Ariana as they welcomed her to New Providence. She was introduced to Charles Vane and Stede Bonnet, both pirates about whom she'd heard horror stories, but both were charming and polite to her.

When they moved out of hearing, Ariana asked, "What success are they talking about, Jeremy?"

Jeremy just smiled and said it was nothing. "Jean Paul, what are they talking about?" she persisted.

"They are congratulating Jeremy on having a woman who looks like you," he laughed.

"Jean Paul, you're going to make her very difficult to live with," Jeremy teased.

"So many of them seem like gentlemen," Ariana said, ignoring his teasing. "They don't seem very different from the men in England."

"A good many of them are gentlemen, or were at one time. In the early 1700s, piracy had virtually died out. Then, this past year, the war between England and Spain ended, and many of the younger seamen who had been privateers for the Crown knew no business other than plundering enemy shipping. Unemployment forced them one step further to the illegal plundering of all shipping, and made most of them far richer than they'd been doing the same thing for the Crown.

"Did all of them come here to settle?" Ariana asked, looking out over the harbor filled with ships.

"The Bahamas are safe and immensely profitable. The location makes it an ideal base from which to prey on the heavy volume of shipping that passes through the Gulf of Florida and the sea lanes between the Spanish Main, the West Indian colonies, and parts of Europe and North America. All they need do is wait for their prey among the shoals, bays, and reefs, and once the ship is sighted, they pounce.

"And pity the poor unsuspecting souls," Ariana said.

"Aye, pity them if they meet up with the wrong pirates. Most of these *gentlemen* are a bloodthirsty lot."

Business was brisk along the quay. Not only were there shop merchants inspecting the goods being unloaded from the pirate ships, but merchant captains representing England, France, and Holland were also bidding on the stolen merchandise.

"But why would they buy stolen merchandise?" Ariana asked. "It encourages piracy."

"Where else can they buy Spanish goods at such excellent prices?" Jeremy answered.

"But that's terrible!" Ariana exclaimed.

"I'm afraid it's an imperfect world, my love. Greed usually overrules righteousness, even in your fine England."

They stopped at a table covered with Spanish muskets and Toledo blades. Jeremy picked up a small silver pistol and balanced it in his hand.

"What do you think, Jean Paul?"

His friend balanced it, then peered down the stock. "Excellent quality."

Jeremy instructed the merchant to deliver it to Devil's Reach with powder and shot, then they moved on. Another table was covered with Spanish lace, Moroccan leather, and other various goods. Ariana picked up a pair of silver-and-pearl combs and admired them.

"Would you like them?" Jeremy asked.

"No, I think not," she answered, laying the combs back on the table. Her hand moved to a fan intricately inlaid with silver and gold. "The workmanship is beautiful," she said. "I've never seen anything like it."

"Aye, it is exquisite," Jeremy agreed, nodding to Jean Paul.

Ariana didn't notice that Jean Paul hung back as they moved to the next table covered with bottles of Spanish wine. Suddenly she heard someone call her name. She felt Jeremy tense at her side. Glancing around she saw

Mason Taylor making his way toward them.

"Oh, Mason, I'm so glad to see you," she exclaimed, restraining herself from throwing her arms around his neck. "I've been so worried about you."

Jeremy leaned against one of the tables, his arms folded across his chest as he patiently waited while they talked. He felt like a heel when he noticed tears in her eyes while they clasped hands. Damn, he should never have brought her into New Providence, he thought angrily. He should have considered the possibility of running into Taylor.

"Captain Corbett," Mason turned to him. "I've tried to see you to thank you, but I could never get past your guards." He held out his hand to Jeremy. "I understand I also have you to thank for providing me with enough gold to stay on the island. I'm very grateful."

Ariana's eyes flew to Jeremy's face, but he avoided them. "I was glad to be of assistance," he said, looking embarrassed.

"I'm more than grateful," Mason laughed, taking Ariana's hand. "I'm going to be married."

"Married . . . but how . . . who?" Ariana asked.

"Her name is Gideon," Mason said, his eyes shining with love. "She'd the daughter of Doc, the man who took care of me."

"I'm very happy for you, Mason, but how are you going to make a living here on the island?"

"I'm going to sign on with one of the pirates. I'll make ten times the money I ever made sailing for the Royal Navy."

Jeremy shook his head. That's all they needed, one more pirate. He should have had the young man shanghaied as originally planned. It would have saved everybody a lot of trouble.

"But what about you, Ariana? Will you be staying on the island?" Mason asked.

Again Ariana glanced at Jeremy, and again he wouldn't meet her eyes. "I don't know yet, Mason."

"If you're through with this touching reunion, I'd like to move on," Jeremy announced.

"Of course, Captain Corbett. Forgive me for delaying you, but when I saw Ariana I had to speak with her. I had been told that she was well and in good hands, and now I've seen it for myself."

"Do come visit me at Devil's Reach," Ariana said. "The guards will be told to admit you this time. Won't they, Jeremy?"

"Yes—of course," he mumbled.

When Mason disappeared in the crowd, Ariana turned on Jeremy. He had expected her to be angry, but instead her voice was calm and her eyes twinkled with amusement.

"He was never in danger from you, was he?"

Jeremy tried to look stern. "That isn't entirely true. Fortunately we didn't have to put my threat to the test."

"And what was this about you giving him gold to stay on the island?"

Jeremy took her arm and smiled. "It wouldn't have done to have him leave here, now would it? I've always found it very ineffective to threaten someone who is on the other side of the ocean."

"And of course you didn't want him to return to England and tell my family where I was."

"That too," he admitted.

"I don't believe you're nearly as bad as you pretend."

"Don't let anyone else hear you say that," he laughed.

Across the square Tia and François watched Ariana and Jeremy with interest. "He never leaves her side," Tia said in disgust. "Perhaps if a fight were to break out. . . ."

"I doubt if he'd leave her alone under any circumstances. It's strange, she doesn't look unhappy," François commented as he watched her walking arm-in-arm with her captive. "Yet she pleaded with me to find a ship going to England."

"I don't care whether she's happy or not. I want her off the island," Tia said furiously. "Don't go soft on me, you bastard, or I'll tell Jeremy this whole thing was your plan."

François turned a deadly smile on her. "You're as sweet as a black widow spider, my cherie. Don't worry about me. I'll hold up my end of the deal," he said, moving across the square toward Ariana and Jeremy.

"Captain Corbett, Lady Wellsley, how nice to see you again," Saint-Gilles greeted. He lifted Ariana's hand to his mouth and kissed it. "Are you enjoying your visit to New Providence?" he asked in French.

"Oui," she answered.

He continued, "I have news of an English ship, but we must talk in private."

"I have changed my mind," she answered in French, glancing at Jeremy's expressionless face.

"But mademoiselle," Saint-Gilles persisted, "everything is arranged."

"You heard the lady, Saint-Gilles. She is no longer interested in leaving New Providence," Jeremy said, smiling calmly at the Frenchman.

Saint-Gilles looked between Ariana and Jeremy, a puzzled expression on his face. "You . . . you speak French?" he asked, dread in his voice.

"That's right," Jeremy answered.

"But you never said anything. . . ."

"Sometimes it is beneficial to keep such things to oneself."

"Of course," he laughed uneasily, wondering if he was going to be able to walk away without a fight.

"Let me give you a warning, Saint-Gilles," Jeremy said, his hand on the hilt of his sword. "If I ever catch you near the lady again, I'll kill you without asking questions. Do I make myself clear?"

"Of course, Captain Corbett. I don't blame you at all," he said, backing away from the group. "I must be on my way now. *Pardon*."

"What was all that about?" Jean Paul asked as he rejoined them.

"It was nothing," Jeremy answered.

"I think I'm ready to return to Devil's Reach," Ariana said, visibly shaken.

"I had planned for us to have supper aboard *Black Moriah*, but if you would rather not. . . ."

"No, I think I would enjoy that. Just anyplace but here on the quay."

"I understand, English. I did try to warn

you."

"I know you did, but I suppose I had to see it for myself."

Jean Paul and Kennedy rowed them in the tender, winding their way through the moorings of the ships until they came out in open water. There, set apart from the others, loomed a large, black ship.

"My God," she whispered in awe. "She is so . . . so. . . ."

"Intimidating?" Jeremy suggested.

"Yes."

"She is supposed to be. That's one of the reasons the Spanish fear her."

When they came alongside the ship's ladder, Jean Paul climbed up and held out his hand to Ariana; Jeremy followed close behind. On the deck another seaman helped Kennedy secure the boat to the ship.

Ariana was amazed to find the crew standing at attention, all looking proud as peacocks. One of them came forward and bowed. "The crew wishes to welcome you back, Lady Wellsley."

"Thank you," she smiled, glancing at Jeremy, who stood with a pleased look on his face. "And thank you all for rescuing me."

After thanking his crew, Jeremy led Ariana

toward the raised quarterdeck where Jean Paul waited. "What do you think of her?" Jeremy asked.

"She is beautiful," Ariana exclaimed. "I wish I had been conscious to enjoy her the last time I was aboard."

Kennedy appeared smiling before them. "Everything is ready, sir."

"Thank you, Kennedy."

"Enjoy your surprise, m'lady," Kennedy said to her, his eyes merry with excitement.

"Surprise?" Ariana asked as Kennedy disappeared. "What does he mean, Jeremy?"

The rattle of the chain in the hawser and the grind of the captan broke the evening silence, and suddenly the crew were all in action. Jeremy called out an order behind her, clear and decisive, and she smiled as she realized what Kennedy had been talking about. They were leaving the harbor of New Providence.

They crept out of the harbor like a ghost upon the water, catching a stronger breeze in the unsheltered water. The ship heeled slightly, her decks aslant. The air was fresh and salty, a relief after the stale air of the quay, and an escort of seagulls rose in the air and followed them.

Jeremy wrapped his arms about her waist as they watched the sails fill with the evening breeze. "Are you happy with your surprise?"

he asked.

"Oh yes," she answered, laughing up at him. "I've never been happier."

He raised an eyebrow in question. "Do you really mean that, English?"

"Yes," she smiled up at him, knowing that what she said was true. She would never trade being with him for all the riches in England. "I am with the man I love. How could I not be happy?"

Let tomorrow take care of tomorrow,
leave things of the future to fate.

Charles Swain

Chapter Nine

They stood at the rail watching the sunset, while Jean Paul directed the course of the ship. The land was a blur upon the horizon as the *Black Moriah* cut through the crystal-clear water turned red by the sun.

"Where are we going?" Ariana asked.

"No place in particular. This is more or less a dry run to be sure the ship is seaworthy after being careened and overhauled."

"I can tell she is," Ariana smiled. "She feels like a living thing beneath my feet."

"Only a real seaman would make a statement like that," he laughed. "I'm glad you feel that way."

"Don't you feel that way about her?"

"*Black Moriah* has always been the means to an end to capture the Spaniard that killed my father, but yes, she has become like a living thing. I trust Jean Paul to captain her, but I could never turn her over to one of my crew to sail without me aboard."

"What do you know about this man who killed your father?" Ariana asked.

"He's a one-eyed pirate named Salizar," Jeremy answered. "For a while I thought he'd already died or been killed, but he was sighted not far from here several months ago. We were searching for him when we discovered you in the water."

"Will you resume your search?"

"Vengeance is a strong emotion—as strong as love or hate, and not easily put aside."

He hadn't really answered her question, but she didn't pursue the subject. Instead she wrapped her arms around his waist and snuggled against him.

"Your crew seems very happy," she commented as singing voices rose on the wind.

"Aye, they all seemed possessed by the sense of excitement at being at sea again. That's what happens when a born sailor stays on land too long."

"Are you a born sailor?"

"Yes," he laughed, "I suppose I am. I could give up pirating in a minute, just as long as I could occasionally go to sea."

"I had a maid who said if men were meant to go to sea, God would have given them fins."

Jeremy laughed. "I would wager she suffered from seasickness."

"She did," Ariana said sadly. "Mother and Lanie were also sick during the storm."

"English, look at me," he gently ordered. "I hadn't meant to tell you until this evening at dinner, but I suppose to keep you from becoming melancholy, I had better tell you now. I received word this morning that your mother and sister were rescued and taken safely to England."

Ariana's eyes widened. "Do you mean . . . my mother and Lanie are alive and well?"

"Yes, love. I talked with the Captain of the *Langston* myself. His was the ship that rescued them."

"Oh, thank God!" she whispered. "And since I have willingly agreed to stay with you, you will let me send a message soon?"

"Soon," he answered, still fearing that something would pull them apart.

Suddenly Kennedy appeared. "Everything is prepared in your cabin, sir."

"Are you hungry?" Jeremy asked.

"Did you bring Helga with us?" Ariana teased.

"No, but you'll find Kennedy does as well."

"Kennedy, I can see now why Jeremy thinks so highly of you. You certainly are a jack-of-all-trades."

"I try, m'lady," he answered with a smile.

"You are very lucky to have a man like that," Ariana exclaimed.

"I know that, but it's a sore point between my father and me, so when you meet Avery, don't mention how wonderful Kennedy is," he laughed.

"I don't understand." Ariana turned questioning eyes on Jeremy.

"I stole him from my father," Jeremy laughed. "He had sailed with Avery for years. As a matter of fact, he was with Avery when he rescued me on that burning ship."

Jeremy opened the door of his cabin to let English enter, but she stood frozen in the doorway. The sun's glow reflected through the large lead-glass windows of the ship's stern, casting the room in a golden haze.

"It's so beautiful," she said, glancing around at the built-in mahogany furniture. A table sat in the center of the cabin covered with flowers and fine china. "Kennedy has outdone himself," she said, picking up a crystal goblet. "How do you keep this from getting broken?"

"We wouldn't be using it if we were in rough seas," he said, holding out a leather-covered decanter. "Would you like a glass of wine before we eat?"

"You do live well, Jeremy."

"Why not. Life is to enjoy, my sweet. You set your mind to what you want and you go after it."

"Is that what you did to me?"

"Somehow I knew the moment they laid you on my deck that you and I were meant to be together. Don't ask me how or why, English, but in that first moment I just knew life would never be the same for either of us."

Ariana touched her glass to his. "To us, then," she smiled.

"To us."

"I have something for you," he said, reaching inside his jacket. Ariana's eyes widened as he produced the beautiful fan she had examined on the quay.

"Oh, Jeremy, it's the fan I had admired. How did you manage that?" she laughed in delight.

"I had Jean Paul purchase it while you were enjoying your reunion with young Taylor."

Ariana smiled at him. "You didn't really mind me talking to Mason, did you?"

"The hell I didn't!" he laughed. "I get jealous anytime you talk to another male—including Jean Paul and Kennedy."

"Oh, Jeremy," she laughed, "I promise, you have nothing to worry about."

They dined on a meal of roast pork and boiled potatoes. Ariana ate with a ravenous appetite which she attributed to the sea air.

"Eat all you want," he laughed. "We won't be able to light the oven if the sea should get rough. If that should happen, then you'll be eating bread and cheese."

"That will be fine, too," she answered, holding out her glass to be refilled. "I can see why you enjoy this life," she said, looking around the room. "It is very pleasant."

"Not always," he laughed. "Sometimes there is a great deal of danger."

"And excitement," she added. "I could feel it just being around your crew."

"Aye, I suppose they are excited for several reasons; being at sea again, the prospect of finding a prize, and having you aboard."

"Why should having me aboard make a difference?" she asked.

"They all want to impress you," he laughed. "You are an added stimulation, and they will all work harder in front of you."

"Then I should sail with you all the time," she said, looking at him over the rim of her wineglass.

"Perhaps you should," he smiled.

While Kennedy cleared away the dishes, Jeremy and Ariana went back on deck to watch the stars come out in the black sky. After relieving Jean Paul so he could get something to eat, Jeremy took the wheel, holding Ariana between him and the spokes.

"This is the most beautiful night I have ever seen," she said, leaning against him. "I never want to go back."

"Ah, how many times I have felt that way when we first go to sea. After a while, though, you yearn to place your feet on solid ground."

"At this moment I cannot imagine yearning for anything but this."

"Here, take the wheel," he said, moving away from her.

"Are you sure?" she asked. "I've never done this."

"Just hold the spokes in your hand and keep the ship on a steady course," he instructed. "Do you feel the wind at the back of your head?"

"Yes," she answered.

"Good, then keep it that way. Don't let it come forward of your right cheek." Jeremy leaned against the rail, casually lighting a long, thin cheroot. "You're doing fine," he commented.

"It feels wonderful," she answered, feeling the movement of the lively hull and the surge as they swept forward, cutting through the seas like a sharp knife. The wind whistled in the riggings, and the sound of humming filled the sails. It was a night she would never forget, she thought. She couldn't remember ever being happier.

Jeremy watched her with pride. Her hair blew in ringlets around her face, and even in the darkness he could see her eyes sparkled with excitement. What a team they would make, he thought smugly, but that wasn't what the future would hold for them, he reminded himself silently. He wanted her and their family to have respectability.

"I am glad to see my faith in you wasn't misplaced," he said, breaking the silence.

"What do you mean?" she asked.

"I never doubted that you could sail a ship this size." He laughed, as he walked away, leaving her alone with the *Black Moriah*.

"Jeremy, where are you going?" she asked, her heart beating rapidly at the thought of being in full control of this great ship.

For at least thirty minutes she was left alone at the wheel. At least she thought she was alone, unaware that Jeremy was never far away if her arms should get tired. She whistled a tune to herself as she studied the stars overhead. So this was what is was like to be a pirate, she thought.

"It isn't always like this," Jeremy said from behind her.

"How is it you can read my mind?" she asked.

"I could read the look of contentment on your face and remembered a time I thought being a pirate must be the the most wonderful profession on earth."

"Isn't it?"

"It is until the ship you plan on capturing decides to fight back. Then it turns into a bloodbath," he answered, "and I don't like to see my men killed. I have been lucky that a false reputation preceeded me, and I've had to murder very few." Ariana's eyes darted to his face. "Do not delude yourself, English; I *have* killed people."

"I can't imagine it," she said, leaning back against him. "I think that is a side of you I never want to see."

"Are your arms tired?"

"They're about to drop off," she admitted.

Jeremy took over, keeping her between him and the wheel. "Somehow, someplace, I will find a way to put my past behind me and make a new life for both of us."

"I will be with you, whatever you choose to do," she said, looking up at him. "I know now

217

that my place is beside you, whether it's living in danger as a pirate, or in peace as a farmer."

Jeremy put one arm around her waist and pulled her against him. "And may anyone who tries to part us rot in hell," he swore before capturing her mouth in a searing kiss.

After throwing everything that wasn't nailed down, Tia turned on François. "How could you let this happen, you bumbling idiot? You were right there talking with them and you didn't know that they planned to sail?"

François sipped at his drink, unperturbed. "I wasn't taken into Captain Corbett's confidences," he answered cooly. "Besides, the *Black Moriah* was just refloated, so I assume he hasn't gotten far."

"You assume?" she screamed, picking up the wine decanter and throwing it across the room. "You assumed Jeremy didn't speak French, too, and now he knows that you planned to help his English harlot. Where does that leave us?"

"You're the one who was intimate with him. I would think you'd know if he spoke French. Surely he must have whispered words of love in French, or was your mating without those small niceties?" François spat sarcastically, tired of being blamed.

"I knew he spoke Spanish and Dutch, but I knew nothing of French. Are you sure you didn't mention my name when you were talking to her?"

"Why would I mention you?" he laughed. "Lady Wellsley wouldn't trust you if her life depended on it."

"I should have killed her when she first came to the island!" Tia spat, pacing the room.

"It isn't as if you haven't tried, cherie. The spider was a nice touch, but the odds of it somehow finding its prey were against you. If it had been me, I would have used poison; it's much more effective. But then, of course, you stood the chance of your lover drinking it too," he laughed smugly.

"Will you just be quiet!" she screamed. "I have to think. Maybe I should send a ship after them. . . ."

"Don't be a fool, Tia. There isn't a ship in the harbor that could go up against the *Black Moriah*."

"Yes, you're right—but they can't stay at sea forever, and when they return I will be waiting," she snarled.

Ariana heaved a sigh of contentment as she slipped between the smooth sheets of the large bed. "Isn't it strange how one's perspective can change so dramatically?"

"How so?" Jeremy asked as he slipped in beside her.

"A short time ago I would have fainted at the idea of being close to a pirate. I can remember that in Bermuda, the ladies at tea would tell stories they'd heard about you and the others. When the name *Black Moriah* was mentioned, I imagined a devil with horns and breathing fire."

He leaned up on one elbow to look into her face. "And now what do you think of me?"

"Oh, I still think you're a devil," she smiled mischievously, "but I don't believe you can breath fire."

"Haven't I told you I could do anything I put my mind to?"

She ran her thumb along his square jawline. "Yes, you've told me that, and I am a believer."

"That's a good girl," he teased.

"I'm not a girl; I'm a woman, Jeremy."

"Just how old are you, love?"

"Are you afraid you're robbing the cradle?" she asked, running her hand down his firm stomach.

"No—I just wondered how old you are."

"I'm nineteen. I'll be twenty in December. How old are you, Jeremy?"

"I'm afraid I'm already an old man, my love."

"Jeremy," she pushed playfully. "How old are you?"

"Twenty-five," he answered, nibbling on her ear.

"My, you really are an old man."

Jeremy looked down into her face. "I'm not too old to turn you over my knee and give you a sound thrashing. As a matter of fact, I might even take great pleasure in doing so."

"I bow to your age, sir," she said running her hand still lower on his stomach.

Jeremy's eyes widened in surprise. "You little vixen, are you trying to seduce me? How do you know I don't want to sleep tonight?"

"Your eyes are becoming smoky gray, Jeremy, and I know that look only too well."

"Do you, now?" he laughed, his voice husky with desire. "And your eyes are the color of the sea at dawn, my love, and when you are at your most passionate, they are the color of emeralds. What do you think about that?"

"I think if you go to sleep and ignore me, I shall be very angry."

"Have no fear, English. Sleep is the last thing on my mind." He leaned over and closed his lips over a coral nipple, then came back to her mouth. "Your skin is like velvet, all warm and soft," he murmured against her lips. He

221

placed kisses on her eyes, then down her jawline and across her chin. "I always have this
craving to devour you when you lie beneath
me," he whispered.

"That is the way I feel after we've made
love," she admitted. "I feel as if I've been
consumed by you."

"And I feel possessed by you," he said, trailing kisses down her throat.

She wound her fingers in his hair as he
moved lower across her stomach. She started
to protest, but only a moan escaped as the
urgency of his desire communicated itself when
she ran her hands over his muscular shoulders.
He was driving her into a frenzy of pulsating
desire. She arched her body upward as wave
after wave of pleasure saturated her.

Afterward he moved on top of her, and she
clutched him feverishly, crying out his name as
he thrust deep inside her.

He smoothed back the tousled hair from her
damp forehead and placed a kiss on her parted
lips.

"Jeremy, do you know this is the first time
I've ever made love on a ship?"

"It damn well better be," he answered, still
kissing her warm skin.

"Is it the first time for you?" she asked
without thinking.

She felt a hesitancy on his part, then he

leaned up on one elbow to look at her. "Don't ask me to answer that, love. Just believe that if I could turn back the hands of time, you would be my first and only love."

Ariana felt as if she'd been hit in the stomach; tears welled in her eyes. "I'm being foolish . . . of course I know you've had other women. You've probably made love to Tia right here in this bed. Oh God, why did I say that," she cried, seeing the look in Jeremy's eyes as she hit on the truth. She suddenly sat up, holding the sheet beneath her chin as words came from her mouth in torrents. "I'm sorry, I don't know why I brought this up, Jeremy. I don't want to know about you and Tia . . . I don't want to know why you cut her wrist and yours to mingle your blood."

"Stop it, English," he said, shaking her. "I have had sex with Tia, but I've never made love to her, and I sure as hell didn't cut her wrist and mine so our blood could mingle. You must believe that I have never loved another woman, English. I was fourteen when I first had sex, and it's never been anything but raw animal lust—until I met you."

Ariana leaned against his shoulder. "I'm sorry, Jeremy—I don't know what got into me. The whole evening has been so beautiful and now I've ruined it."

"You haven't ruined anything, love. You've

only said things that were in the back of your mind and needed to be said. I will never tire of convincing you how much I love you. Now lie back in my arms. We're both tired and need to get some sleep before morning."

She did as he suggested, feeling his heart beat against her breast, but she could not sleep. She was ashamed of the way she'd acted. Jeremy's past was his own business, and she had no right to hurl angry accusations at him for anything he'd done. God, she was no better than Tia Bouché, she thought in disgust. She closed her eyes and tried to sleep, but images of Tia Bouché in Jeremy's arms kept invading her mind. Did he do the things to Tia that he did to her? She clenched her fists, knowing that he must have. It was no wonder the woman wanted him back, but she wasn't going to get him, she thought determindly as she finally fell asleep.

Nothing was said the next morning about her outburst. Instead, Jeremy teased and cajoled her about being a sleepyhead and missing the sun coming up.

"Stay in bed until Kennedy brings you coffee," he suggested, kissing her on the nose. "I'll be up on deck for a while." Before he opened the door he turned and smiled. "The clothes on the chair may be more to your liking as a deck hand."

Ariana glanced at the chair and saw her riding clothes. "You think of everything," she smiled warmly. "Thank you."

"I'll see you on deck," he said, blowing her a kiss.

Flexing the muscles in her arms, Ariana realized she was sore from her turn at the wheel. She wouldn't dare let Jeremy or Jean Paul know that, she decided as she climbed from the bed. They'd tease her unmercifully. She'd just finished dressing when there was a knock at the door and Kennedy entered carrying a tray of steaming coffee and honey pastries.

"Good morning, m'lady," he greeted cheerfully. "I trust you had a good night."

"Yes, thank you," she answered, feeling the heat rise to her face. "It looks like it is going to be a beautiful day."

"I'm sure of it," he said as he held a chair out for her. "Will there be anything else, m'lady?"

"No, thank you, Kennedy. This will be fine. I plan to join your captain on deck as soon as I've eaten something."

"Very good, m'lady. May I say, the crew was very proud of the way you handled the ship last evening. They've talked of little else since."

Ariana had to giggle. "I would have thought

they'd have been quaking in their boots."

"Not at all, m'lady. They know if the Captain trusts you, they can trust you."

"Thank you, Kennedy. That means a great deal to me."

After enjoying the strong black coffee and pastries, Ariana joined Jeremy and Jean Paul on deck. The sun that had been so bright only minutes before was now covered by a massive black cloud. She turned in the direction of the wind and realized it had changed. There was a tang about it that was familiar, a wet salt smell. A chill came over her as she remembered it was the same just before the storm hit the *Huron*.

"I'm afraid the weather is going to foul our plans, love," Jeremy said as she joined him.

"Is it going to be bad?" she asked, her voice trembling.

"Nothing like the storm you were shipwrecked in," he said, putting his arm around her. "I think this one will be mostly rain and perhaps a little wind. And don't forget, the *Black Moriah* rode out the last storm without any problems."

"That's true," she smiled. "The *Huron* didn't have a captain like the *Black Moriah* has, either."

"Ah, you are finally learning," he laughed. The rain began to fall as they spoke. "Will you weather the storm with me, English?"

She turned her face up to the rain, feeling a surge of excitement. "There's no place I'd rather be," she answered.

"What have you done in your life to deserve such a woman?" Jean Paul asked.

"It must be my good deeds," Jeremy laughed.

"Ship ahoy!" the lookout shouted.

Kennedy handed Jeremy a spyglass and he studied the ship. "Damn, it looks to be Spanish!" he said. He handed the spyglass to Jean Paul. "Take a look."

Jean Paul whistled. "She's riding mighty low in the water."

"Exactly," Jeremy said. "She's probably loaded with gold."

"You're liable to have a mutiny on your hands if you deny your crew this one."

"I'm well aware of that," he growled.

"Jeremy, if you're hesitating because of me, please don't. I'll be fine."

Jeremy put the spyglass to his eye and studied the ship again. The crew waited, their faces full of expectation. "All right, Kennedy. Command the men to battle stations. Let's get this over with quickly."

She feared no danger, for she knew no sin.

Dryden

Chapter Ten

Jeremy snapped out orders one after the other, his face tense and alert. Ariana shivered for no reason. Without a word she moved to stand against the rail. She suddenly felt like an intruder, a foolish woman who was among men who had serious work to do. Jean Paul was at the wheel while Jeremy shouted orders. Men were running everywhere, each with a job that he had done many times before.

The deck beneath her shifted slightly as the port guns were hauled into the gunports. Goosebumps rose on her arms and at the back of her neck as they moved closer to the Spanish vessel.

"English, it's time you get below deck," Jeremy said at her shoulder.

"No, please — let me stay here. I won't get in the way."

"Absolutely not. They may decide to stand and fight, and I won't have you in danger."

"I won't be in any danger, Jeremy. If that happens, I promise I'll go below."

Jeremy grabbed her shoulders in an iron grip. "Damn it, I have too much to worry about without worrying that you could be hurt. Now do as I tell you."

Ariana flinched at the stern tone of his voice. "You needn't shout at me!" she retorted angrily.

"Then do as I say!" he shouted back.

Ariana could see the three-masted vessel clearly now, and she knew he didn't need to be worrying about her. "All right, Jeremy. I'll go below . . . please be careful."

He leaned over and quickly kissed her, then turned her around and smacked her on the derrière. "Get moving!" he ordered.

She hesitated as she reached the companionway, turning to take one last look. They were abreast of the Spanish ship now.

"Stand by your guns for a warning shot," Jeremy shouted.

Ariana was thrown backward as two cannons went off in unison, belching white smoke into the air.

She waited like the rest of the crew, her heart pounding as she wondered if the ship would surrender or return their fire. Many of the crew members stood by with grappling hooks, ready to swarm over the rails of the Spanish ship.

"Rendir, el capitan!" Jeremy ordered the surrender in Spanish. "Lay down your arms and no one will be hurt."

Without warning a puff of smoke came from one of the guns on the Spanish ship and a hail of shot rattled onto the deck of the *Black Moriah*.

A shower of oak splinters fell all around Ariana. She felt a burning sensation in her thigh and looked down to find a long, thin piece of wood had penetrated her leg.

"Open fire!" Jeremy ordered.

One volley from the thirty guns on *Black Moriah* was all that was needed. The Spanish ship waved a white flag.

"Look lively, men," Jeremy ordered as his men swung aboard the Spanish ship.

In less than an hour the bounty from the Spanish prize had been loaded aboard the *Black Moriah*. Jeremy bade the Spanish captain good-bye and ordered his men to cast off.

Swiftly they put the open sea between them and the Spanish galleon.

"I'm damned glad I came along," Jean Paul laughed, slapping Jeremy on the back. "It was amazing—not a single drop of blood shed."

"Kennedy, break out a barrel of rum. The men deserve a celebration. I'm going to get English. I'm surprised she didn't come on deck when the shooting stopped."

Jeremy headed for the companionway, then stopped at the top of the stairs and bent down to examine a small puddle of blood. "Kennedy! Did anyone report an injury?"

"No sir . . . not even a broken fingernail."

"There's blood here on the deck and on the steps . . . Jesus!" he swore, leaping down the stairs. He swung open the door of his cabin and froze in his tracks.

Ariana stood clinging to the desk, the leg of her pants soaked with blood. "Oh God, English," Jeremy gasped, seeing the wicked piece of wood embedded in her leg.

"I'm sorry, Jeremy. I've gotten blood all over everything," she said before fainting dead away.

"I'll get Doc," Kennedy said from the doorway.

Jeremy picked English up and gently laid her on the bed. Swiftly he tore her pant leg away and grimaced at the sharp wood protruding from her leg. She opened her eyes and looked at him.

"I was going below, Jeremy. I really was . . . I just stopped for a moment."

"Damn it, English, I should give you a sound thrashing, but for now it's going to have to wait."

"I know. I deserve as much," she smiled faintly. "Is it very bad, Jeremy?"

"No . . . Doc will take care of it, but I warn you, it's going to hurt like hell." Jeremy didn't tell her that gangrene was what they worried about most in the tropics. He knew Doc wouldn't have any trouble removing the piece of wood, but keeping infection from the wound was a complicated matter.

"What have we here?" Doc asked as he entered the room. "Did you go and spoil our record, little lady?"

"What record was that?" Ariana asked, her face white with pain.

"We thought we'd plundered that ship with nary a drop of blood being shed."

Ariana closed her eyes and gritted her teeth when he touched the splinter of wood. "Please tell the crew I'm sorry," she gasped in pain.

"The young lady needs a good stiff drink, captain. Maybe even a couple, Doc said."

Jeremy poured a water glass full of whiskey, then lifted her head and put the glass to her mouth. She swallowed the fiery liquid, then choked and gagged. "Can't I have wine?" she asked when she'd caught her breath.

"Wine won't do, little one. We need something to dull the pain quickly." Jeremy poured more whiskey into the glass and held it to her mouth. "Drink up, English."

"I don't think I can. It tastes so terrible."

"Terrible! This is the best Irish whiskey made. Come on now, you have to drink it," he encouraged. Again she swallowed it, and again she choked and coughed.

"Just take the splinter out of my leg," she said in exasperation. "It can't be any worse than trying to drink this awful stuff!"

Jeremy had to laugh. "I know you're tough, but this is for your benefit, love."

Ariana finished the last gulp, then shivered and made a terrible face. "How can a person enjoy something that tastes like that?" she asked, her speech already somewhat slurred. "It's like drinking poison."

"Captain, she is going to have to be tied down," Doc whispered. "I can't have her moving when I'm trying to cut out that piece of wood."

"I'll hold her," Jeremy insisted, "and Kennedy can hold her legs. It's going to be a bad enough experience without frightening her to death."

236

"What's wrong, Jeremy?" Ariana asked, hearing them whisper.

"Nothing, love. Doc is just deciding how he wants to do this. How about taking one more drink?" She shook her head and hiccuped. "This isn't going to be the most pleasant thing you've ever been through, love, but it will be over with quickly."

"I understand . . ."

While Kennedy held her legs, Jeremy held her in his arms, her face buried into his shoulder. Her muffled scream rang out in the cabin before she fainted in his arms.

"It looks clean," Doc said, examining the nasty-looking piece of wood. "I don't think any of it chipped off in her leg." He picked up the bottle of whiskey, took a slug, and then poured some over Ariana's leg. Even unconscious, she rose off the bed and cried out in pain.

As Doc began to bandage her leg, Ariana opened her eyes and stared at Jeremy. "Do you have any more of that stuff?"

"The whiskey?" Jeremy asked in disbelief.

"Yeah, that terrible tasting stuff," she said, trying to focus her eyes.

Jeremy poured another glass and held it to her mouth. She took a long drink, then fell back on the bed, unconscious. "I hope I haven't created a monster," he smiled.

"It's all for the best right now. If I were you, captain, I'd try keeping her that way until we get back to port," Doc suggested. It won't hurt her none."

Ariana slept most of the evening while the ship was on a course back to New Providence. Jean Paul paid a visit to the cabin to find Jeremy hovering over Ariana like a mother hen.

"Stop worrying, mon ami, Doc said she's going to be fine."

"This is what I was afraid of," Jeremy said, running his hand through his tousled hair. "I should never have allowed her to come along. What if the wound becomes infected? Christ, what a fool I am! I should have let you take the ship out, and I should have stayed at Devil's Reach with English."

"Jeremy, hindsight is fine, but it doesn't change anything. What happened can't be undone. Now calm yourself . . . English will be much better off if you remain calm."

"If anything were to happen to her . . ."

"Do you remember how to pray, mon ami?"

Jeremy stared at Jean Paul. "Of course I remember."

"Then I suggest you spend your time doing that instead of blaming yourself. I'm going back on deck to make sure everything continues to run smoothly. Let me know if you need anything."

"Thank you, Jean Paul. You're a good friend."

"Of course, mon ami, and good friends have to look out for each other."

Jeremy poured himself a drink, then pulled a chair up next to the bed. He sat staring at Ariana, praying she would be all right. He didn't know how he'd go on if something happened to her.

"Jeremy," she whispered.

"I'm right here, love."

"Was I hit in the head, too?"

"No, of course not," he laughed. "Why?"

"It feels like it," she sighed.

"I think that's because you don't know how to hold your liquor," he laughed.

"Was the Spanish ship loaded with gold?"

"Yes, but I'd give all of it back if it would take your pain away."

Ariana stared at him. "Do you really mean that?"

"Of course I mean it. I've made a very important decision while I've been sitting here watching you."

"What is that?" Ariana asked.

"I'm giving up piracy."

"But why? You seem to be very good at it.

239

I was thrilled watching you in action," she said, her voice still slurred.

Jeremy rubbed his thumb along her jawline. "I'm the best, but I met this wench who makes me want to lead a respectable life."

"A wench?" she repeated.

He nodded grinning. "She drives me crazy. Every time I look at her, my pulse races, and when she smiles, oh God, when she smiles at me, I'm lost."

"It sounds like she wields a great deal of power over you."

"Oh, she does, English, but I can't let her know that. I fear it would be my undoing."

"Most certainly," she smiled. "She is a very lucky woman," she sighed before closing her eyes and sleeping.

"No, I'm the one who is lucky, English," he whispered, pulling the covers up to her chin.

"The *Black Moriah* has returned," Tia announced as she rushed into François' room. "Now we can get on with our plan and get rid of that English bitch."

"*Your* plan," François corrected.

"If you want out, just say so," she shouted. "I can always find someone else to help me. I'm sure Stede Bonnet would be interested in sharing the ransom."

"Don't get excited, my little wildcat. I did not say I wasn't interested."

"Captain," Dobson interrupted, sticking his head in the door. "You've got big trouble."

"I know," François answered. "The *Black Moriah* has returned."

"More than that, Captain," the sleazy-looking pirate grinned.

"Well, get on with it, man."

"Lady Wellsley's parents and a fiancé just arrived on the *Dove*. Captain Quigley is keeping them aboard until he hears from you."

"Oh God, no!" Tia exploded. "What are we going to do? They are bound to run into each other on the quay. This is going to ruin everything."

"Just calm down, Tia," François ordered. "This may work out better than you think."

"Dobson, tell Captain Quigley to inform his passengers that there is a quarantine on the island and they will have to stay aboard his ship for a few days. It may even be better if he anchors outside the harbor."

"Right ye are, Captain," Dobson said, holding out his hand.

"What is this going to accomplish?" Tia asked after Dobson left.

"It will give us some time, my dear."

"I'm fine, Jeremy," Ariana assured. "Please, you can put me down now," she insisted as they followed Helga into the bedroom.

"Not yet," he said, placing kisses all along her slender neck.

"Please, Jeremy, you will embarrass Helga."

Helga smiled as she turned the covers down. The young woman was good for her captain, she thought.

"Helga approves," Jeremy grinned, seeing the pleased look on his housekeeper's face. "Helga, we have missed your cooking," he said in Dutch. "I have particularly missed your conch soup. Do you think you can make some for us to have this evening?"

"Ya, ya," she said, laughing as she left the room."

"What did you say to her?" Ariana asked.

"I told her we were going to make love all afternoon and we didn't want to be bothered."

"Oh, Jeremy, you didn't! Please tell me you didn't," she begged as he laid her on the bed.

"I didn't," he laughed. "But what difference does it make? Helga knows how I feel about you."

Ariana leaned back against the pillows Helga had propped up on the bed. "I just wish . . . I mean, it's embarrassing when everyone knows . . ."

Jeremy sat on the side of the bed. "Everyone knows what, English?" he forced her to explain, even though he knew what bothered her.

"Everyone knows that I am a kept woman!" she cried out.

Jeremy's deep laughter filled the room. "Is that all that's bothering you?"

"It's no little thing, Jeremy," she pouted. "I was raised to believe a woman who gave herself to a man she wasn't married to was a . . . a whore."

"Are you trying to force a marriage proposal from me, English?" he asked, a wicked grin on his handsome face.

Ariana's eyes widened. "I meant no such thing . . . it never even crossed my mind. Just wipe that smug look off your face, Jeremy Corbett. I would never try to force you into any such thing!"

"That's good, because I don't hold up very well under pressure. Who knows, I may just break down and ask you to marry me," he teased.

Ariana stared at him angrily. "This is not a joking matter, Jeremy."

Jeremy had every intention of marrying her, but he wanted to wait until Mary and Avery returned. "Stranger things have happened, English."

"You're not making any sense, Jeremy." She

243

turned from him as her eyes filled with tears. "I'm suddenly very tired. Can we talk about all this later?"

"Of course, love. While you're resting, I'm going to check on the unloading of the ship. Kennedy will be here at the house if you should need anything. I'll be back in time to eat with you."

"I'll be fine," she sighed, closing her eyes.

When Jeremy was gone, Ariana opened her eyes and stared at the closed door. What did the future hold for them, she wondered. Would he ever marry her, or just expect to keep her as his woman until he tired of her? She wiped a tear away. It didn't really matter, she thought bitterly. She loved him and would stay with him, no matter if she were his wife or his whore.

"They say she was injured when they attacked a Spanish galleon," Dobson explained, breathing heavily from running to Tia's villa. "My friends say the governor loaned Captain Corbett a carriage to take her to Devil's Reach."

François rubbed his chin in thought. "This may be to our advantage," he mused.

"I don't see how, damn it. He'll never leave her side now," Tia fumed.

"Dobson, spread the word that the one-eyed pirate was seen anchored off one of the out islands. Be sure Corbett's crew hears of it."

"Is that all, Captain?" Dobson asked.

"Yes, for now," Saint-Gilles said, dropping some coins into Dobson's outstretched hand.

"What makes you think Jeremy will fall for that?" Tia asked when they were alone.

"He knows Salizar was in the area a few months ago. Why not again?"

"I don't know," Tia paced, "it's dangerous."

"Do you have a better idea for getting him out of our way for a while?"

"No, I suppose not. I just wonder if he'll leave her. Particularly if she's hurt."

"Corbett has been looking for this man since he was old enough to sail. I can't imagine his hatred for the Spaniard being any less just because he has a woman in his bed. If he should fail to take the bait, we'll have to come up with some other way . . . perhaps a bullet through the head."

"No! He is *not* to be hurt. I don't give a damn what you do to that English bitch, but I'll kill you if you harm Jeremy."

"What will you do when he turns on you, cherie?"

"He won't do that. If everyone keeps their mouths shut, he'll never know. And speaking of that, can we really trust Dobson?"

"Of course we can. He hates Corbett enough to do this without pay, but loyalty is always better assured if gold crosses the palm."

"I hope you're right. Jeremy has always been a good judge of character, and it worries me that he had cause to throw Dobson off his ship."

"We have other things to worry about, Tia. Right now I think you should have your men take your ship out of the harbor."

Tia turned around, her eyes blazing angrily. "What the hell are you talking about? My ship doesn't go anyplace without me."

"Think, my dear: Corbett would be quicker to leave the lady if he thought you were away from the island."

Tia couldn't argue with that. "I suppose it's true."

"Besides, if you'll do as I suggest, we can make Corbett think Lady Wellsley left him of her own accord, and we can make the lady think Jeremy had been holding her for ransom all along."

"Perfect," Tia agreed, pouring them both a drink. "To our success!" She raised her glass.

When vain desire at last, and vain regret
Go hand and hand to death, and all is vain,
What shall assuage the unforgotten pain
And teach the unforgetful to forget?

Dante Gabriel Rossetti

Chapter Eleven

Jeremy noticed the *Sea Witch* sailing out of the harbor as he headed for the quay. Perhaps he'd have some peace for a while, he thought as he passed the area where the taverns and brothels were, returning the greetings called out to him.

"I hear you was lucky again, Captain Corbett," an old seaman called out.

"It wasn't luck, my friend, it was skill," Jeremy laughed.

"Naw, it was the luck of the Irish," another laughed. "You and your father both have it."

Jeremy waved and kept on walking. *The luck of the Irish,* he thought bitterly. Corbett was Irish, but he doubted his real father was.

"Captain, have you heard?" Landers, one of his seamen shouted as he approached him.

"Heard what?" Jeremy asked.

"I was just heading to Devil's Reach to tell you." He struggled to catch his breath. "That one-eyed Spaniard has been sighted off one of the out islands."

"Where did you hear that?" Jeremy asked.

"Everyone at the Tiger's Den was talking about it, captain. They all wanted to know if you knew."

Jeremy kept walking, his mind in turmoil. "When was he sighted?"

"Day before yesterday. We might have sailed right past him, captain," Landers said as he ran to keep up with Jeremy's long stride.

"I doubt it," Jeremy said, sure he would have known if he'd been close to the Spanish bastard.

"What are you going to do, captain? Are we going out after him?"

"I don't know," Jeremy answered.

"You don't know . . . but captain, he's so close! This time we'll get him, I'm sure of it."

Black Moriah was still at the dock where she was being unloaded. Jeremy went up the gangplank shouting for Jean Paul and his

250

quartermaster, Tom Fairfax.

"Have you heard the story Landers is telling?" he asked when Jean Paul appeared.

"I've heard," he answered. "What are you going to do?"

Jeremy ran his hand through his hair in frustration. "Hell, I don't know. Damn, why did this have to happen now?"

"If I were you, I'd forget the bastard. You have more important things in your life now."

"That's easier said than done, my friend. My quest for revenge has been a part of my life for so long that I'm not sure I can put it aside."

"Then tell English what you have to do and get it over with. If you don't, it's going to be a bone of contention between you for the rest of your life."

"I know," Jeremy said pacing the deck. "Damn! I wish Mary and Avery were back. What the hell is taking them so long? They could have sailed around the world by now."

"Captain, everything is divided as ordered," Tom Fairfax interrupted. "The men are waiting to see what you want to do about going after the one-eyed pirate."

Jeremy stared out to sea as if he could see the Spaniard's ship. "Ask them to stay close tonight. I'll make a decision in the next few hours."

"Right ye are, captain. Just give us the word and we'll be ready."

"Thank you, Tom."

"I saw Tia leave a little while ago, if that's any help," Jean Paul said as they walked down the gangplank to the quay.

"I know. I saw her sailing out of the harbor. At least I don't have to worry about her for a while."

Jean Paul stopped, placing a hand on his friend's arm. "Jeremy, if you decide to go after Salizar, I'd like to go with you."

"Thanks, my friend. I would be honored to have you at my side. Listen, Helga is preparing a welcome-home dinner this evening. Why don't you join us?"

"Are you sure you want company this evening?"

"I'm sure. Besides, I'm probably going to be lousy company for English this evening. Maybe you can help."

"I'll do my best, but I'd strongly suggest you explain what is going on as soon as possible."

"Aye, I suppose I should," Jeremy agreed as they headed in the direction of Devil's Reach.

After bathing with Helga's help, Ariana slipped into a buttercup yellow gown of soft cotton, then tied back her chestnut hair with a yellow ribbon. When Helga left her alone, she took a hesitant step away from the bed, testing the strength of her leg.

"Not too bad," she mumbled to herself. It was sore, but she could put her weight on it.

Hearing Jeremy's voice, she quickly sat back on the bed and waited for him to come to her. After a few minutes she decided he wasn't coming so she'd go to him. Hobbling across the room, she opened the door and called out, but no one answered.

"Where is everybody?" she shouted as she slowly made her way down the hall.

"Ariana, what are you doing out of bed?" Jean Paul asked as he took her arm and helped her to the veranda.

"I thought I heard Jeremy."

"You did. He decided to take a swim before dinner."

Ariana looked out over the veranda and could see Jeremy swimming offshore. "Something is bothering him."

"I'm afraid you're right. It seems Salizar, the Spaniard who killed his father, was spotted in the area."

Ariana's fingers gripped the stone wall. "And Jeremy is torn between taking care of me and going after his father's murderer."

"You're very perceptive. But you must understand that Jeremy has been driven by his desire for revenge since he was a small boy. It isn't something he can easily set aside."

"Will he be in great danger?" Ariana asked.

"It is possible."

"But you still don't think I should try to discourage him. . . ."

"To be honest, I think you would do your relationship great harm if you did, but I wouldn't blame you for trying."

"Thank you for your honesty, Jean Paul." Ariana noticed that Jeremy was heading back toward the house. "Let's keep this conversation between ourselves. I'd rather give Jeremy the opportunity to tell me what he's going to do."

"Of course. Perhaps I shouldn't stay this evening."

"No, please stay. Jeremy is going to need his friends around him tonight."

He strode quickly toward the house, his head down as if he had the weight of the world on his shoulders. Ariana's heart went out to him, but she knew this was a decision he was going to have to make.

He looked surprised to see her when he reached the house. "Hello, love. I didn't realize you were up," he said, kissing her. "Did Jean Paul carry you out here?"

"No, she didn't give me the chance," Jean

Paul answered. "She walked out here on her own."

"English, you're suppose to be off that leg," he reprimanded her.

"I'm fine, Jeremy. It doesn't even hurt now."

"I'm glad to hear that," he smiled at her, but she could tell he was preoccupied. "Give me a few minutes to get cleaned up," he said as he headed for the door.

They were both silent for a long moment, staring at the door Jeremy had disappeared through. "I could go with him," she finally said. "That would solve his problem, wouldn't it?"

"I don't think he'd hear of it," Jean Paul shook his head, "Particularly after you were hurt on this past trip."

"I suppose you're right," she sighed. "Well, I'm a big girl. I can take care of myself."

Jean Paul thought of Tia and wondered how Ariana would fare against such a devious and dangerous opponent. Well, at least she was out of the way for the time being.

"Did the gold get divided among the crew?" she asked, trying to keep her mind off Jeremy.

"Yes. I suppose they are all in town spending it at this very moment," Jean Paul laughed. "My crew will be furious when they learn I was in on the capture and shared in the prize."

"I wondered about that," Ariana said. "Where is your ship?"

"I'm afraid she was a casualty of the same storm that almost took your life. We limped back into port, but the damage was extensive. They are having to practically rebuild her, and work here on the island moves at a snail's pace."

"Can't your crew help with repairs?"

Jean Paul laughed. "Pirates don't want to do physical labor. That's why most of them are pirates . . . all they want is the gold and plunder."

"You sound disillusioned."

"I suppose I am. I'm tired of having no purpose in life. Enough about my boring existence," he laughed. "Would you like a glass of wine? This is a concoction Kennedy made up with fruits and berries in it."

"Yes, I'd love to try some of it. It sounds refreshing."

"But she prefers Irish whiskey," Jeremy said as he joined them.

"Oh please, don't even mention that stuff," Ariana said, holding her head.

"I thought you learned to like it," Jeremy teased. "You were begging for it by the time we reached port."

"I was not myself, and it's very ungallant of you to mention such a thing." She pretended to be insulted.

"You're right, English, and I am sorry. I promise I shall make it up to you," he winked.

He was trying too hard to be cheerful, she thought silently. She just wished he would bring it up and tell her what he was going to do. His tension was almost a visible thing, showing itself in nervous motions that he didn't usually have.

"Where is Helga with dinner?" he asked, drumming his fingers on the table. "I'm starved."

"I'll check on her," Jean Paul volunteered, meeting Ariana's eyes.

Jeremy didn't miss the look that passed between the two of them. "I suppose he told you what has occurred? The bastard has been seen in these waters again."

"Yes," she answered. Seeing the look of pain in Jeremy's eyes, she knew she could not dissuade him. He had witnessed his father's death at the hands of this Spaniard, and if he didn't have his revenge, it would destroy him—or at the least, destroy their relationship, because she would be the reason he'd put it aside.

"I don't know why it's a problem, Jeremy. You've been looking for this man all your life. Why should anything be different now?"

"You're what makes it different," he answered impatiently. "Your safety is my concern now."

"Jeremy, you saved me from drowning at sea. That does not mean you have to hover over me for the rest of my life. Do what you have to do and get it over with."

"Damn it, you don't understand, English. I can't just leave you here unprotected."

"Then I'll go with you."

"No! Not this time, or the next," he answered tersely.

"You're being unreasonable. Is your anger supposed to make it easier for you to go? Fine, then strike out at me if it helps."

"I'm sorry, English," he said, holding his head in his hands. "I'm driven to seek my revenge, yet I'm putting everything that we have in jeopardy." He looked up at her, his eyes filled with turmoil. "I have to risk it all to be able to live with myself. Do you understand that, English? I swore to my father when he was dying that I'd kill the bastard that did it. If I fail when I have the chance, then I'll be worthless to you and to myself. Take honor from me and my life is done."

Ariana forced a smile and wrapped her arms around his shoulders. "I understand, Jeremy. If this is what you must do, then do it and come back to me quickly."

Jeremy pulled her into his lap. "I should

have known you would understand."

"Yes, you should have."

"I'll have to sail at dawn. . . ."

"Then we shall have to make the best of our time until then," she smiled seductively.

Jeremy raised one dark eyebrow. "Are you telling me that you would be able to . . . to. . . ."

"Are you getting coy on me, Jeremy Corbett?" she laughed. "Of course, I'm telling you I want to make love with you."

"I think that's my cue to leave," Jean Paul said as he rejoined them.

"No, stay for dinner, Jean Paul," Ariana pleaded. "Jeremy and I will have time together later."

"If you are sure."

"We're positive," Jeremy assured him. "Besides, after dinner I would like you to round up my crew and tell them we will be sailing at dawn."

"It will be my pleasure, mon ami."

The feasted on conch soup, oysters, and baked chicken. Over the meal they discussed who should be left behind at Devil's Reach to watch over English. Jeremy decided he'd feel safer with Kennedy guarding her, and Kennedy was quick to agree.

"You sound as if you're tired of going to sea," Jean Paul laughed.

"Aye, I am a bit, captain. My family has grown up and I've hardly had any time to spend with them."

"He has been talking about retiring," Jeremy commented, "and he certainly deserves to. He was with Avery for many years before he joined me."

"What will you do, Kennedy?" Ariana asked.

"Fish, and just lie around the beach watching my children," he said as he picked up the dishes.

"That sounds wonderful," she smiled.

"Kennedy doesn't have any financial worries," Jeremy mentioned. "He has more gold saved than any of us."

"Not true, sir," he said as he headed for the door. "But I have enough to live comfortably for a long time," he threw over his shoulder with a hint of laughter.

"I must be on my way," Jean Paul announced. "I have a lot to do if I'm sailing with you."

"I'll see you at the ship in the morning," Jeremy said.

Jean Paul leaned over and kissed Ariana on the cheek. "Take care of yourself, English, and I'll take care of this lovesick fellow for you."

"Thank you, Jean Paul," she said, squeezing his hand. "I shall miss both of you."

"Don't forget, one of these days you're going to introduce me to that beautiful sister," he teased.

"I won't forget," she promised.

Ariana and Jeremy sat on the veranda holding hands and sipping brandy while Kennedy and Helga finished up in the house. After a while, it became very quite.

"Good night, sir, m'lady," Kennedy said from the doorway. "I'm going to walk Helga home. I'll be back before you leave in the morning."

"Thank you, Kennedy."

"Good night, Kennedy," Ariana smiled.

Jeremy stood up and stretched. "Dawn will come early. I suppose I should get some sleep."

"You will have to sleep when you're on your ship, Captain Corbett. I have other plans for you tonight."

He gazed at her, a mischievous grin on his handsome face. "Am I to understand, English, that you have need of my body?"

She really felt like crying and begging him not to go, but she knew that that would only make him feel worse. Instead she decided to try to lift both their spirits. "That is exactly what I had in mind, my handsome pirate, and well you know it."

"Yes," he said pulling her gently to her feet,

"but I do enjoy hearing you admit it, and it's also nice to be pursued."

"So you want to be pursued," she smiled wickedly. "Come with me, said the spider to the fly."

"Not a black widow spider, I hope," he laughed deeply, following her into the house. "Don't you want a cup of tea or something before you turn in?" he teased.

"I want nothing but your body, Captain Corbett," she said, leading him to the bedroom.

"Do you wish me to carry you to our room?" he asked, aware of her slight limp.

"How can I be the pursuer if you're carrying me?" she protested.

"I just hope I can perform under this pressure," he grinned in the darkness.

"I have no doubt that you will be able to," she said, amused. Leaning over, she removed the knife he carried in a sheath in his boot. "But if I should have to use force, I will," she said, brandishing the silver blade.

"I am quaking in my boots, English. This is a side of you I've never seen," he said, trying to keep from laughing.

"You're always telling me how when you see something you want, you go after it. Well, so do I."

"It's an admirable quality," he chuckled,

"one I heartily recommend."

"I thought you would. Now take off your clothes."

He laughed deep in his throat. "Take off my clothes?" he repeated.

"That's right, captain. Take everything off."

He shrugged. "Very well." He lifted his shirt over his head and tossed it on the floor.

"Hurry up," she ordered. "I wouldn't want to have to cut those breeches off you," she threatened, remembering his words about her dress before he destroyed it.

"I shouldn't want you to have to do that either," he retorted. "A slip of a knife in the wrong place can be very dangerous, and I do recall you threatened to make me a eunuch once before."

"It would be to your benefit to keep that in mind, captain," she warned with laughter in her voice.

Jeremy sat on the side of the bed and removed his boots. Then slowly he stood up and pushed his breeches down. Her eyes followed the downward movement of his pants until his pulsating member was exposed. Her heart was racing and her hand trembled.

"Do you approve, m'lady?" he asked, his voice deep with desire.

She had to take a deep breath before she could answer. "I approve," she said huskily.

"I was hoping you would. Now, how about your clothes. . . ?"

"All in good time, captain."

"English," he growled. "This is what every man dreams of, but I'm only human, and I'd hate to accidently feel that blade."

Ariana looked down at the knife blade she forgot she held. Tossing it across the room, she moved to stand in front of Jeremy. "No, don't touch me," she ordered. "I want to inspect the goods first."

"The goods?" he laughed in disbelief.

She ran her hands over his hard shoulders and down his muscular arms. "Very nice," she whispered.

"Thank you, m'lady."

Wrapping her arms around his waist, she moved her hands up his back and then down over his buttocks. "Oh yes, very nice," she moaned, wondering how much longer she could carry out this charade.

"Enough," Jeremy exploded. "I am not made of stone, my love. Now I suggest you remove your clothes before I throw you on the floor and take you with your skirt pulled up over your head."

"You wouldn't," she laughed.

"Don't tempt me," he growled.

"But my leg," she whimpered.

"You haven't thought about that leg for the

264

past fifteen minutes," he replied, "but granted, it would be easier on you if we were in bed. So undress!"

"I suppose it is only fair," she said, removing her hair ribbon to let her chestnut tresses fall free. "Would you unbutton me, captain?" she purred.

"You do put a man to the test, my love. Do you have any idea how much willpower I'm exerting here?"

"Why, whatever do you mean, captain?" She pretended innocence.

"You know damn well what I mean," he growled, finishing the last of the buttons with unsteady fingers.

Ariana smiled sweetly as she slipped one strap of her chemise off her shoulder, then slowly ran her finger across the top of the lacy material.

"Why the hell did I ever give in to the underwear?" he swore.

Dropping the other strap, she slowly stepped out of the undergarment. "Is that better, captain?" she asked, one finger placed coyly to her mouth.

"Woman," he moaned, picking her up. "I have created a monster," he laughed as he laid her on the bed.

"Come to me, love," she said holding out her arms. "Make this night last forever."

"It will certainly be one that haunts me when I'm away from you," he confessed as he lay beside her.

"You will never be out of my thoughts," she whispered, placing kisses along his neck and shoulders.

His lips grazed her breasts, teasing the already taut nipples, as her desire grew almost unbearable.

"Jeremy," she moaned, "Please, I can't bear another moment. Enter me now. . . ."

"My thoughts exactly," he laughed softly as he knelt above her. "Look at me, English," he ordered gently, entwining his fingers in hers above her head. "I love you," he whispered hoarsely.

Both were engulfed by the searing flames of desire. Ariana went rigid beneath him as an exquisite shattering explosion consumed her. She felt his body tense and his breath catch as he spilled his seed deep inside her.

Afterwards there were no words between them. They clung to each other, the reality of his impending journey again on both their minds.

Doubt is brother-devil to Despair.

John Boyle O'Reilly

Chapter Twelve

At dawn Ariana stood on the veranda, the spyglass to her eye as she waited to catch a glimpse of the *Black Moriah*. Kennedy poured her a cup of tea, then watched through his own spyglass.

"Anytime now you should be able to see them," he commented.

Ariana saw the black topsail as the ship sailed out of the cove of New Providence harbor. "There it is," she exclaimed as the rest of the black sails came into full view.

There was something strange and eerie

about the ship in the early morning light. It seemed to hang there between the sea and the sky. Ariana shivered suddenly, an ominous feeling settling over her. "She looks like a ghost ship," she whispered.

"Aye, that she does," Kennedy agreed. "Let's hope she puts that same fear into the Spaniard."

When the ship was but a speck on the ocean, Ariana sat at the small table on the veranda and reread the note that Jeremy had left. It said that no matter what happened, his time with her had been the best in his life. He would live to regret this nondescript message.

"There is something else, m'lady," Kennedy said as he laid a small silver pistol in front of her. "The captain wanted you to have this. He said it was for your protection and to keep it loaded at all times."

"I can't imagine having to use it," Ariana said, admiring the pistol, "but I will do as he asks."

"I'll get your breakfast now, m'lady."

"I'm not really hungry, Kennedy. I believe the tea will be all I'll want this morning."

"Very well, m'lady. Will there be anything else?"

"Why don't you sit with me for a few minutes?"

"Of course, m'lady." Kennedy looked uneasy

but did as she requested.

"If you are going to be my companion until Jeremy returns, we should get to know each other better. Jeremy mentioned that you had been with his father before sailing with him."

"I sailed with Captain Avery Corbett for nearly fifteen years, m'lady."

"Were you with him when he found Jeremy?" she asked.

"Aye, it was a terrible thing that Spanish bastard did to those people, and that poor little boy witnessed it all."

"He was lucky to have had Avery and Mary to help him get through those early years," Ariana commented.

"Aye, they were all lucky. Mary Corbett couldn't have children, and they both wanted a child terribly. Jeremy filled that void for them."

"I look forward to meeting them." Ariana smiled. "They must be very special people."

"Aye, they're good people," Kennedy agreed, fidgeting in his chair.

Ariana felt sorry for him, knowing he was very uneasy with his new responsibility. "Kennedy, I know Jeremy left you to watch over me, but you needn't worry about me. I won't be leaving Devil's Reach, so you can relax. Go visit with your family if you'd like."

"Oh no, I couldn't do that. Captain Corbett

271

trusted me to stay right here."

"Then perhaps you would like to bring your family here. You and I will both be more comfortable if we're not in each other's way all the time."

"I understand," Kennedy agreed, "but I have my orders from Captain Corbett."

"I think I will lie down for a little while," Ariana said, having gotten very little sleep during the night.

"Very good, m'lady." He pulled her chair back. "I will have Helga prepare you a hearty noon meal, since you ate no breakfast."

"Not too hearty," Ariana laughed. "I wouldn't want Jeremy to come back and find me pleasingly plump."

"I cannot imagine that," Kennedy smiled politely.

Mid-morning, in the harbor of New Providence, François Saint-Gilles boarded the *Dove* and introduced himself to Ariana's family as Captain Jean Paul Moreau.

"I apologize for the condition of our little village." He bowed over Lady Denise Wellsley's hand. "I decided that perhaps it would be safer if our transaction was made aboard the ship. That way you will not be exposed to the fever."

"Where is my daughter?" Lord Wellsley demanded.

"And where is this Black Moriah bastard?" Brett Leighton stepped in.

"Now, please, let us act like gentlemen," François said, pulling a lace handkerchief from his sleeve and mopping his brow. "I have been sent as an emissary for the Black Moriah. As soon as I collect the ransom money, I shall go immediately to Devil's Reach for your daughter."

"How do we know we can trust you?" Lord Wellsley asked, his face red with anger.

"You have come a long way on that trust, sir. I suggest you continue to show your faith and you shall have your daughter safe and sound by this afternoon."

"Is she well?" Lady Wellsley asked, still unable to believe that her daughter was alive after all these months.

"She is quite well." He patted her hand. "You shall see for yourself soon. Her host has taken very good care of her. As a matter of fact, he became so fond of her that he considered not asking for ransom and just keeping her for himself, yet then he knew he would tire of her sooner or later, as he does all the hostages he holds."

Brett grabbed François by the shirt front. "If she's been harmed. . . ."

273

"Now, sir, there is no reason to take offense with me . . . I am just a messenger here. But you must understand that your daughter has been living with the Black Moriah. It would be cruel of me to tell you that she is the same innocent you knew in England."

"That damned bastard," Brett swore, shoving François against the rail of the ship. "I want you to take me to him. We have a matter of honor to settle."

"Stop it, Brett," Lady Wellsley cried. "It doesn't matter what Ariana has been through. I just want my daughter returned to us."

"And you shall have her, if this unruly fellow will contain himself," François said, brushing himself off.

"Brett, perhaps it would be better if I handled this alone," Lord Wellsley suggested. "Why don't you take Denise below?"

When they were alone, Lord Wellsley turned to François. "I am not afraid of this plague you have on the island, Captain Moreau. If you expect to see any of this money, then I suggest you take me to my daughter now. The money will stay in my possession until we arrive at this Devil's Reach place."

"I can see I'm dealing with a very wise and careful man," François said.

"Yes, you are, Captain Moreau, and let me warn you: if you cross me, I'll return and

274

blow this whole damned island off the map. Do you understand me?"

"I understand perfectly, Lord Wellsley, and I must say it's good doing business with a man who gets right to the point. Now, if you don't mind, I'd like to at least see the money. . . ."

When Ariana woke from her nap, she was surprised to find she was alone in the house. She decided Kennedy must have taken her suggestion and had gone to get his family. She was peeling an orange when she heard movement behind her. She turned around with a start, dropping the orange, she had just peeled.

"Didn't mean to startle you," a scruffy-looking seaman said, standing inside the door with his hat in his hand. "My name is Dobson. I sail with Captain Corbett, but I wasn't in the village when he and Captain Bouché sailed this morning. I just wondered if you knew when they'd be returning?"

"Captain Bouché?" Ariana repeated. "You must mean Captain Moreau," she corrected.

"Him too," Dobson said. "I suppose it seems strange to you that two men should share the same woman, but in a place like this the men outnumber the woman, so it isn't unusual."

Ariana stared at him, trying to digest what he was saying. "Do you mean that Tia Bouché sailed with Captain Corbett this morning?"

"Aye. She's his lady, you know. She's sailed with us before. The two of them is quite a pair," he laughed. "Damn, what bad luck not to have been there this morning. I understand they were going after the one-eyed pirate."

Ariana was having trouble breathing. She was feeling anger, blind, unreasoning anger. "Have you seen Kennedy?" she asked, storming past the seaman.

"No, ma'am. Didn't he go with the captain?"

"Find me Kennedy!" she screamed.

Dobson looked surprised at her outburst. "Yes, ma'am, I'll try," he said, backing out of the room.

It wasn't possible, she kept telling herself. He wouldn't have taken Tia . . . she had to calm down and think this out . . . Kennedy would tell her the truth. He would tell her that Dobson had been mistaken.

"Kennedy," she screamed. "Helga. . . . Damn it, where is everybody?"

Ariana ran from room to room shouting for Kennedy. Oh God, where is he, she thought. She leaned her head against the bedroom door as tears streamed down her face. It wasn't like him to leave her alone, even if she had sug-

276

gested it. She took a deep breath, determined to find him and straighten out this whole matter. Hearing a knock at the door, she ran to answer it. "Kennedy, where have you been?" she shouted as she flung the door open.

Her eyes widened in shock and her knees turned to jelly as she clung to the massive door. "Father," she whispered. "Oh God, it really is you," she cried, throwing her arms around his neck. "It's you," she sobbed. "I didn't think I'd ever see you again."

William Wellsley was surprised to find her in a pale yellow muslin dress, looking so fit and tanned. "I know." He stroked her hair. "I can't believe I'm standing here with you, either. God, your mother is going to be so happy!"

"Is she with you? Is she well? Is Lanie all right? It was just recently that I heard they made it back to England. . . ."

"They are both well, and now you are. . . ." he laughed with relief. "Your mother wouldn't let me come without her, but Lanie is still in London. Brett is with us, though. That poor man has been so concerned."

"Brett . . . he's here on the island? Send for them, Father. They must come to Devil's Reach so I can explain everything. You see, things have changed . . . I can't marry Brett," she rambled on, close to hysteria.

277

"We can talk about that later," her father assured her as he led her into the house. "You just can't imagine how relieved I am to see you. My Lord, girl, do you realize we thought you were dead until we got the ransom note?"

"I know, I was so worried about mother and Lanie. . . ." Suddenly she pulled away from his embrace. "The ransom note?" she repeated in a choked voice.

"We need to get to the ship as soon as possible. Your mother will be going out of her mind until she sees you. She wanted to come with me, but this Moreau fellow thought it better if they weren't exposed to the fever epidemic in the village."

She stared at him, hearing his words, but nothing made any sense. Jean Paul . . . fever epidemic. "I don't understand any of this," she screamed, clenching her fist to her side. "You said ransom note? What are you talking about? I wasn't held for ransom," she insisted, praying her father would agree with her.

"My dear, I know this has been a harrowing time for you," he said sympathetically, "but everything is going to be all right as soon as we get away from this place and back to England. Now go get whatever you want to take with you and let's get off this island."

"No, Father! Not until I know what you're talking about."

William Wellsley knew his daughter must have suffered at the hands of this blackguard pirate who held her for ransom, but he was now wondering if she'd lost her mind as well. He took her hands in his and patiently tried to explain. "My dear, we received a ransom note from this pirate who calls himself the Black Moriah."

"Did you see him, Father? Did you talk to him?" she asked, tears running down her face.

"No, dear, I didn't talk with him. He sent this fellow named Jean Paul Moreau to do his dirty work. Mr. Moreau collected the money and brought me here to get you. I'm afraid that's all I can tell you."

"No!" she screamed. "This can't be! Somebody has made a mistake. He wouldn't do this to me . . . I know he wouldn't . . . he loved me. . . ." she sobbed hysterically.

William Wellsley stared at his daughter, a look of confusion on his face. He had a sick feeling in the pit of his stomach as her words registered and he realized his daughter apparently cared for the man who had held her prisoner. "Ariana, I'm sorry if this is hard to understand. I don't know what has happened here, and I don't want to know right now. We must get out of here and back to the ship before this pirate changes his mind about letting us leave."

279

Ariana stared at him, her eyes glazed with pain. "Jean Paul ... did he have a French accent?" she asked, still looking for a flaw in his story.

"Yes, dear. A very thick French accent. I would say he had been a gentleman at one time."

Ariana shook her head. "Kennedy ... that's why Kennedy disappeared. He was only guarding me until you came ... Oh God, the note ... the note said if anything happened ... why Jeremy?" she sobbed. "Why did you do it?"

Wellsley put his arm around his daughter's shoulder and led her to the door. "It's going to be all right, Ariana. Your mother will know what to do for you," he assured.

"Wait," she suddenly froze. "I have to get something." She rushed back into the house and moments later came out carrying the silver pistol, and the Spanish fan.

"My dear, you won't have any need of that. . . ."

"They are mine," she said sharply, "they are all I have and I'm taking them with me."

There was a tearful reunion at the ship with her mother, but Ariana could not bring herself even to acknowledge Brett's presence.

Once in the safety of her cabin, she collapsed tearfully in her mother's arms.

"Do you want to talk about it, dear?" Denise asked, stroking her daughter's hair.

"I can't . . . not yet. . . ." She sobbed. "I thought he loved me, Mother. . . ."

"I know, dear. Try to calm down now," her mother said, placing a damp cloth to Ariana's forehead. "We will talk later when you're not so upset."

"He saved my life . . . was so wonderful . . . I don't understand how he could do this . . . he said we'd be together . . . start a new life in the Carolinas . . . there was this sea witch . . . she was the one . . . it had to be her."

Tears ran down Denise's face as she listened to her daughter ramble on. "Please rest, Ariana," she pleaded. "Things will look better once we're home."

"What the hell is going on, William? She didn't even acknowledge that I was here," Brett said angrily.

"Just give her time, Brett. She's been through a terrible ordeal."

"It wasn't quite the reunion I had imagined," he continued to rant. "I thought she'd at least be glad to see me."

"My God, have some feelings for her," William snapped. "I don't think she was even aware of where she was, or who was around her. It's going to take time."

"Of course, William," Brett answered. "I apologize for my behavior. I knew it wouldn't be the same, but I suppose I was just shocked that she wasn't happy to see me."

"She has calmed down a bit," Denise said as she joined the two men. "The ship's surgeon had laudanum aboard, and he's given her a strong dose. I'll just be so glad when we're back in England," she shivered.

"I'll go see why it's taking so long to get under sail," Brett said. "Captain Quigley said we'd be sailing as soon as Ariana was aboard."

Denise and William Wellsley stood staring at each other when they were alone. "It's a different situation than we'd expected, William."

"I had assumed that. Has she said anything?"

"She keeps saying that she thought he loved her," Denise whispered, her eyes filling with tears again. "Oh, William, what do you think has been going on here?"

"I have no idea, but if I could get my hands on this Black Moriah, I'd ring his neck."

"How could Ariana fall in love with a . . .

282

a pirate?" she asked, a stricken look on her lovely face.

William put his arm around his wife's shoulder and led her toward the rail. "Perhaps it was the only way she could deal with the situation, dear. We can only guess at what she has been through, but we know this man has used her."

"Oh, William, I can't bear the thought of it!" Denise cried. "If only we hadn't been separated," she sobbed, leaning her head against her husband's strong shoulder. "If only we hadn't been shipwrecked. . . ."

"You can't brood about his, Denise. We all have to be patient and understanding with Ariana. She has never needed us more than now. We have to make her see that her life isn't over and that she can pick up the pieces once we reach England."

"I know, William . . . I know, but I'm so afraid. It's almost as if she's a stranger."

Ariana opened her eyes. There was movement . . . she was on a ship. She tried to sit up, but everything began to spin. She fell back against the pillows. It must have been a bad dream, she thought wildly. She was still on the *Black Moriah* with Jeremy. Her head was spinning. What was wrong with her? Why did everything seem so disjointed? This wasn't Jeremy's beautiful cabin. . . .

"Jeremy!" she cried out. My God, had that been her slurred voice? she wondered. Damn, she wished the cabin would stop spinning. If she could just get up and get some fresh air. . . .

Somehow she managed to stumble to the cabin door. Fumbling with the knob, she finally opened it, but once in the companionway, she was exhausted from her efforts and had to lean against the wall for support. "Jeremy!" she called again, "Oh God, why won't you answer me?" she sobbed.

"Ariana, what are you doing out here?" a stern male voice asked.

She tried to focus on him. He had called her "Ariana" . . . Jeremy wouldn't call her Ariana . . . her name was "English". . . .

"I suggest you go back in your cabin, my dear. You wouldn't want to fall overboard in your condition."

"Who are you?"

"I'm your loving fiancé," he answered, his voice cold and unsympathetic.

"Brett—"

"Yes, my dear. I'm surprised you remembered my name."

"I'm sorry, Brett. I don't know why I can't think straight. Where are we?"

"You are on the good ship *Dove* sailing back toward England and home."

"Where is my mother?" she asked, feeling weaker by the moment. "Is she all right?"

"Of course she is. If you will return to your cabin, I'll go find her for you," he volunteered.

"Thank you," she said, hesitantly moving away from the wall that held her up. "Brett, what is wrong with me?" she asked, tears running down her face. "I can't seem to make my legs move."

At the sight of her tears he softened. Picking her up, he carried her back inside the cabin. "The ship's surgeon gave you something to help your nerves. Apparently he gave you too strong a dose."

"I don't need anything," she said, lying back against the pillows. "All I need is. . . ."

"Yes," Brett said, his eyes hard and cold. "What, or should I say who, is it you think you need, Ariana?"

"I can't think," she whimpered.

"What did he do to you, Ariana? Tell me! I want to know what hold that bastard has over you. I will kill him, I swear it!"

"I don't know who you're talking about," she lied. "Please, just let me sleep. I'm so tired."

"You won't be able to escape into this

laudanam-induced stupor forever, Ariana. Before we reach England I want to know what happened to you on that island. I deserve to know what I'm getting," he said angrily.

"I release you from your obligation to marry me," she whispered. "I can't marry you ... I'm going to marry ... no, I forgot, he doesn't want to marry me anymore...."

"Ariana, what are you talking about?" Brett asked. He shook her when she didn't answer, but realized that she was in a dead sleep again. He spoke nonetheless.

"I will have my answers sooner or later, Ariana. I don't intend to be made the laughingstock of London—no matter how much I desire you."

For everything you win
There is something lost.

Unknown

Chapter Thirteen

They had been searching for four days, and still there was no sign of the Spaniard's ship. Jeremy impatiently paced the deck, his hard gray eyes scanning the horizon as the red glow of the setting sun reflected off the water.

"Where the hell is he?" he shouted to no one in particular. "Another day is ending and we still haven't sighted him."

"Do you want to turn back?" Jean Paul asked.

"No! Not yet," Jeremy answered in angry frustration. "Damn it, Jean Paul, if I don't find him this time I may never find him. I can't spend the rest of my life in limbo waiting to have my revenge."

"I understand, mon ami, and of course things have changed recently for you. There is something more important now, eh?"

Jeremy laughed. "I can't bear another sermon about how you wouldn't have left English if she were your woman."

"I was just telling you how I feel," Jean Paul said.

"If this weren't so damned important to me. . . ."

"I understand, mon ami. I'm sure if this Salizar had killed my father, I too would be seeking my revenge."

"Sail ho!" a loud shout rang out from the ship's rigging.

"Where away?" Jeremy shouted back.

"Dead ahead," the seaman in the rigging replied.

"What flag does she fly?" Jeremy asked.

"No flag, captain."

Jeremy picked up the brigantine through his spyglass. "I have a feeling my search is finally over, Jean Paul. I can feel it in my bones."

"I hope you are right, mon ami."

"Full sail," Jeremy shouted, the excitement in his voice transfering itself to his crew.

They gained on the ship minute by minute, each seaman at his assigned post.

When they were broadside he could see the captain standing on the deck. Even though Tia's story had been a ruse, as Fate would have it, Jeremy had found his one-eyed pirate.He was naked to the waist, his barrel chest covered with black hair.

Jeremy's heart was pounding and he could feel the blood pulsing through his veins. After all these years he was going to come face to face with the murdering bastard who had killed his father and the crew of the *Heron*.

He cupped his hands to his mouth and shouted, "Salizar, we have a matter to settle."

The Spaniard smiled a toothless grin, confident that his ship was in no danger. "So you're the Black Moriah. I've heard you were looking for me, but why, señor? We have never met." His hand went to his cutlass as Jeremy's men threw grappling hooks over the rail of the Spanish ship.

"What are you doing, señor? We have no wish to fight you," the Spaniard shouted angrily.

Jeremy was the first to land on the deck of Salizar's ship. Brazenly he unsheathed his cutlass. "My fight is with you, Salizar. Shall we settle this between us and leave our crews out of it?"

"You must tell me why you wish to die," Salizar said, an evil glint in his black eyes.

"Twenty-two years ago you boarded an English ship and killed everyone on board — everyone except me. I watched you murder my father, Salizar, and I swore that one day we would meet and I'd have my revenge."

"I regret that I overlooked you," Salizar snarled, "but then you must have been a child. . . ."

"Aye, I was a child, and you thought you had killed me. You left me on a burning ship, you bastard," Jeremy said, circling the pirate like a wild animal ready to pounce. "Do you remember that black day, Salizar?"

"I have had many such days," Salizar laughed. "Why should I remember such an insignificant incident? Come, you make too much of this," he laughed uneasily. "I have admired your work, Señor Black Moriah. You have spirit and gall. I like that in a man. I do not wish to kill you."

"But I wish to kill you," Jeremy snarled. "What do you say, Salizar? Shall we keep this between us? It's up to you. My men would like nothing better than to send your ship and crew to the bottom of the ocean."

Salizar glanced around at his crew, now already surrounded by the seamen from the *Black Moriah*. "Stay out of it," he shouted in Spanish. "This is between this young fool and myself." Then he laughed diabolically. "After I

292

kill him you can do whatever you wish to his seamen."

"I am going to cut you into little pieces," Jeremy warned. He quickly maneuvered Salizar around so the setting sun was in his eyes. The cutlass became like a living thing in his hand, flicking at the pirate's bare skin like a viper's tongue. In less than five minutes, blood was dripping from a dozen shallow cuts on Salizar's upper body and arms. "You cut my father open from the back of his neck to his spine, Salizar. Your death won't be as quick."

"I am an old man, Señor Black Moriah. I'm afraid I'm a little slower than I used to be."

"The captain of the *Heron* showed you a white flag and asked for quarter," Jeremy snarled. "You cut him down savagely."

Salizar's cutlass flashed in the dying sunlight, forcing Jeremy to step backward, but the tip of it caught him along the jawline, drawing a thin trail of blood. "I believe I do remember the *Heron,*" he said in a ragged gasp. "You leaped upon me after I killed this man you called Father. Ah, yes, I do remember: your Father tried to fight me," he laughed, slashing out at Jeremy as he taunted.

The sharp-edged blade whistled past Jeremy's left ear, cutting a glancing blow to his shoulder. "Perhaps I am not too old after all," he said, regaining some of his confidence.

Jeremy renewed his effort, thrusting and parrying, leaving his mark on the Spaniard with every advance. Salizar's face was red and he was breathing hard as he tried to avoid each thrust and slash of Jeremy's cutlass. Salizar moved backward against the rail, tarrying the cutlass as Jeremy moved in for the kill: he swung the cutlass up and across the pirate's chest, opening a gash from shoulder to shoulder.

"Did you think you were going to die just then, Salizar?" he asked, his cold, gray eyes deadly. Hate siezed him, choking off all reason. "I want you to pray for death, you bastard," he said, raising the cutlass to slash an ugly wound in the pirate's thigh, then another to his upper arm.

Salizar stumbled around, no longer able to lift his cutlass and defend himself. "I should have killed you on the *Heron*," he said between gritted teeth. "It mattered not to me that you were a child."

There was a mumble of voices behind Jeremy as the onlookers circled the two opponents. "Jeremy, finish him!" he heard Jean Paul's voice. "Your father would not want you to stoop as low as this bastard."

He had become an animal, he realized as he still circled his prey. He had waited so long for his revenge. "Damn you to hell," he growled, running Salizar through with a final thrust.

"Sweet Jesus," someone exclaimed, then there was a cheer from his crew and Jean Paul was there, clasping him in a bear hug.

"It's over, mon ami. You've had your revenge," Jean Paul shouted.

Laughter and tears mingled with Jeremy's feelings of elation. He had avenged his father's death. He could put it to rest now and get on with his life.

"Come, let's get back to the *Black Moriah*," Jean Paul urged. "You have wounds that need tending."

The Spanish crew stood silently as the members of Jeremy's crew went back to their own ship. "Tell your people they have seen the last of the *Black Moriah*," Jeremy said before swinging back to the deck of his ship.

They cast off from the Spanish ship, the sails filling with the evening wind. Jeremy leaned against the rail, watching the ship become smaller as the distance widened between them. Salizar was dead, he thought with satisfaction; it was finally over. Suddenly he was tired and hurt all over. All he wanted to do was get to his cabin and have a good stiff drink and lie down.

It was several days before they reached the harbor of New Providence. As they approached the mooring, Jeremy spotted Avery's ship sailing into the harbor from the opposite direction.

"Get ready to be my best man," he shouted, practically swinging Jean Paul off his feet. "There's going to be the biggest wedding this island has ever seen."

Jeremy couldn't wait for Mary and Avery to reach shore. He borrowed a longboat and rowed out to where they had anchored.

"Where the hell have you been?" he shouted, grabbing Avery in a bear hug from behind.

Avery laughed, returning his son's embrace. "How is everything?"

"It couldn't be better, but I want to tell you and Mary about that together."

"Oh-oh, what have you done now?" Avery laughed. "I notice a new scar on that handsome face."

"It's nothing," Jeremy said, touching the wound, "and believe me, it was worth it."

"Jeremy!" Mary exclaimed as she came up on deck. "Oh, it's so good to see you."

Jeremy swung her up in his arms and kissed her. "It's good to see you too, Mother. I thought you had decided not to come back to

New Providence."

"Your mother has been worried about you," Avery commented. "She's had a feeling ever since we left here that something was wrong."

"And I see my fears weren't unwarranted," she said, touching the new scar on his cheekbone. "Things haven't been going well, have they?"

"On the contrary, Mother, everything is perfect. I'm going to get married."

"Married," Mary repeated, the thought of Tia Bouché as her daughter-in-law was too much to bear.

"That's right. You haven't met her, but you did see her."

A big smile broke out on Mary's face. "It isn't Tia?"

"Please, Mother, give me credit for having some sense," Jeremy laughed. "I'm going to marry English."

He laughed at the puzzled look on both their faces. "The girl I fished out of the sea. She's the most beautiful, most sensitive woman I've ever met. Her real name is Lady Ariana Wellsley, but you'd never know she's from London aristocracy. She's sweet and down to earth."

"It seems a lot has happened while we were away," Avery laughed.

"It has," Jeremy agreed. "I'm head-over-heels in love, and you're going to adore her, too.

"I'm sure I will," Mary said, hugging her son.

"There is something else," Jeremy said. "My search for Salizar is over; I killed him several days ago."

Tears welled up in Mary's eyes and she clung to her son. "Thank God it's over!"

"That's right, it is over, and now I can get on with my life."

"How did you finally find him, Son?" Avery asked.

"Someone on the island spotted his ship around the outer islands. I thought for a while we were on a wild goose chase, and was about to give up; then, on the fourth day we spotted his ship. We settled our differences while our crews watched. Now enough about that. Tell me, what did you think about the Carolina coast?"

Mary and Avery looked at each other and smiled. "We loved it," Avery declared. "It was everything you said it was and more. We looked into the land you talked about and it's almost two thousand acres, running from the ocean and going back into miles and miles of prime fertile land and forests. It also includes the inlet you mentioned."

"It sounds wonderful."

"We returned with the hope that you would settle there with us," Mary said. "New Providence is not the place to have a family, Jeremy."

Jeremy hugged his mother. "You don't have to convince me. English and I have already talked about it. I'm just glad you found it to your liking. There was so much wilderness there, I was afraid it wouldn't appeal to you."

"It's exactly what we were looking for," Avery said, hugging his wife.

"Particularly if you and your English settle there too," Mary smiled.

"Well, why are we standing here? Come to Devil's Reach with me and meet her. She doesn't know I'm back yet."

Jeremy went through the house calling out her name, but no one answered. "She and Kennedy must have gone for a walk," he said, obviously disappointed that she wasn't there. "I thought Helga would be here, but she isn't either," he commented.

"Why don't we go home and open the house up?" Mary suggested. "We'll come back this evening to meet English."

"All right," he agreed. "I think I'll take one of the horses and see if I can find them. I know she enjoys walking on the beach."

Jeremy rode as far as he thought English would walk, but still there was no sign of them. He stopped by Kennedy's house and was told Kennedy hadn't been seen since he went to Devil's Reach to stay with Lady Wellsley. That didn't really surprise Jeremy; he wouldn't have expected Kennedy to leave English alone to go home, but still something nagged at him.

It was nearly noon. Surely they would return to Devil's Reach for the noonday meal, and even if they didn't, Helga would probably know where they were.

But no one showed up at the house. Jeremy paced the veranda, then each room. Something was wrong; he could feel it in his bones. It was nearly two o'clock and even Helga hadn't shown up. Frustrated, he decided to go to her house. She didn't live far and he ran all the way, his panic rising the closer he got.

"Helga, where is English?" he asked in Dutch as she opened the door.

"I don't know," she answered. "No one has been at the house since the day you left."

Jeremy leaned against the door, a sick feeling in the pit of his stomach. "Kennedy must have been there. . . ."

"No . . . no one," she answered. "I went to

300

make dinner and the house was empty."

Mary and Avery were surprised to find Jeremy's house empty when they returned a few hours later.

"Where could he be?" Mary asked, concern in her voice. "I hope he found English."

"So do I," Avery agreed. "I haven't seen him so excited about anything since I gave him *Black Moriah*."

After waiting several hours for Jeremy to return, Avery decided to go into town to see if he could find him. Halfway there he met his son and Jean Paul. Jeremy was singing a bawdy song while Jean Paul tried to keep him on a steady path toward Devil's Reach. Even from a few yards away, Avery could see that Jeremy's face was cut and bruised.

"There's my good old Papa." Jeremy stumbled towards Avery. "You should have been in town with us. We really tore up the place, didn't we, mon ami?"

"What happened?" Avery asked. "I thought we were going to celebrate your upcoming marriage this evening."

"Marriage?" Jeremy laughed bitterly. "There isn't going to be a marriage," he said, stum-

301

bling ahead of them.

"Do you know what happened, Jean Paul?"

"Apparently the lady waited until Jeremy left, then she took off. A couple of seamen in town saw her heading out to the *Dove* with an unknown man. Jeremy checked, and the *Dove* sailed for England the evening we left. Since then it has been all downhill. He tried to take on anybody and everybody in town."

"How could he have been so wrong about this girl?" Avery asked.

"She had us all fooled, Avery. I would have bet my life that she loved him as much as he loved her."

"How long has he been drinking?"

"Since shortly after noon. He broke up the Tiger's Den pretty good. I promised Liam he'd take care of everything when he was sober."

"I'll take care of it. Come on, we better stick close to him," Avery said, noticing that Jeremy had passed the bend in the road.

Mary met her son at the door. She gasped as she saw his condition. "My God, what happened to you?"

"Some bastard said something I didn't like," Jeremy said, falling in the door. "I'm sorry, Mother, I shouldn't talk that way in front of you," he said, stumbling toward the liquor

302

cabinet. "But they shouldn't have said what they did. I can tell you this," he said in a slurred voice. "They look a whole lot worse than I do. Isn't that right, Jean Paul, old buddy?"

"That's right," Jean Paul agreed.

Jeremy poured a glass full of whiskey and then fell into a chair. "I'm the Black Moriah, and nobody better cross me." Suddenly he threw the drink across the room, then held his head between his hands. "I'd rather be alone. I'm sorry, but I'm not fit company for anybody tonight."

Mary glanced at Avery, shaking her head no. "He needs someone with him tonight," she insisted.

"It's all right . . . I'll stay with him," Jean Paul volunteered. "I know you both must be exhausted."

Reluctantly Mary and Avery left. When they were alone Jeremy began to talk. "I really thought she loved me, Jean Paul. Everything was so perfect. We talked about starting a new life in the Carolinas. She said she wanted to be with me. . . ."

"I know, mon ami," Jean Paul said, hoping that as Jeremy talked he would get Ariana out of his system.

"She wanted to go with me . . . was that all a ruse? Was she just waiting for her chance to escape? Oh God, how could I have been such a fool? But why is Kennedy missing? He wouldn't have gone with her and left his family. Hell, for all I know, she's probably using him too. She probably promised him a lot of money to help her get away."

"I don't think Kennedy would betray you, mon ami."

"No, I didn't think so, but hell, what do I know? I didn't think English would either."

Jean Paul had seen Jeremy angry and hot-tempered, but he had never seen him helpless with tears in his eyes. He didn't know what to do for his friend.

"I want another drink," Jeremy said, unable to get out of the chair.

Jean Paul hesitated but then decided to let him go on drinking. Soon he would be unconscious, and perhaps that was the best thing for him . . . let him drink away his pain.

Anger is a short madness.

Horace

Chapter Fourteen

"I don't want any more of that vile stuff, Mother. I am not sick," Ariana said sharply.

"It was only to help you calm down, my dear. You were in a frightful state when your father brought you aboard."

"I know you mean well, Mother," she replied contritely, "but I'm walking around in a trance, and I don't like the feeling. I will never be able to accept what happened if I can't distinguish between reality and this drug-induced dream world."

"Are you ready to tell me what exactly happened on that island?" Denise asked, her eyes filled with sympathy.

Ariana looked away, still unable to think about Jeremy and the island. "How is Lanie? Who is she staying with?"

Denise sighed, knowing how stubborn her oldest daughter could be. "She is fine. She stayed in seclusion for weeks after we arrived back in London, insisting no one was to see her while her skin was peeling."

"I know the feeling," Ariana laughed bitterly. "I'm still freckled."

"But the real reason she didn't want to see anyone was because she wouldn't admit that you were dead and she didn't want people giving her their sympathy. That was a very difficult time for all of us."

Ariana spun around. "Oh, Mother, I'm sorry. I wanted to get a message to you, but . . . there just wasn't any way to do it." She turned back around and began to flip the pages of a book lying on the table. "You didn't say who Lanie was staying with," she said, hoping to change the subject.

"Brett's aunt invited her to stay at Rockglen. Rachel has not been in very good health lately, so she was looking forward to Lanie's company."

"I can't wait to see her. For a long time I thought all of you had drowned too. Then finally I heard that you'd made it safely back to London." Ariana sniffed, wiping a tear from her cheek.

Denise raised Ariana's chin, forcing her to look into her eyes. "Ariana, talk to me. Tell me what happened to you on that island. We've always been able to talk and work things out. I promise it will help if you just get it out into the open."

"I can't, Mother," she cried. "I don't think you'd understand."

"You don't think I will understand that you fell under the spell of this pirate who held you?" she asked softly.

Ariana sat on the side of the bed rubbing her forehead. "I fell in love with him, Mother. I fell in love with him, and slept with him, and then he betrayed me. And do you know what, Mother? I still love him. How can I expect you to understand that when I can't understand it myself?"

Denise sat beside Ariana, taking her hands in hers. "Perhaps you just thought you loved him, to enable yourself to cope with the circumstances."

"If that were true, why wouldn't I be glad to be away from him? Instead I have this terrible empty ache inside every time I think about him. Oh, Mother, how could he have betrayed me? He said he loved me . . . he said we would start a new life. . . ."

Denise wiped a tear from her daughter's face. "Greed is sometimes stronger than love, Ariana. I'm sure he loved you in his own way. We can be thankful that you weren't harmed in any other way," her mother put in delicately.

"No, I only lost my heart and my virginity," she said bitterly. "Oh, Mother, what am I going to do? I can't marry Brett, even if he still wanted to marry me. I realized while I was on the island that I didn't love him."

"This is not the time to make any drastic decisions, dear. There will be plenty of time to decide what you want to do once we are home."

"I'm afraid neither time nor home will alter the facts," Ariana mumbled.

"Perhaps not," Denise hugged her daughter, "but humor me for now. I have many more years of experience, and I know things like this can be worked out. It isn't the end of the world."

In less than a week, Jeremy's self-pity turned to anger. No one could reason with him, so they decided the best thing to do was leave him alone to exorcise his demons.

Jeremy knew better than anyone that he had

to get hold of his life. He'd been drinking for nearly a week, and his head throbbed violently. The worst thing was, he still had not been able to forget her. He'd spend one minute cursing her and the next longing for her.

He closed his eyes and leaned against the stone wall that surrounded the veranda. He could imagine her there with him, her voice soft and full of laughter, teasing him, seducing him. Oh God, English, why did you do it . . . why did you leave me? he wondered.

His eyes snapped open as he felt someone wrap their arms around his waist. "I came as soon as I heard," Tia said, rudely breaking into his reverie.

He removed her arms and turned around to stare out to sea hoping if he ignored her she'd go away.

"I tried to tell you she wasn't the type to stay on this island. She was London society, darling. It isn't a surprise to anyone that she fled the first chance she had. I'm just sorry to hear that poor Kennedy disappeared in the process. I pray nothing has happened to him."

"Nothing better have happened to him!" he growled. "I'll kill her if any harm has come to Kennedy."

"I don't blame you, darling. I know Kennedy has been a friend to you since you were a boy."

Jeremy clenched his fists, still unable to believe that English could have brought any harm to his friend.

"I am sorry if you are hurting."

"I'm sure you are," he mumbled.

"She must have been out of her mind to leave you," she purred, rewinding her hands around his waist. "You are all I think about, day and night."

Jeremy jerked away from her. "If I didn't know you were away from the island, I'd swear you had something to do with her disappearance."

"Well, I was away," she retorted. "I've never lied about wanting her off the island and out of your life, but I had nothing to do with her leaving you. You must accept it, caro. She wasn't any good for you. Now we can pick up the pieces and begin again. I can make you forget her. We can resume your search for Salizar together."

"Salizar?" Jeremy laughed. "I've already taken care of the Spaniard."

Tia's eyes widened. She had been hiding out at her place in the hills and hadn't heard. "But when . . . how did you find him?"

"I don't feel like going into it with you, Tia. As a matter of fact, I don't care to discuss anything with you."

"But you shouldn't be alone, caro."

"I'm alone because I want to be."

"I refuse to believe that. I know you, and I know by now you probably need me."

Jeremy's harsh laughter surprised her. "If I took you right now, I'd probably kill you," he growled. "That's how I feel about women. Now get out and leave me alone."

"I'll go for now, darling, but I'll be back. I know you'll need me sooner or later."

He waited to hear the door slam, then with a shaking hand he poured himself another drink and downed it. He didn't need any woman, he told himself. They were all lying, cheating whores. Damnit, he'd been good to her. Why would she run from him like a scared rabbit the first time he turned his back? "Damn her . . . damn her to hell," he swore, pouring another glass of liquor. He had to stop thinking about her, he thought, regarding the amber liquid in his glass. "Jesus, this isn't helping anything," he said, throwing the glass across the veranda to shatter off the stone wall.

"That's the first smart thing you've done in weeks," Jean Paul said from the doorway. "Are you ready to get on with your life?"

"I'm ready to do something," Jeremy replied bitterly. "I know I can't keep this up without going crazy."

"Why don't we see if we can find us a nice,

rich Spanish galleon?" Jean Paul suggested.

Jeremy had to laugh. "Don't tell me all your gold is gone already."

"No; I'm just bored. I'm beginning to wonder if they will ever have my ship repaired. Lately I've had this feeling that I'm going to be stranded here the rest of my life, and it isn't a pretty prospect."

"I thought you were happy here with Tia."

"No," Jean Paul shook his head. "She is back, as you probably already know, but for some reason I have no desire to be with her."

"I know the feeling, my friend. She is poison for both of us. Leave her to Saint-Gilles . . . they deserve each other."

Jean Paul laughed. "Even Saint-Gilles deserted her—he sailed for Tortuga the day you returned."

"Good riddance," Jeremy said.

"So what do you say, mon ami? Do we sail for the open sea and forget New Providence for awhile?"

"Hell, why not? It will take a few days to get the ship ready. That will give me time to make Mary and Avery understand why I can't go with them to the Carolinas."

"They will be disappointed," Jean Paul commented.

"Aye, but I have no reason to start over in that godforsaken wilderness," he said bitterly, remembering his plans with English to start over there. "I'm a pirate, and a damned good one. I may as well stick to what I do best."

Her father and Brett stayed behind to see that their trunks were removed from the ship, leaving Ariana and her mother to travel alone in the cumbersome coach. Ariana was greatly relieved that Brett wouldn't be going on to Wellsley Manor with them. He had tried to be pleasant and polite, but the tension in the air was almost palpable when they were together.

The air was cool and damp as they stood on the docks of the Thames River, preparing to depart in the coach. Ariana shivered, unused to the cooler temperature. Denise wrapped a shawl around her daughter's shoulders. "I'm sorry, dear. I should have remembered you wouldn't have any appropriate clothing. We'll take care of that as soon as we get settled. Madame LeFleur can whip you up a few things to tide you over, and then we'll have her work on an entire new wardrobe."

Ariana nodded her head but said nothing. She stared out the coach window, thinking nothing had changed in London. The streets were clogged with farmers herding their cattle to market and with vendors crying out their singsong pitch. The stench of open sewers and

315

gutters blended with the odor of garbage, almost making her gag. The memory of the sweet-smelling flowers at Devil's Reach came to mind. No, no—she had to put everything that reminded her of Jeremy out of her mind.

"Here, dear, this may help," Denise said, handing Ariana a delicately scented handkerchief to hold to her nose.

This was where she was going to spend the rest of her life, she thought bitterly as she inhaled the fragrance of the handkerchief.

"We will go on to the manor and then send our carriage for Lanie," her mother said. "She will be so glad to see you."

"I'll be glad to see her also," Ariana said, staring out the window as they passed a gibbet with some unfortunate man hanging from it. "My God, Mother, how can you stand to live in a place like this after living in Bermuda?" Ariana exclaimed.

"This is home, dear. You learn to adapt to your surroundings. Isn't that what you did in New Providence?"

"Yes, I suppose so," she answered, pulling her shawl closer around her shoulders.

Nothing had changed at Wellsley Manor; it was as if she'd never been away. James, the butler, answered the door of the big brick mansion, his usual disciplined features changed only by the smile on his face. Mattie and Peggy stood at the foot of the steps, both beaming. Ignoring James's look of shock, Mattie ran to Ariana and hugged her.

"Oh, Miss Ariana, I'm so relieved to see you. It has been so dreadful around here without you.

"Thank you, Mattie," she smiled through her tears. "As you can see, I'm very much alive."

"Mattie, why don't you take Ariana to her room while Peggy prepares a bath for her."

"Yes, mum," the girl curtsied.

Ariana stood in the center of the room, glancing around at the beautiful blue and pink decorations. She had to admit she loved this room, she thought, running her hand over the big featherbed.

"Nothing has been changed, Miss Ariana. The servants kept it immaculate while we were in Bermuda.

"I had forgotten how beautiful it was. . . ."

"You shouldn't have. I remember you and your mother going round and round about the colors. She wanted it to be yellow and white and you wanted pink and blue," Mattie laughed. "Lanie ended up with a yellow and white room, so your mother was appeased."

A procession of servants entered the room carrying hot water for the big brass tub. Within minutes the tub was filled and Mattie was laying out perfumed soap and soft towels.

Ariana slowly lowered her body into the steaming water. She tried to close her mind to the times she had bathed with Jeremy. Violently she began to scrub her legs and arms.

"Easy, Miss Ariana—you'll take the hide off. Here, let me shampoo your hair," Mattie said. "My word, isn't it amazing what the sun can do to your hair," she commented as she lathered Ariana's sun-streaked chestnut locks. "The only thing it did to my old gray head was to make me look older."

"You don't look a bit older!" Ariana exclaimed. "Neither does Mother. We were all very lucky to have been saved, Mattie."

"Indeed we were. It's just a shame we were separated. It has been very difficult on your family, and on your young man."

"I'm surprised he hasn't already found someone else," Ariana commented, watching her maid's face.

"A sweet thing like you would be very difficult to replace," Mattie said, pouring water over Ariana's head. "Now, why don't you get out and dry, and I'll get you some tea?"

"Thank you, Mattie."

Ariana wrapped herself in a heavy velvet robe, then curled up on the bed to have her tea. She heard a commotion in the hallway and knew right away it must be Lanie. She jumped off the bed and swung the door open, coming face to face with her sister.

"Oh Lanie," she cried, hugging her. "My God, you've grown up in the few months I've been away!"

"I'll have you know I turned seventeen while you were gone," she sniffed.

"I know, and I turned nineteen."

Lanie wiped at her tears with the back of her hand. "I can't believe we are all together again," she sniffed as the two sisters sat on the bed and talked. "Oh Ariana, it was so terrible to be separated."

"I know, love, I felt the same way," Ariana said through her tears. "I shall never forget that terrible moment when the boat you and mother were in broke away. It was the most helpless feeling I have ever had. I kept thinking we would get back together."

"I know, we thought the same thing, but the rough water carried us away so swiftly."

"How did you ever get into a boat? I thought they had all left the ship," Lanie asked.

"I didn't get into a boat," Ariana explained. "Do you remember the young Lieutenant Taylor? Well, he and I floated on the top of a hatch cover for days. When a ship picked us up, we were both more dead than alive."

"Well, you look wonderful now," Lanie exclaimed. "Your hair is beautiful with those sun streaks. I shall have to try that," she laughed. "It is so different. You'll probably set a fashion trend among the London ladies," she chuckled.

"I doubt that," Ariana laughed.

"Well, I may try to get mine to look like that," Lanie said, sweeping her hair up on her head.

"You don't want to get it the way I did," Ariana said, clasping his sister's hands. "Besides, you're beautiful just the way you are."

"Thank you," she laughed, bouncing on the bed like a child. "Oh God, Ariana, I'm so glad you're home! I've missed having you to talk to. I know Brett must have been out of his mind with joy when he found you safe and alive," she exclaimed. "Now you two can get married as planned, and it will be so much fun!

Ariana stood and moved to the window, twisting the delicate handkerchief she held in her hand. "Things have changed, Lanie. I'm not sure there is going to be a wedding between Brett and me."

"Oh, Ariana, don't even say such a thing,"

Lanie scolded. "Brett would be heartbroken if you called off your engagement, and so would his Aunt Rachel. She's been as excited about you coming home as we have."

"You are not a child." Ariana turned angrily on her sister. "You should understand that I am not the sweet, innocent girl Brett wanted to marry."

Lanie stared at Ariana as if she had sprouted horns. "But you were forced. . . ."

"I was forced the first time, Lanie. From then on I was a willing participant. I fell in love with Jeremy. I thought he was in love with me—until he ransomed me to our parents. Do you really think Brett or his aunt would ever understand that?"

Lanie rushed to Ariana and hugged her. "Please forgive me for being so insensitive, Ariana. I knew you had changed . . . I could see it in your eyes, but I didn't realize what it was. Sit back down and tell me about it."

"I'd rather not," Ariana said, reluctantly letting Lanie pull her back to sit on the bed.

"Come on, Ariana, tell me what he looked like. Was he very handsome?"

"Yes. He had curly black hair and wore it shorter than the men in London."

"And what color were his eyes? Was he thin or stout?"

Ariana laughed at her sister's curiosity. "He

had gray eyes, Lanie, and he wasn't thin or stout." She sighed, knowing her sister wasn't going to leave her alone until she heard everything. "He had wide shoulders that tapered to a narrow waist, and he was muscular . . . not like the dandies in London." Ariana fell silent, remembering the way he looked when he came out of the water, his body bronzed and glistening.

"You are leaving something out," Lanie persisted.

"He was a magnificent specimen, Lanie. Does that satisfy your curiosity?"

"Oh, Ariana, it sounds so exciting! Why did I have to be picked up by an English ship with a starchy old captain who was old enough to be my grandfather?" she pouted.

Ariana had to laugh. "I'm not sure London society will look on my experience as exciting. They will probably consider me a fallen woman."

"London society doesn't have to know what really happened, Ariana."

"Oh, they will know, love. I'm sure by now word has spread that poor Lady and Lord Wellsley went to the pirate's lair and rescued their pitiful, ravished daughter."

"It doesn't matter what they say or think, Ariana. We know better. You loved your pirate, and the days you spent with him will probably remain in your memory for the rest of your life."

"For the rest of my dull, boring life," Ariana corrected. "Yes, you are probably right, Lanie. I can't imagine ever forgetting Jeremy—even if I wanted to."

At her family's insistence, Ariana tried to get back into a routine. With Denise, she and Lanie spent several afternoons at the dressmaker, having new wardrobes made. Then Denise invited several of Ariana's friends to tea, but the afternoon was strained; Ariana couldn't wait to escape to her room. They had all expressed sympathy for her plight, telling her they knew how terrible it must have been. She had been tempted to describe her real adventure just to see the shock on their righteous faces, but she knew it would also shock and upset her mother.

Brett came often and showed an immense amount of patience that Ariana wouldn't have thought he had. He told her often that she was being ridiculous to think he wanted out of their engagement, but she noticed he couldn't look her in the face when he said it. She would have been devastated if she'd known that Brett's aunt had threatened to disinherit him if he called off his engagement to her.

The only time she could honestly say she was happy was when the family was alone. Her parents couldn't have been more understanding of her reluctance to rejoin her circle of friends, and they spent more time together than they ever had before. She felt she was really getting to know them for the first time.

And then there was Lanie . . . dear sweet, Lanie. Ariana found it difficult to find time to mope during the day with Lanie always finding some outrageous thing to do to make her laugh. She found she could talk to her sister about Jeremy, and it seemed to help.

Yes, the days had become bearable, but then there were still the nights when one moment she would remember Jeremy's touch and the way he had made love to her, and the next she would tell herself she had been used and discarded like a whore. She wondered if she would ever regain her self-respect. It was foolish of her to feel soiled and unworthy just because Jeremy no longer desired her, she told herself, but still she found it difficult to go out in public and hold her head high — and even more difficult to stop thinking about Jeremy Corbett.

I had rather have a fool to make me merry than experience to make me sad.

Shakespeare

Chapter Fifteen

Ariana stayed close to home the first few weeks, preferring to avoid people as long as possible. That way she didn't have to listen to the whispers or try to ignore the curious stares. But then an invitation to tea came from Brett's Aunt Rachel, and Ariana knew it was time to make a decision.

The next afternoon she presented herself to the Dowager Duchess alone, as had been requested. The majordomo took her wrap, then led her into the parlor where the Duchess waited in a large wingback chair before a blazing fire.

"Come in, my dear," Rachel Leighton greeted her. "Forgive me for not getting up, but it becomes more difficult all the time."

Ariana was shocked at how ill the Duchess looked. She leaned over and kissed the old woman on her wrinkled cheek. "Mother told me you were feeling poorly."

The Duchess snorted. "Poorly is putting it mildly, my dear. I'm afraid my days are numbered," she said, patting Ariana's cheek with a shaky, blue-veined hand.

"Oh, Rachel, I'm so sorry. I didn't realize—"

"Now, I don't want your pity, my dear," the old woman smiled. "I've lived a long life . . . too long, to be honest. I've outlived two sons and a grandson, not to mention several daughters-in-laws. That's the deepest hurt there is," she said, the remembered pain in her voice. "A parent should never outlive her children," she said, wiping a tear from her faded gray eyes.

"I know the pain you've suffered must have been terrible, Rachel, but you still have Brett."

"So I do, my dear, and that's why I've asked you here. I would like to see my grandson married before I die."

"Rachel, there are circumstances . . ."

"Now I know you've been reluctant to resume your plans, my dear, but neither your family nor I see any reason for it."

Ariana stood up and warmed her hands before the fire. "Things have changed, Rachel. I don't believe I'm suited for Brett."

"Nonsense! I picked you for him myself. Of course, it was Charles' son I first had in mind when I made arrangements for your father's first daughter to marry my grandson, but no matter."

"Those arrangements were made years before I was even born," Ariana protested.

"That's the way it is done in old families, my dear . . . blood is the important thing. Wellsley and Leighton blood would mingle very nicely and your offspring would be beautiful, intelligent children."

"What if my father had had only sons?" Ariana queried.

"But he didn't, my dear. Now tell me what's on your mind."

Ariana began to pace. "Even before I went to Bermuda with my family, I wasn't sure Brett and I were suited for each other."

"That's nonsense," the Duchess persisted. "Of course you are suited for each other. You make a beautiful couple."

"No, you don't understand," Ariana tried to explain as she knelt next to the Duchess. "Things have changed, Rachel. Something happened while I was away that would make it very unfair of me to marry Brett."

"Tell me what it is, my dear. I'm sure it can't be all that bad."

Ariana stood again and stared into the fire. She took a long breath. "I am no longer a virgin," she said bluntly.

Ariana stared in shock as the Duchess laughed in delight. "Oh pooh, that's not important. Virginity has always been vastly overrated, in my opinion."

"Not important?" Ariana asked in shock. "I'm afraid your grandson may disagree with you."

"Of course he agrees with me, my dear. We have already discussed it. Neither of us thought you could be held by pirates for several months and not be deflowered."

"Deflowered," Ariana repeated bitterly. "Rachel, I'm afraid there was a little more to it than just being *deflowered*."

"Oh, my dear, you're not pregnant? Now that may upset the apple cart," the Duchess mused.

"There is always that possibility," Ariana considered. "I've been home less than a month, but it isn't just that. Rachel, I fell in love with the man who saved me."

"My dear, I am sorry." The faded gray eyes were sympathetic. "Come sit next to me and tell me about it," she encouraged.

330

"He saved my life after the shipwreck," Ariana began. "He was very gentle and caring, nursing me back to health. I'm not sure when I fell in love with him, but I had never been happier than I was on that island, Rachel. He didn't look like most people's idea of a pirate. He was tall and handsome, with curly black hair and beautiful gray eyes . . ."

"I'm sorry, Rachel," Ariana suddenly shook her head. "Forgive me for going on that way."

"Nonsense, dear. I find it all quite interesting. What drove the young man to piracy? Was he one of the Crown's privateers during our troubles with France?"

"No, he was saved by one of the pirates from a sinking ship when he was just a child and was raised as one of them. He's very intelligent, though, and was considered their leader. I was amazed when I found out he could speak four languages, and he was very well read."

"He sounds like a very interesting man," Rachel agreed. "Why in the world did you leave him, my dear?"

"I thought my affections were returned," Ariana said, her eyes bright with tears, "but I was wrong."

"Oh, I am sorry, my child." Rachel patted her hand. "Then you must put it behind you now and go on with your life."

"Yes, I'm trying to do just that," Ariana agreed.

"Then we're back to where we started. Pour yourself a cup of tea, my dear, and I'll have some blackberry brandy. We have plans to make," she said, rubbing her hands together in anticipation.

"I dislike having my life interfered with," Brett said angrily. "You may not care that Ariana is no longer a virgin, but I do. She is the talk of London society."

"And that is why you should be willing to marry her, my dear grandson. It would put a stop to those wagging tongues," the Duchess answered irritably.

"At my expense," he snorted. "It will only serve to make me the center of their gossip."

"Are you concerned that your degenerate friends at the gaming houses will look down their noses at you?" she laughed bitterly. "I hardly think so, my dear Brett, since your losing keeps them in money—my money, I might add."

"Is that what this is all about, Grandmother? I admit that my losses have been heavy lately, but that will change."

"That's not what this is about, Brett, and you know it," she said in exasperation. "I

332

want to know that Rockglen will stay in the hands of our descendants. We owe that much to our ancestors who built this great place and brought honor to the name Leighton. I want children to fill these halls," she said, slamming her cane on the hard wood floor. "You would be lucky to marry a woman like Lady Ariana Wellsley, after some of the bawdy whores I've heard you associate with."

"Now, Grandmother, you shouldn't listen to gossip," he said, pouring himself a drink. "I must admit, I've always desired Ariana, but really Grandmother, under the circumstances I would rather take her as a mistress."

"How dare you!" the Duchess exploded before having a coughing fit. "Lord Wellsley and I made these arrangements more than twenty years ago and you will abide by them — or suffer the consequences," she managed to sputter.

"Don't threaten me, Grandmother," he warned, his pale blue eyes narrowed with malice. "I don't wish to seem goulish, but all I have to do is wait until you die and I'll have it all without being forced into marriage with a woman who's been disgraced."

The Duchess snorted, a satisfied look on her face. "I'm one step ahead of you, my greedy, young fool. I've already had my solicitor place a clause in my will stating that if you aren't married to Lady Ariana Wellsley at the time of my death, all my money is to go to charity."

Brett laughed bitterly. "I must admit, Grandmother, your mind is still working brilliantly, but tell me this: even if I'm forced into this marriage, how do you plan to keep me faithful to my lovely, but soiled wife?"

"You would be a fool to be unfaithful to Ariana," she said in disgust.

"Ah yes, but marriage was your only stipulation," he said triumphantly. "I bow to your wishes, my dear Grandmother. I'm sure you have already made the plans."

"You will reannounce your engagement two months from today, on Ariana's twentieth birthday," Rachel Leighton said. "You will be married a month after that."

"So soon?" he laughed sarcastically. "Is my bride already with child?"

"I sometimes find it difficult to believe you are my grandson," Rachel said in disgust.

"Ah, but I am, dear Grandmother, and your only living relative to boot."

"I've asked Lord Wellsley to forgo the appropriate waiting time because of my ill health," Rachel continued, undaunted. "He has graciously consented to do so."

"The good Lord Wellsley is not only rich, but wise," he said snidely. "He knows a good thing when he see it."

"You will be lucky if he doesn't put a bullet through your heart before your honeymoon is over," Rachel warned.

"I'll keep that in mind," he said coldly. "I must depart your charming company now, dear Grandmother. I have a young lady waiting for me."

The Duchess stared after her grandson, worried that she was doing Ariana Wellsley a disservice. No, she told herself, Lady Ariana Wellsley had enough spirit to tame her wayward grandson. Besides, Brett couldn't be all bad. He had Leighton blood in him. She took a deep breath and shook her head. It was just a shame he was such a greedy young man. She was afraid one day it would be his downfall.

"I believe you've made a wise decision, Ariana," her mother said as her daughter paced in frustration. "You cannot continue to be a recluse. I'm sure you'll find that once you are married the talk about what happened will die down."

"And will I live happily ever after?" she asked sarcastically.

"Ariana, we only want what is best for you," her mother sighed. "Brett is willing to go through with the marriage ... why shouldn't you be?"

"Because I don't love him!" Ariana shouted.

"I know that, dear," Denise said calmly. "You're in love with a man who betrayed you. I know this is going to seem harsh, but it appears to me that you have several choices: you can return to that island and beg him to take you in; you can become a spinster and never leave Wellsley Manor; or you can marry Brett and have a satisfying life filled with family and children. And who knows, you may come to love Brett again."

"If I had ever imagined finding myself in such circumstances, I would never have returned. I would have stayed on the island and fought it out with Jeremy. I would have made him realize that he really did love me. Oh God, why didn't I do that? I know he cared for me."

"You didn't do it because you had pride, Ariana," her mother insisted.

"Pride!" Ariana snorted. "That's as bad as honor or revenge. What good do any of them do you?" she spat.

"The fact is, you *did* return to England, and now the only way you can save your reputation is by marrying Brett."

Ariana was silent for a long time. Finally she turned to her mother. "All right, make the plans," she said, rubbing her temples. "Do whatever has to be done, but please don't expect me to be enthusiastic about it. I suppose I shall have to content myself to remember my time with Jeremy as the one brief, shining moment in my life. At least no one can take that from me."

Denise hugged her daughter. "No one wants to take that from you, dear. There is really nothing any of us wants more than to see you happy."

"I know, Mother. This is just so difficult. If I only had more time . . ."

"Unfortunately, that is not something Rachel Leighton has a lot of, and she fervently wishes to see her grandson married to you before she dies. That is why she has asked that the engagement be announced two months from today, on your birthday. It is just a formality, since most people already know you've been betrothed since birth."

"I know, Mother. Did you know she wants to give the party at Rockglen, since it is difficult for her to get about?"

"Did you agree?" Denise asked.

"Yes, I agreed. It broke my heart to see Rachel as she was. I had no idea her health had declined so."

"I was rather shocked myself when we returned from Bermuda," Denise agreed. "I'm told she was always a vibrant woman when she was young, but she has suffered a great deal in her life. I can empathize with her after thinking I had lost a daughter."

"Poor Rachel has lost two sons, two daughters-in-law, and a grandson. No one should have to suffer so much," Ariana sympathized, remembering Jeremy's loss at such an early age. "We have been very lucky, Mother."

Denise hugged her daughter. "Yes we have, my dear. Very lucky, indeed."

Jeremy returned home richer, but no happier. It hadn't helped getting away, and he was beginning to wonder if anything would help. They had captured a Spanish ship the first week out, then had celebrated the following two weeks in Bermuda. He visited every whore on the island and drank at least a barrel of rum, but nothing helped. Now as he stood on the deck of *Black Moriah* staring at the harbor filled with people, he realized he had never been more alone. There was no one he was returning to, and it was a damned empty feeling that he didn't like.

"Jeremy, isn't that Avery's ship still in the harbor?" Jean Paul pointed out.

"I'll be damned," Jeremy exclaimed, his spirits lifting. "I thought for sure they'd be gone by now. I wonder what kept them here? Hell, no matter; it will be good to see them."

Jean Paul studied his friend, wishing there were something he could do to lift his spirits. In Bermuda Jeremy had tried to have a good time, but Jean Paul could tell it was forced for the benefit of his crew. It was a terrible thing to see a grown man brought to his knees by a woman, he thought sadly.

"Why don't you go ashore? I'll look after things here," Jean Paul suggested.

"No, come with me. I'm not going to stay there long, and we'll go to the Tiger's Den for a drink afterward. Fairfax can take care of things here."

"If you are sure that's what you want to do," Jean Paul said.

"I'm sure. Come on, I'm curious to see what delayed their departure."

Avery opened the door and warmly greeted his son and Jean Paul. "I saw *Black Moriah* enter the harbor, and I started to meet you on the quay, but then I decided it was better if we talked in private," he said, leading the two men toward his library.

"Is Mary all right?" Jeremy asked with concern in his voice.

"I'm fine, son," Mary said as she joined

them. "How was your trip?"

Jeremy hugged his mother. "It was fine. I'm surprised to see you still here."

"Something came up and we thought we should stay around," Avery said. "There is someone here to see you. . . ."

Jeremy's heart leaped, half expecting to see English, but instead Kennedy stood up as they entered the room.

"By God, I'm glad to see you," Jeremy exclaimed as he embraced his friend.

"I'm surprised you don't want to slit my throat, sir," Kennedy said, unable to look Jeremy in the eye. "I let you down, I did, and I wouldn't blame you for wanting to run me through."

"Don't worry about it, Kennedy. I'm just glad you're alive. I'm afraid Lady Wellsley was more devious than any of us thought," Jeremy said bitterly. "She had us all fooled."

"I don't know about that, sir. All I know is that somebody didn't want me around her."

"I don't understand," Jeremy shrugged.

"Well sir, Lady Wellsley and I watched your ship leave the harbor. She was very sad and worried about you, and had been up nearly all night. When you were out of sight, she decided to lie down for a while. I went back on the veranda to pick up a bit, and the next thing I know, I've got a knot the size of an egg on my skull and I'm on a ship heading for the Canary Islands. Fortunately the captain was an understanding chap and put me off on the first ship we met so I could work my way back here."

"I don't know how she managed it, or why," Jeremy said angrily. "This whole thing is just beyond my reasoning. . . ."

"Sir, I don't want to be disrespectful, knowing you're an intelligent man, but I think you've got this all wrong. I don't think the lady had anything to do with it. When I was being thrown in the hold of that ship, I could have sworn I heard someone mention Dobson's name."

"Dobson?" he said in disbelief. "Why the hell would Dobson have anything to do with this?"

"Well, sir, your father and I went to Dobson to ask a few questions, but he wasn't talking."

"The bastard will talk for me!" Jeremy swore.

"I'm afraid nobody can make him talk, son. When we found him, somebody had blown a hole through him."

"Why would anyone want to kill that worthless bastard?" Jean Paul asked.

"Probably to keep him from talking," Avery answered.

"From talking about what?" Jean Paul

asked, confused.

"Wait a minute." Jeremy spoke in a choked voice. "Are you saying that English was kidnapped?"

"No, I've already looked into that. The *Dove* arrived in England with your lady and her parents aboard."

"It doesn't make any sense. Why would her parents kidnap Kennedy and ship him off to the Canary Islands just to get their daughter back?"

"It *doesn't* make any sense," Avery agreed, "but there had to be a reason why someone wanted Kennedy out of the way."

"I'd be willing to bet Tia could give you some answers," Jean Paul suggested.

"I think you might be right, my friend," Jeremy growled.

"That's entirely possible, if she were here," Avery commented. "She very conveniently left the island the day Kennedy returned."

Jeremy paced the room. "I don't know why I'm getting all excited. This really doesn't change anything between English and me. Even if she left with her parents, if she'd cared anything about me she'd have left a note."

"If someone went to such lengths to get Kennedy out of the way, perhaps they also convinced English that you didn't want her

342

around any longer," Jean Paul suggested.

"No," Jeremy said, his mind in a turmoil.

"I have to agree with Jean Paul," Mary said. "I have a strange feeling it isn't as it seems."

Jeremy stared out the window overlooking the sea. "It seems to me that the only way I'm going to get any answers is to go to England."

"Oh, Jeremy, please, don't even think of such a thing," Mary begged. "You can't just sail the *Black Moriah* up the Thames. They'd hang you on sight."

"Your mother is right, Son. It would be foolhardy to go as the *Black Moriah;* but if you went using you real identity, you wouldn't have any problem being accepted."

Everyone in the room stared at Avery, waiting for him to explain.

"Years ago I decided never to tell you who your father was, Son, but now I think it's necessary in order to keep you alive. Your father was Lord Charles Leighton, the Duke of Rockglen. I have the log from the ship you were on."

"My God!" Jeremy gasped.

"After I brought you to the island, I made some inquiries through a contact in London and found that your mother had died just a short time before you and your father took that ill-fated trip. At the time the only living

343

relatives you had were a grandmother on your father's side and an aunt by marriage who had a small son."

Jeremy ran his hand through his hair and swore softly. Mary touched his shoulder, tears in her eyes. He turned around and hugged her. "Your mother never knew your true background, son. I felt it best not to tell anyone. You can hate me if you want, but I truly felt that you'd be better off with Mary and me, and I've never regretted that decision. I may have deprived you of wealth and social standing in London, but I think you've become more of a man on this island than you could ever have become in London."

Jeremy pulled his father into his embrace. "You made the right decision, and I'm grateful to you. You and Mary are the only parents I know and the love I feel for you both couldn't be more if I was from your seed."

O lost, and by the wind grieved,
ghost, come back again.

Thomas Wolfe

Chapter Sixteen

Ariana sat on her mare watching Brett check the hoof of his horse. He was of slighter build than Jeremy, she thought, and for the first time she realized how dissipated he looked in the light of day. Jeremy always looked so tanned and healthy. Damn, she had to stop comparing Brett to Jeremy, she told herself.

She closed her eyes tightly for a moment and tried to put Jeremy out of her mind.

"It seems to be all right," Brett broke into her thoughts. "Why don't you dismount and we'll sit over there on the hillside and talk for a while."

Ariana started to protest, but this was the first time she and Brett had been alone, so she supposed they should discuss the upcoming party to announce their engagement.

He held his hands up to assist her down from the sidesaddle. "We haven't really had a chance to talk," he said casually.

"No, we haven't," Ariana agreed.

"Have you found London to your liking?" he asked as they sat down on a grassy slope.

"I really haven't gotten back into the social circle yet."

"No, I suppose it's difficult for you."

"It has been," she answered, studying a piece of grass she had picked.

"Everyone seems to think the gossip about you will cease as soon as we're married."

Ariana cringed at his words. "What do you think, Brett?"

"Oh, I suppose it will die down once they have something else to talk about."

"Does it bother you?"

"I won't lie to you, Ariana—of course it bothers me. But there are more important things in life than worrying about what people say." He was thinking about his aunt's money, but Ariana couldn't know that.

Ariana was surprised and relieved to hear his opinion. "Thank you, Brett. I know this

348

whole situation has been difficult for you also."

"I assume you will be worth it."

Ariana's eyes searched his face, wondering what his meaning was. "If you have any doubts about this marriage, I will understand. I've told you before that I will release you from any obligations you feel you have."

Brett laughed bitterly. "You're supposed to be a woman of the world now, my pet, but still you are so naive."

She was getting angrier by the minute. "What is that supposed to mean?"

"Come now, I don't wish to make you angry, my dear," he smiled, but it never reached his eyes. "I don't wish to be released from our arrangement, so stop worrying about it." He ran a finger along her jawline, then clutched her chin between his fingers and pulled her toward him. "I have desired you since you were a little child, my sweet Ariana. Did you know that? I've watched you grow into a beautiful young woman, and for years I fought every urge I had to teach you what it was like to be a woman, knowing that someday you would be mine." His fingers tightened on her chin. "Then, damn it, you go off and let some bloody pirate rape you," he spat between gritted teeth.

She was tempted to tell him it wasn't rape,

but she decided it wiser not to say anything.

"Did you enjoy what he did to you, Ariana?" he demanded sharply.

Ariana pushed his hand away. "This is not something I wish to discuss with you or anyone else."

"I'm going to be your husband," he persisted. "I have a right to know. Tell me what he did to you," he pressed.

"How dare you?" she slapped him hard.

Brett grabbed her by the shoulders and pushed her back on the grass. He kissed her roughly, bruising her soft mouth.

Ariana struggled against him and was able to push him off her. "How dare you!" she said, brushing the grass off her velvet riding habit.

"Come now, Ariana, let me sample what I'm getting, to see if it's worth ruining my reputation. You aren't a virgin, so what harm is there?"

"I may not be a virgin, but I'm not a whore," she spat as she stood up, "and you needn't worry about your reputation. I wouldn't marry you if you were the last man on earth."

Her statement suddenly reminded him what was at stake. "I'm sorry, Ariana—please forgive me," he said, leaping to his feet. "I don't know what made me act that way. I didn't mean any of the things I said. I've wanted you all my life, and I've dreamed about the moment that you would be in my arms. I suppose just knowing that someone else had you first has made me a little crazy."

Ariana stared at him, not quite comprehending what was going on. "I'm going home now," she said, heading toward her horse.

"Ariana, wait," he said, catching her arm. "Please, you must forgive me, love," he begged, forcing tears into his eyes. "I never meant to insult you. I want to marry you. I know you had no control over what happened. Please, say you'll marry me, Ariana."

She wanted to tell him to stop acting like a babbling idiot, but instead she forced a smile. "It's all right, Brett. I understand. We have all been distressed by recent events."

"That must be what it is, Ariana. I swear to you, I'll be a gentleman with you from now on. I'll never again mention what happened when you were away."

"Fine," she said, pulling away from him. "Now let's go back to the house. If we are going to the Mendleson affair this evening, I need to start getting ready."

"Of course, dear," he said, following after her like a pup.

Something is definitely wrong here, Ariana thought silently. This was not the arrogant,

351

decisive Brett Leighton she had remembered. He actually acted as if he were afraid she would call off their marriage, but why, she pondered.

As soon as she reached her room, Ariana threw herself across the bed. Oh God, how could she marry Brett Leighton? She could barely stand the man. Compared to Jeremy he was a fop. Oh, Jeremy, why did you do this to me? she thought as she clutched the coverlet. "I hope you rot in hell for your betrayal," she cursed, and began to cry.

As Mattie dressed her hair for the occasion, Ariana stared at herself in the mirror, remembering the evening of Tia's party. She shivered as she recalled the passionate night of love she had spent with Jeremy.

"Are you cold?" Mattie asked.

"No — just remembering something."

"Put those bad thoughts from your mind, dearie. You're at home safe and sound now."

"I know," Ariana said squeezing her hand.

"Your mother and father are going to be so proud of you tonight. You look absolutely beautiful in that pink gown."

Ariana stared at the pale pink silk with its frosting of lace and ribbons. "I hope the neckline isn't too low," she said, pulling up on it.

"Nonsense. I always say, if you've got it, you might as well take pride in it," her maid laughed cheerfully.

"Are you almost ready?" Lanie burst into the room. "Brett is pacing downstairs. He looks very handsome. What do you think of my dress, Ariana?" she asked, spinning before her sister. "Do you think Roger Wainwright will approve?"

"Roger Wainwright?" Ariana laughed. "Pray don't tell me you're interested in that dandy." A moment passed.

"Oh, I'm sorry," Ariana said, after she saw the look on her sister's face. "I had no idea you were really interested in Roger. I haven't seen him in years, but I remember a chubby young man who dressed just like a cherub and never left his mother's side."

Lanie suddenly laughed. "He hasn't changed much."

"Mattie, would you tell Lord Leighton that we'll be down shortly," Ariana asked dismissing her.

"Come sit with me," Ariana laughed. "There was a Frenchman named Jean Paul Moreau on the island who wanted to meet you. He was actually from French aristocracy, but he had turned to piracy. He kept asking me if I had a sister at home and swore one

353

day he'd come to England to meet. you."

"Oh, Ariana, you must have had such an exciting time!"

"It certainly makes life in London seem boring," she admitted. "The men here all seem like dandies to me, and I didn't use to feel that way. I always thought Brett was handsome and charming."

"And now you don't?" Lanie asked, her eyes wide with surprise.

"Not compared to . . . no, as a matter of fact, I find him rather repulsive."

"Oh, Ariana, that's terrible!" her sister exclaimed. "How can you marry a man you find repulsive?"

"I was wondering that myself," she sighed.

Ariana accepted a glass of champagne from Brett, then glanced around the room. Perhaps a score of people had gathered in the salon after dinner. The Mendlesons had been friends with her parents for years, and she knew that that was the reason for the dinner party. But even they couldn't keep from giving her curious glances all during the evening.

Lanie was occupied with several people her own age, including Roger Wainwright, who wasn't as bad as Ariana had remembered. Still he didn't compare with Jean Paul, she thought with a sigh.

"Can I get you anything, my dear?" Brett asked, never leaving her side.

"No, nothing," she answered. "I am growing weary; I hope this affair doesn't go on too much longer."

"Look over there," he pointed. "Lady Adamsley has fallen asleep on the sofa. That goes to show you what an exciting party it is."

Ariana had to laugh behind her hand. "I'm afraid if I were sitting I'd do the same."

"I wish we could leave here and go to one of the gaming houses, but I know that's impossible. Your reputation would only suffer the more for it."

In truth, she didn't care what people thought, but she knew her parents did. "Yes, I'm afraid it would; but please don't stay on my account. I can return home with my mother and father."

"Absolutely not!" he gasped. "I wouldn't think of leaving you here."

"If you would like to go. . . ." she persisted.

"Not another word," he scolded. "Brace yourself; here comes Lady Litchfield."

"There you are, my dear girl," the woman said, patting Ariana's hand. "I've been waiting for a moment to talk with you all evening. I would like to give you and Lord Leighton a reception at North Shore next week. I've already made all the arrangements with your mother."

"That is very kind of you, Lady Litchfield," Ariana said, annoyed that no one had consulted her.

"I think if you can put the unfortunate incident behind you, then we should make every effort to also do so."

"I am grateful for everyone's concern," Ariana said wearily.

"Ariana and I are both grateful," Brett added, giving Lady Litchfield one of his most charming smiles.

"Let me give you a little advice, my dears. Each social gathering that the two of you attend will end a little of the gossip," she continued annoyingly. "In time a new scandal will come along to divert attention."

"I do hope so," Ariana answered, trying to keep the bitterness from her voice.

And that was the way of it for the next few weeks: boring, tedious gatherings at which people would tell her how happy they were to see her getting back into the social circle, then whisper and snicker behind her back. The hardest thing to accept was the fact that everyone thought Brett was a martyr. *What a wonderful man he was to be able to put aside the*

356

fact that she had been soiled, and still do the honorable thing by her.

God, that made her furious. She still hadn't been able to figure out just why Brett was willing to marry her, but it certainly didn't have anything to do with his honor or his love for her. She had even questioned his aunt about it, but if Rachel Leighton knew why, she wasn't saying.

Ariana picked up the fan Jeremy had given her and touched it to her lips. What was he doing at this moment, she wondered. She flicked the fan shut with a snap. Damn him, he was probably with the Sea Witch, laughing at what he had done to her, and at how much money he had gotten from her father. "Damn you, Jeremy. Why can't I hate you?" she shouted, throwing the fan across the room. "It would be so much easier if you weren't always in my thoughts. . . ."

"Madam." Simmons, the majordomo, of Rockglen interrupted the duchess while she was having her tea. "There is a young man here who insists on seeing you."

"Tell him I see no one at this hour of the afternoon," she said, annoyed. "I'm an old woman and I don't take kindly to strangers coming here unannounced."

"I've tried to explain that to him, madam," the old man said, "but still he insists. He says since you are alive, he will not budge from the reception area until you see him."

"Of all the gall," she exclaimed, slamming her cane down hard on the floor. "Where is Brett? Tell him to evict this bounder immediately."

"I'm sorry, your ladyship, but the young lord is off someplace and didn't say when he would return."

"This is probably one of his creditors trying to collect from me," she said in disgust. "All right, show him in. Let's get this distasteful visit over with," she grumbled.

Lady Leighton was surprised when a handsome, velvet-clad young man entered the room. There was something familiar about him, but she wasn't sure just what. Perhaps she'd seen him with Brett, she thought. "All right, young man, I will give you exactly two minutes to state your case."

"Two minutes isn't very much time," he smiled.

"How much does my grandson owe you?" she asked impatiently.

"I beg your pardon?"

"Brett . . . does he owe you money?"

"I haven't the faintest idea who Brett is, m'lady. I've just arrived in England."

358

The Duchess stared into his gray eyes. The feeling of déjà vu was very strong. "What brings you to Rockglen, young man?"

"It seems we are related, m'lady."

"Nonsense, I would know if I had any living relatives other than Brett," she stated emphatically. "What kind of a cruel trick is this?"

"It isn't a trick at all, m'lady. Some twenty years ago my father and I were returning to England from the Indies. A pirate ship attacked us, and I was the only survivor."

Rachel's eyes widened and she put a hand to her breast. "Go on," she ordered.

"I was saved by another pirate who spotted the burning ship. He and his wife raised me as their son. Just recently he gave me this log book from the *Goodwill*. It was the first time I knew who my father was."

She stared at him as if she'd been turned to stone. Jeremy stepped forward, fearing the old lady had taken her last breath.

"Oh my God. . . ." she gasped. "Charles . . . oh my God, you look so much like him. . . . You are Jeremy. . . ."

"That's right," he smiled warmly. He hadn't expected it to be so easy. He still held in his hand the log that he'd hoped would convince her.

"Kneel down here," she ordered. "Let me

see you up close. Yes, yes, you have the Leighton eyes. That is one thing that Brett doesn't have."

Jeremy knelt before Rachel and took her hand. "I wasn't sure I would find you," he said softly, his own eyes blurred with tears. "My father . . . I mean, the man who raised me told me I had a grandmother, and the log book mentioned Rockglen."

Tears rolled down her wrinkled cheeks. "This is truly a miracle," she sniffed. "You left here a little child," she dabbed at her eyes, "and you return from the grave a grown man."

"You should look at this book," he suggested. "I wouldn't want there to be any doubt in your mind."

"There is no doubt in my mind, Jeremy," she whispered. "All I have to do is look at you and I see my son Charles. You are tall and dark, just as he was."

"I remember very little about him, except his death."

"Oh, my dear grandson, how terrible that must have been for you."

"Yes, well that's behind me now. I finally found and killed the man who murdered my father and all those other people. Now I'm ready to get on with my life. I must be honest with you, m'lady. . . ."

"Please, call me Grandmother," she smiled.

"Grandmother, I won't be staying in England any longer than necessary to take care of . . . of some business. I have no idea how long it will take."

"But where will you go? You can't leave now that I've finally found you. You are a Duke, Jeremy, a nobleman of the highest rank. You are the first son of my first son. No, I can't let you go," she clutched his hand. "Just stay with me for a while. We have so much to learn about each other."

Jeremy didn't have the heart to refuse. "I can't promise how long, but I'll stay long enough for us to get to know each other," he smiled. "But you may not like what you learn about me, Grandmother."

Rachel nodded her head, certain that this was no ordinary man she was accepting as her grandson. He had lived a life most would shudder to think about, and yet standing here in front of her, he gave no indication that he was raised as anything but a gentleman of London society.

"My dear, perhaps it would be wise if you didn't mention your previous way of life. Let's just say you were raised by planters or shipbuilders."

"Whatever you wish, Grandmother," he agreed.

Suddenly she chuckled. "This is going to

upset your cousin considerably."

"My cousin?" Jeremy asked.

"Yes, dear; I have another grandson. He's the offspring of Harrison, my second son. He's been living with me since he returned from school. He's a passable young man, but he's very arrogant, and very greedy, I'm afraid. He's going to assume the worst when he meets you," she smiled mischievously. "I'd be willing to wager he won't accept this revelation on your word, so do leave the log with me. I will put it in a safe place."

"Just to set the facts straight, Grandmother, I want nothing from the Leighton family except the use of the name and title while I'm in London."

"But I am a very wealthy woman, Jeremy—"

"I'm also a very wealthy man, Grandmother," Jeremy said kissing her on the cheek. "I don't wish to deprive your other grandson of anything."

"Well, just between you and me, let's not mention that just yet. We'll let him squirm for awhile."

Jeremy laughed. "I can tell already that I have a very crafty grandmother."

"Simmons," she shouted as she rang the bell on the table. "I must try to find Brett," she said to Jeremy. When the old servant entered the room, the Duchess introduced Jeremy as

362

her grandson.

"Grandson?" he repeated, his tired old eyes looking Jeremy up and down. "You're Lord Charles's son. I should have known."

"Simmons has been with me forever," she laughed. "There isn't a secret in this family he doesn't know," she chuckled.

"Now m'lady, you'll have the young man thinking suspicious thoughts about me. Shall I take his bags upstairs?"

"Of course," the Duchess exclaimed. "I want him to have the room next to mine."

"But, m'lady. . . ."

"The room next to mine," she repeated.

"I won't be putting anyone out, will I?" Jeremy asked, seeing the look that passed between them.

"No—it was my husband's room, and no one has used it since he died. I want you close to me so we can talk to all hours of the night. I don't sleep very well, and you'll find I keep very odd hours."

"I will be honored," Jeremy bowed.

"Oh my, I'm so excited," the Duchess said, clapping her hands. "We are having a party here tomorrow night to announce Brett's engagement. What a surprise I shall have for all my friends," she laughed gleefully.

Ariana was spending the evening at home with her family, while Brett was enjoying a night out on the town with his friends. They were all surprised when the Duchess' major-domo arrived, flustered and excited.

"I must find the young Lord," Simmons exclaimed breathlessly. "My God, you wouldn't believe what has happened." He shook his gray head.

"What is it, Simmons?" Ariana's father asked. "Has something happened to Rachel?"

"Something wonderful, sir. I still can't believe it, but there is no doubt when you see him—"

"See who?" William Wellsley asked impatiently.

"Lord Charles's son, sir. He just showed up on the doorstep, insisting on seeing the Duchess."

"Oh, that's wonderful," Ariana exclaimed. "I know she must be so happy."

"She is, m'lady. Her eyes just sparkled when she introduced us."

"Is she sure it is really Charles's son, and not some impostor hoping to be included in her will?" William asked suspiciously.

"When you see the boy, you'll have no doubt, sir . . . no doubt at all. He's tall and handsome just like his father. Polite, too. I don't know where he's been, but he's a fine

364

young man. He'll make the Duchess very proud tomorrow night. Well, if you don't know where Lord Leighton is, I guess I'll have to look elsewhere. There's no telling where he is, and the Duchess is anxious for him to meet his cousin."

"I don't imagine Brett is going to be very happy about having to share the Leighton fortune," Ariana chuckled when she and Lanie were alone.

"Can you imagine coming face to face with someone you thought was dead all these years?" Lanie shivered. "I wonder where he's been?"

"I suppose we will find out all about him tomorrow night. At least he will be the topic of conversation instead me," Ariana yawned.

Lord of himself—that heritage
of woe.

Byron

Chapter Seventeen

Jeremy stared at the young man his grand-mother introduced as his cousin. He hadn't made the connection before, but he knew as soon as Rachel said his entire name just who Brett Leighton was. This was the young man English was going to marry, and the party this evening was to announce that.

Rachel Leighton leaned on her cane and studied her two grandsons. They were sizing each other up like adversaries. She had expected Brett to be defensive, but she was surprised to see the look of hatred in Jeremy's eyes: it was as if he knew Brett. Brett, on the other hand, had been drinking all night and was annoyed at being summoned to join her for breakfast. It was obvious he was still trying to understand the situation.

"What do you mean, *cousin?*" Brett asked, his annoyance obvious. "I have no cousin."

"You didn't listen to me, my dear grandson. Perhaps you'd like a cup of coffee and I'll start over," Rachel smiled.

"Just explain to me why you're allowing this . . . this impostor to claim to be a relative. For God's sake, Grandmother, what were you thinking of to let a perfect stranger come into our home? As soon as I get rid of him, I'm going to have the doctor check you. I am afraid, dear Grandmother, that senility has crept up on you."

"Perhaps we should discuss this later, when you are sober," Jeremy said, looking up from his breakfast.

"Sober?" Brett shouted. "I can handle the likes of you drunk *or* sober. Now get out of this house before I throw you out!"

"You will throw no one out!" Rachel cried angrily.

"I will not allow you to be taken in by this man's lies. My God, Grandmother, Charles and his son disappeared over twenty years ago. Can't you see this man is only here because he knows you don't have long to live?"

Jeremy glanced at his grandmother, realizing that what Brett said was probably true. "Let me explain something to you," he started.

"No," Rachel said, interrupting him. "I don't want you to explain anything. Brett, you may as well make the best of this. This is my grandson, the Duke of Rockglen."

Brett's eyes widened in disbelief. "You can't do this, damn it. I've earned that title. This impostor is no more than an opportunistic fortune hunter."

"Jeremy brought proof with him of his birthright, but I didn't need it. He looks exactly like his father," she said squeezing Jeremy's hand.

Brett's face paled and he clenched his fist. "Damn it, old woman, can't you see this is a trick?"

Jeremy had had enough. He shoved his chair back and picked Brett up out of his chair by his collar. "Apologize to your grandmother," he ordered.

"Who do you think you are?" Brett asked as he dangled an inch off the floor.

"I'm your cousin, whether you want to accept it or not. Now apologize!" he said, cutting off Brett's air passage.

"I'm sorry, Grandmother." Brett gasped for breath. "But it changes nothing," he said as

Jeremy released him. "I'm still not convinced this man is who he says he is, but he and I can discuss it in private," he said, glaring at Jeremy. "Perhaps our solicitor should be present." He gave Jeremy a suspicious look.

"That will have to wait until after the party tonight," Rachel advised. "I have plans for Jeremy today."

Jeremy glared back at his cousin. "Perhaps it would be better if we had our discussion before the party."

"Nonsense. There will be time for discussions later," she insisted. "Go back to bed, Brett. My God, you certainly don't want Ariana to see you looking like that."

Brett swayed where he stood. If his head didn't ache so badly, he'd wouldn't leave her alone with this intruder, but he decided it would be better to face the man when he felt better. He stumbled toward the stairway, mumbling something about taking up the matter later.

"I'm afraid you didn't meet Brett at his best," she chuckled. "I've spoiled him terribly, and now I regret it. He thinks nothing of gambling or staying with harlots for days at a time. I know I should have put a stop to it long ago, but he was all I had. I'm afraid he's going to be in for a rude awakening when he gets married next month."

"I'm afraid he's going to be in for a rude

372

awakening before that," Jeremy commented coldly.

Excusing himself after breakfast, Jeremy went to the inn where Jean Paul had taken a room. It was near the docks, where he could keep an eye on the ship and the sparse crew that had chosen to sail with him. Jeremy's plan had been to face English as soon as he'd introduced himself to his grandmother, but he hadn't intended to like the duchess so much. Now he was finding it difficult to leave as quickly as he'd planned.

He found his friend in the dining room with a barmaid on his lap. "You don't waste any time," he laughed.

"Be a good girl and get my friend a mug," Jean Paul said. "Your introduction must have gone well," he said to Jeremy.

"It went very well. I found that my grandmother is still alive."

"And she accepted your story right off?" Jean Paul asked in surprise.

"Apparently I look very much like my father."

"That's convenient."

"She's a dear, sweet lady."

"Most grandmothers are," Jean Paul agreed.

"There are several problems, though. You're not going to believe this, but English's fiancé is my cousin." At this juncture Jean Paul roared with laughter. "I'm glad you find that amusing," Jeremy said sarcastically.

"I'm sorry, mon ami, but of all the damned luck! Have you met him?"

"Oh yes, I've met him," Jeremy laughed bitterly. "I would probably want to strangle the spoiled dandy even if he wasn't engaged to my woman."

"He's that bad?"

"He's lived too easy all his life. He's younger than I am, but he looks pale and sickly. I can't imagine what English sees in him."

"Of course, you are hardly an impartial judge of character in this case."

"I suppose you're right."

"Does your grandmother know about English?"

"No, I'll be introduced to her tonight at her engagement party," Jeremy said curtly. "I thought it better if I talk to English before showing my hand."

Jean Paul whistled. "Ah, what a tangled web we weave. . . ."

"There's more," Jeremy said, tossing the girl a coin as she sat a mug of ale on the table. "I've promised my grandmother that I would stay in London for a while. I'm afraid she doesn't have long to live. She has a terrible cough, and last night I noticed blood on her handkerchief after she had suffered a bout."

"I'm sorry to hear that, mon ami. Well, I can entertain myself as long as you want to stay. I'm sure the crew feels the same way—you're paying them well."

Jeremy took a long drink of his ale. "How would you like to witness the fireworks tonight?"

"What do you mean?"

"Come to Rockglen. I have a feeling I'm going to need your support tonight. Besides, you wanted to meet English's sister, didn't you?"

"I'm not sure this is going to be the appropriate time, but hell, why not? Are you sure they'll let me in?"

"I'll arrange it. The affair starts at eight," Jeremy said as he stood up. "The majordomo's name is Simmons. Tell him you're my guest."

"You must have made quite an impression," Jean Paul exclaimed.

"I'll see you there," Jeremy said.

"That is the Van Fleet Manor," Rachel Leighton pointed out to her grandson as they rode around London. The Van Fleets will be at the party this evening. "Harrison Van Fleet was a good friend of your father's."

"And that's the Rathbone place," she pointed out. "They have a lovely unmarried

375

daughter."

"Where does Lord Wellsley live?" Jeremy asked in a disinterested voice.

"I didn't realize you knew Lord Wellsley."

"I heard someone mention it was their daughter who was going to marry Brett," he explained without really lying.

"Oh yes, of course you've heard the nasty rumors, I suppose. Ariana is a lovely girl. Don't pay any attention to what you've heard. She had a harrowing experience and really hasn't been herself, but I think this marriage will help. At least I hope it will keep the tongues from wagging."

"I didn't hear any rumors," he said, trying to keep his voice steady.

"The poor girl was held by pirates for months after being rescued at sea. Somehow after Denise and William found out where she was, word got out that she'd been held against her will, and used rather poorly, I'm afraid. You can imagine the gossip that followed. Lady and Lord Wellsley are decent people, and it's been very difficult for them to know their daughter has been the topic of such shameful conversation."

Serves her right, Jeremy thought bitterly. *She should have known what she was coming back to.* "I'm surprised your grandson is still going to do the honorable thing and marry the young lady."

"I wish I could say that he hadn't needed a little prodding," Rachel admitted. "This marriage was arranged before Ariana was born. My first grandson, and William's first daughter."

Brett is not your first grandson, he thought silently. He stared at his grandmother, considering telling her the truth, but she seemed so happy with the way things were going. Besides, if English tells him she left the island on her own accord, what the hell difference did it make?

"What do you mean, he needed prodding?" Jeremy asked.

"I'm ashamed to say he preferred to take her as his mistress rather than his wife. I had to threaten to disinherit him."

"I'm beginning to dislike that cousin of mine more each minute," Jeremy said angrily.

"There it is, dear: Wellsley Manor. Beautiful place, isn't it?"

"Yes," Jeremy answered, his tone distracted. How could anyone not want to marry English? He stared out the coach window at the large stone house. "It looks like a fortress."

"I suppose it does. Would you like to stop in now and let me introduce you? I'm sure they would be pleased. William and Denise have been such good friends."

"Perhaps it would be better if we waited until this evening," he quickly suggested.

"I suppose you're right." She smiled at him. "I do need to rest awhile this afternoon. Even at my age a lady needs her beauty rest," she chuckled.

"You are quite beautiful already," he said, kissing her hand. "I'm sure this evening you will outshine all the other ladies."

"My, my what a gallant I have for a grandson. I shall have to find you a wife, my dear."

"That won't be necessary, Grandmother."

"Oh my, you aren't already married, are you?"

"No, but I've already decided who I want to marry."

"Is she in London?"

"As a matter of fact, she is," he said, glancing out the window as they drove away from Wellsley Manor.

"You shall have to bring her by and introduce us. I'm sorry I didn't know sooner or I would have invited her to this evening's affair."

"That wasn't necessary," he smiled. "I shall introduce you the first chance I get."

Simmons met them at the door and announced that the Duchess' grandson was in the library with her solicitor.

"I should have known he wouldn't listen to me," Rachel said angrily. "Come, Jeremy. It's time you were introduced to my old friend

Nigel Blake. He's worked for me for more years than I want to remember," she said, leading the way to the library.

Simmons stared after them, thinking it was amazing how much better the Duchess seemed since her long-lost grandson arrived. She was walking with spirit in her step again. He shook his head, knowing what young Lord Brett was up to. It would certainly be a shame if anything spoiled her newfound happiness.

"Darling Nigel, what brings you to Rockglen this early in the day?" Rachel greeted.

Her friend looked uneasy, his eyes darting from Brett to Jeremy. "I am sorry, Rachel, but Brett said it was imperative that I come here this afternoon. I knew you would be tied up with preparations for this evening's affair, but I thought I should stop by."

"I'm glad you did." She smiled. "I want you to meet my other grandson. This is Lord Jeremy Leighton, Duke of Rockglen," she introduced.

Jeremy smiled sardonically, his gray eyes meeting Brett's hard blue gaze. "I'd rather just be know as Jeremy Leighton," he said, shaking the solicitor's hand.

"My word, I can see it," Nigel gasped. "It's eerie standing here looking at you. It's like seeing Charles when he was your age."

"I didn't bring you here to add to this foolishness," Brett snapped. "I want you to look over this proof he claims to have," he ordered.

"I'm sorry, Brett—it's just the startling resemblance," the solicitor said, still unable to stop staring at Jeremy. "Your father was a good man. . . ."

"We don't know that Charles was his father," Brett raved. "Would you please just check this proof he claims to have."

Nigel shrugged his shoulders and smiled apologetically at the Duchess. "It's up to you, Rachel . . . whatever you wish me to do."

"Of course, check the proof," she smiled confidently. "I have it in my desk," she said, unlocking the top drawer. She took out a black faded log from the ship *Goodwill* and handed it to Nigel. "I'm sure you'll find everything in order."

They were all silent at Nigel flipped the pages and read silently.

"You see, there isn't any positive proof," Brett squirmed uneasily. "He's a fortune hunter."

"I don't want your money or your title," Jeremy growled.

"Jeremy, please—let's just let Nigel finish reading," Rachel interrupted. "Perhaps we can put this matter to rest once and for all."

For perhaps a full minute, gray eyes locked with blue. Brett had the distinct impression that there was more here than anyone was

380

saying. Why did this bastard keep saying he didn't want the Leighton fortune or title? If he didn't want them, then what was he doing here? And why did there always seem to be a challenge in those icy gray eyes? With a hint of boredom in his voice, Brett said, "One day you will thank me for being cautious, Grandmother."

"And one day you will thank me for trying to make a man out of you," she snapped. "You should be delighted to have found your long-lost cousin."

"Senility," he shook his head sadly. "This is what I was talking about, Nigel. I'm afraid I'm going to have to protect her from herself."

"Quiet," Nigel ordered. "I am almost finished."

A few minutes later Nigel closed the log and looked up. "Well this doesn't prove *without a doubt* that Jeremy is who he says, but it does tell that he was on the ship with his father. Since he looks so much like Charles, and since you have no reason to doubt him, I'd accept his word."

"No, damn it," Brett burst out. "You said it doesn't prove anything."

"Just a moment," Rachel said. "My grandson had a scar on his wrist from falling on a sharp object when he was just a baby." She put her finger to her lips in thought. "It was the right wrist, I believe."

Jeremy stared into the gray eyes so much like his own. He wanted to laugh at her ploy, but instead he held his scarred wrist out for inspection—the wrist that Tia had cut.

"There, didn't I tell you?" she exclaimed triumphantly. "Now, Brett, I don't want to hear another word of doubt—do you understand me?"

"Yes, Grandmother," he said, but his pale blue eyes narrowed with malice as he glared at Jeremy.

"If we are all in agreement, then I shall be on my way," Nigel said, thinking the problem was solved. "Until tonight, Rachel." He kissed her hand. "I know you shall enjoy this evening introducing your grandson," he smiled.

"I'll see you to the door," Brett said.

"You are a very clever woman," Jeremy laughed when they were alone.

"I apologize for the deception, dear one, but I know you're my grandson, and I felt it was the only way I could convince Brett."

"I'm not sure he's convinced yet, but it doesn't matter."

"Oh, it matters very much, Jeremy. Perhaps he'll learn a lesson from this. I think you could probably teach him to be more of a man," she said, thinking how much Brett could learn from Jeremy.

"I have neither the time nor the inclination to teach Brett how to be a man, even if I could," he said lazily. "Tell me, how did you know about the scar?"

"I noticed it when we were in the coach today. I started to say I remembered the scar on your face, but that looks to be a recent injury, and it wouldn't have been such a dramatic revelation," she laughed.

"Yes, this scar is from a recent fight. I received it from the man who killed my father—just before I killed him."

Rachel shivered. "I'm afraid there is a side to you that I would be better off not knowing," she said.

"You are very clever and very wise," he commented. "You must remember, I didn't grow up in London society, Grandmother."

"Yes, I know, my dear; but when I see you and Brett together, I wonder which one of you suffered because of that."

"Didn't you say you wanted to rest before this evening's gathering?" Jeremy reminded her.

"Yes," Rachel sighed. "It's been an exhausting day. But I must admit, I haven't had this much fun in ages."

Jeremy walked his grandmother to the stairs. "You will save a dance for me this evening?"

"Oh, Jeremy," she laughed delighted. "I

haven't danced in years."

"Tonight you shall dance," he said, kissing her on the cheek. "By the way, I hope you don't mind, but I invited a friend. He traveled to England with me."

"Of course not, dear, but why didn't you bring him to Rockglen to stay?"

"He preferred staying at an inn near the ship. His name is Jean Paul Moreau," he said, waiting to see her react to the news of a Frenchman coming into her home.

"A Frenchman, eh? Well, Ariana's mother is French, so perhaps they will have something to talk about," she said, climbing the stairs. "Until tonight, my dear grandson," she waved her hand.

"Until tonight, Grandmother."

Jeremy went back into the library and poured himself a drink. "Until tonight," he raised his glass in salute. "It should certainly prove interesting."

"You haven't won yet," Brett said from behind him.

"I didn't know this was about winning or losing," Jeremy said before downing his drink.

"You'll not get Rachel's money. I have earned it," he said coldly. "Do you have any idea what it's like living with an old woman all your life?"

"I would say you're a very lucky man," Jeremy said calmly. "I find Rachel charming, warm, and amusing. Perhaps you haven't taken the time to notice such things."

"I find her a domineering old woman who won't let go of the purse strings," Brett said coldly.

"I thought as much," Jeremy commented.

"Listen to me, you bastard, I don't know what you want, but I won't stand by and see you rob me of my inheritance and my title," Brett threatened. "There are other ways to deal with people like you."

"I don't want your title or your inheritance. And I suggest you not start something you can't finish," Jeremy warned, his gray eyes flashing like shards of glass.

Brett's face paled and he clenched his fists. "Then what do you want?"

"What I want is none of your damned business," he said, walking past him to the door. "At least not for the moment," he threw over his shoulder as he left his cousin alone and confused.

"Well, I suppose I may as well face the inevitable," Ariana sighed as the seamstress marked the hem of her wedding gown. "I understand invitations will go out tomorrow."

"I wish you could be excited about it," Lanie said.

"I wish I could too, my sweet, but at the

moment, the last thing in the world I want is to be subjected to all the pomp and circumstance that goes along with a wedding — especially since it's a wedding I don't even want."

"Try to think about the fact that you will be the mistress of Rockglen in a few years."

"That doesn't help," Ariana sighed. "And I don't think a knight in shining armor is going to come whisk me away to live happily ever after, either."

"You never know, Ari," her sister said sympathetically.

Ariana smiled at her sister. "You haven't called me that since we were little girls."

"I don't know why not . . . it suits you."

It suits you . . . wasn't that what Jeremy said about calling her English? The image of him sitting on the side of her bed feeding her soup came to mind, and a flood of disturbing emotions gripped her.

"Leave me," she said to the stunned dressmaker who knelt on the floor. "Please, just leave me for a few minutes," she repeated, tears running down her face.

The dressmaker backed out of the room in stunned silence while Lanie went to her sister's side. "What's wrong, Ariana?" she asked, taking her hands. "My God, your hands are as cold as ice. Are you feeling all right? Come sit down."

"I can't go through with this farce. I'd

rather be a spinster for the rest of my life than pretend to love Brett."

Ariana, you don't mean that . . . you've always talked about having children. Brett will give you them. You can wrap yourself up in your family. You know we all love you. Haven't you ever heard that it is better to have loved and lost, than never to have loved at all?"

"Oh, Lanie, what would I do without you?" Ariana cried. "Help me get through this nightmare . . . I can't do it alone."

"I will help you, Ari. I promise. I want you to find happiness."

I am the master of my fate;
I am the captain of my soul.
                    William Ernest Henley

Chapter Eighteen

Jeremy listened politely to the woman his grandmother had just introduced, but his eyes were on the entrance as he heard Simmons announce Lord and Lady Wellsley. He felt his heart skip a beat as English appeared in the doorway, a vision of beauty dressed in an emerald green satin gown.

Damn, he swore beneath his breath. How could she still have this effect on him even after she had played him for a fool? He was only there to get the facts from her, yet all he could think about was taking her in his arms.

He watched Brett kiss her hand briefly, then move on to the mother, and another young lady. That must be her sister, he thought, noticing how much they resembled each other. He glanced across the room to where Jean Paul stood conversing with some men, but he noticed he was looking past them to Ariana's family.

"There's our guest of honor," Rachel exclaimed. "Come," she said, looping her arm through his. "Let me introduce you to Brett's fiancée and her family."

Rachel felt her grandson's muscles tense as they approached the Wellsleys, but she assumed it was because of his dislike for Brett, who was with them. Then she saw the look in Ariana's eyes and she knew something was very strange: Ariana looked as if she'd seen a ghost. She turned deathly white, then a rosy flush marked her high cheekbones.

"Lord and Lady Wellsley, I'd like to present my grandson, Jeremy Leighton, Duke of Rockglen," Rachel introduced with pride.

Ariana stared in disbelief as her father placed a hand on Jeremy's shoulder and told him how happy they were that he and his grandmother were reunited. "Simmons told us last night of your arrival. We've all been anxious to meet you."

"Thank you, sir. I've been anxious to meet

your family also," Jeremy said in honesty. "This is my wife, Denise; my daughters, Ariana and Elaine."

Jeremy bowed over each hand. Then when he took Ariana's hand, he met her eyes with a concerned look. "Your hand is like ice, m'lady."

She quickly pulled her hand away and clasped both of them in front of her. Jeremy was saying something else, but her brain was too numb with shock to hear it. She knew they were all staring at her.

"Ariana, are you all right?" her mother asked.

"What? Oh, yes . . . it's suddenly so close in here. . . ."

"Will you be staying in London long, Lord Leighton?" Ariana's father was asking.

"Please call me Jeremy," he said, wondering why Ariana's sister was staring at him as if she knew who he was. "I'm not really sure how long I'll be staying, sir. I have some business to take care of, then I'll see. First I want to get to know my grandmother," he said, giving her a hug.

Jeremy noticed Brett whisper something to Ariana and she nodded. "Will you excuse us? We're going to get a breath of fresh air."

"Perhaps she should be in front of a fire instead of outside," Jeremy commented.

"I think I know what's best for Ariana," he answered, contempt in his voice.

"Brett, please don't be gone too long," Rachel pleaded. "I would like to make the announcement soon."

Ariana's sister was still openly staring at Jeremy as he talked to her mother and father. When the music began, he turned to her.

"Would you honor me with this dance, Lady Wellsley? I'm afraid I don't know anyone here."

She laid a hand on his arm and followed him to the dance floor. "Who are you?" she asked once they faced each other.

"I beg your pardon?"

"My sister knew you."

"What makes you think that?" he asked coolly as they danced.

"My sister is not a faint-hearted woman, m'lord, but I thought for certain she was going to faint when she saw you."

"How odd," he commented.

"Don't play games with me, m'lord. I think I know who you are from her description. But what I don't understand is why you are pretending to be the Duchess's grandson."

Jeremy suddenly laughed. "English said you were prettier than she, but that she was smarter. I'm beginning to think she was wrong."

Lanie's eyes widened in shock. "You are her

pirate. . . ."

"Yes, I am; but let me explain something. I am not pretending to be Rachel's grandson. I recently discovered that I am the son of the late Charles Leighton."

"Then you're not here to stop Ariana from marrying Brett?" she asked, disappointment in her voice.

"I didn't say that, but that's between you and me."

"Ariana is terribly unhappy, and it's all your fault. How could you have treated her so badly?" she asked accusingly.

"I wasn't aware I had treated her badly. As a matter of fact, it's the other way around."

The music stopped and Jeremy bowed deeply. "Thank you, m'lady. It was most interesting."

"What are you going to do?" Lanie asked, referring to her sister.

"I am going to introduce you to a friend of mine who's been looking forward to meeting you. I hope you will be as kind to him as you have been to me."

Jean Paul seemed thunderstruck as he was introduced to Lady Elaine Wellsley. "Your sister didn't do you justice," he said, kissing her hand.

"Thank you," she smiled shyly. "I could say the same."

Jeremy noticed English and Brett as they returned to the room. "Excuse me, but I think I'll see if my cousin will allow me to dance with his fiancée."

He noticed Ariana pale again as he approached. "Dear cousin Brett, will you allow me to dance with your lovely fiancée?"

"But even I haven't danced with her yet," he protested, then noticed everyone looking their way. "Of course, *cousin,*" he said between gritted teeth.

Ariana's heart beat so loudly that she was sure everyone could hear it, and when Jeremy's hand touched hers she felt as if she'd been burned.

"You are looking lovely, my dear, but a bit pale. What you need is to be in the sun again."

With an effort she finally found her voice. "I can't believe you would show up here pretending to be Rachel Leighton's grandson. What cruel game are you playing now?" she spat.

"Believe me, English, this is definitely not a game," he said, looking down into her green eyes now bright with tears. God, why did he want her so badly when she didn't want him?

"How could you play such a cruel joke on Rachel and Brett? Have you no feelings for anyone?"

"I have feelings for you, but that didn't

make any difference to you, did it? I was nothing but a pirate. Surely pirates don't have feelings," he said bitterly.

"I don't know what you're talking about." She glanced around to see if anyone was looking. "If you are here to extort more money from my father, just forget it. I will not allow it!"

Jeremy stopped dancing. "More money? What the hell are you talking about?"

Ariana's green eyes flashed angrily. "And let me warn you about something else: if you dare hurt Rachel, I'll tell all England who you are, and I'll be the first to cheer when they hang you from the gibbets."

Ariana stormed away, leaving Jeremy standing alone on the dance floor with everyone staring. He met his grandmother's inquisitive stare and shrugged his shoulders.

"I thought you weren't going to cause a scene," Jean Paul said as Jeremy joined him.

"I had no intention of doing so, but she never gave me a chance. Something very strange is going on here, Jean Paul."

"That's an understatement, mon ami. Just the fact of our being here is very strange."

"True, but she asked me if I was here to extort more money from her father."

"Ransom?" Jean Paul asked in disbelief. "But who? Could we have underestimated our friend Dobson? Surely he didn't have the intelligence to pull off something like this?"

"Perhaps with help," Jeremy mused. "I think that's where Tia comes into the picture."

"I wouldn't be a damned bit surprised if Saint-Gilles didn't have something to do with it too," Jean Paul exclaimed.

"Somehow I have to get English alone so we can talk."

"That may not be easy. Even your grandmother is watching you with a suspicious eye."

"I know. I'm going to have to explain things to her soon, but not just yet," Jeremy said, glancing around to see where English was. "Damn," he hissed, seeing that his grandmother was preparing to make her announcement.

"As you all know, I have two reasons for celebration this evening. By now you have all met my grandson Jeremy, who has returned to me after all these years. Well, now I have another announcement to make, and I want to thank Lady and Lord Wellsley for allowing me to do this at Rockglen on Ariana's birthday. Most of you probably know that years ago the Wellsley and Leighton families betrothed Ariana and Brett, but tonight we are making it official. One month from today Lady Ariana Wellsley and Lord Brett Leighton will be married at Wellsley Manor.

398

Everyone clapped except Jeremy and Jean Paul. "Did you know this was her birthday?" Jean Paul asked.

"I knew."

Ariana's eyes met Jeremy's, and for a moment it was as if they were back on the island. Her mouth went dry and she felt as if she were suffering from a fever. But she wasn't delirious. He was here, standing not twenty feet from her, looking for all the world like the titled gentleman he pretended to be. My God, he made all the other men in the room look like dandies, she thought. The beauty of his snugly fitted black velvet suit and white silk shirt was simplistic, yet he stood out from all the others in their golds and lavenders. What an actor he was, she thought bitterly. Hadn't she been one of his biggest followers, she thought in disgust. He could make anyone believe whatever he wanted.

A servant passed glasses of champagne as first Lord Wellsley and then the Duchess toasted to a happy, fertile marriage.

"Over my dead body," Jeremy growled. "There will be no marriage to Brett Leighton! I am going to put a stop to this right now—"

"Jeremy, wait," Jean Paul restrained him by the arm. "This is not the time. You should talk to English alone."

Jeremy took a deep breath. "I suppose

you're right."

"Give me a chance to occupy your cousin," Jean Paul suggested.

"How are you going to accomplish that?"

"You did say he liked to gamble."

"Yes, and I hear he does it very badly."

"Give me a few minutes to interest him, then you can talk to English in private."

When Jeremy saw English alone with her sister, he decided to make his move. As she saw him approaching, she turned and quickly left the room. He caught up with her just outside the library.

"We have some matters to settle," he said, taking her by the arm.

"We have nothing to discuss." She jerked her arm away.

"Listen to me, English—we can go into Rachel's library and discuss this calmly, or we can make a scene right here in the hallway. It's up to you. Either way, I'm going to have some answers."

"You're going to have some answers?" she asked in disbelief. "You really do have a lot of nerve."

"Into the library," he said, shoving her ahead of him.

"Weren't you satisfied making a fool of me

on New Providence?" she turned on him angrily. "Do you have to come here and ruin my life in England, too? Brett is willing to marry me, even knowing that I am no longer a virgin."

"How magnanimous of him," Jeremy answered sarcastically, "but he needn't have sacrificed so."

"What is that supposed to mean?" she asked, moving to the other side of the desk.

"You won't be marrying cousin Brett," he said bluntly.

"What right do you have . . . I can't believe you!" she sputtered. "First you tell me you love me, then the next minute you ransom me back to my family. My God, haven't you caused me enough shame? I'm already the laughingstock of London."

Jeremy couldn't bear seeing her tears. He reached out for her. "English, I've been trying to tell you. . . ."

Suddenly the door opened and Rachel Leighton entered, closing it quickly behind her. "Do you mind telling me what's going on?"

"It's a long story, Grandmother," Jeremy said, moving away from Ariana.

"Then let me make it a short one," Rachel said angrily. "You are the pirate who held Ariana."

"How did you know that?" he asked, reluctant to lie to her further.

"It wasn't hard to guess after noticing the look on Ariana's face when she saw you. I'm surprised everyone in the place hasn't figured it out."

I'm sorry, Rachel," Ariana said. "I had no idea he would come here."

"What else have you been lying to me about?" Rachel asked Jeremy.

Jeremy's lips tightened grimly as he faced his grandmother's wrath. "I haven't lied to you about anything. We did not discuss English . . . Ariana."

Rachel lowered herself into a chair, suddenly feeling very tired. "Do you think deliberately skirting the fact makes it any better than lying?" she asked angrily.

"I came here to find English. I had no idea I was going to find any relatives here. I was told that twenty years ago I had a grandmother living in London, so I decided I would be safer if I came to England using my title, instead of announcing I was a pirate. I was delighted to find you alive, and I had every intention of telling you exactly why I was here, but then Brett came into the picture, and I find that he's engaged to my woman. And on top of that, I still haven't had a chance to talk with English," he said, growing impatient.

"Who you are and why you're here is no

longer important to me," Rachel exploded. "What I want to know is how you could use this child so shabbily and then toss her aside?"

Jeremy's eyes met Ariana's. "It wasn't that way. . . ."

Suddenly the door flew open and Brett stared at Jeremy, his fists clenched at his side. "So this is what you're after?"

"What is he after?" Rachel asked from the chair on the other side of the room.

Brett seemed stunned to find his grandmother there. "I'm sorry, I didn't see you there, Grandmother."

"That's obvious," she answered, annoyed that they had been interrupted.

"Someone told me they had seen Ariana come in here with my *cousin*," he said, glaring at Jeremy.

"You may as well know," Jeremy started, but as usual, Rachel interrupted him.

"I wanted to discuss an appropriate escort for Jeremy with Ariana," she said, daring him to dispute her. "I thought she might know of someone who could attend some of the social functions of the wedding with him."

Brett glanced at Ariana, then at Jeremy. The three of them were certainly acting strangely. "You should have asked me," he said arrogantly. "I know more people in London than Ariana does."

403

"I hadn't thought of that, dear. Of course you are right. Who would you suggest?"

A sly smile came over Jeremy's face. "What about Lady Ratcliff's daughter?" he suggested, remembering how she chattered incessantly about nothing.

"Penelope? No, I don't think so," Rachel mused. Though it would serve him right, she thought silently.

"I think she would be perfect for him."

"Thank you both, but I can find my own escorts," Jeremy said, still irritated that he hadn't been able to talk to Ariana. She kept her eyes down and wouldn't look at him. Damn her, he thought angrily. What do I have to do to make her talk to me?

"I will introduce Jeremy to Penelope and let him make his own decision," Rachel said. "Why don't you and Ariana go on and dance and have a good time? I'd like to talk with Jeremy for a few minutes."

"Rachel," Jeremy said, a warning tone in his voice.

"I know, dear—you want to get back to the festivities also. I shan't keep you but a moment."

"Why didn't you let me tell him?" Jeremy asked angrily. "I have no intention of letting him marry her."

"You have no say in the matter!" She

slammed her cane on the floor. "You haven't answered me yet. How could you do such a thing to her? You may have been raised a pirate, but you have Leighton blood in you."

"It wasn't the way you think it was. I was in love with her and she with me. I never had any intention of letting her return to England. I intended to marry her and settle in the Carolinas."

"As a pirate's wife?" she asked in a choked voice.

"No. As a planter's wife," he muttered.

"Then why did you ransom her to her family?"

"I didn't! I didn't even know until tonight that she was under that impression. I risked my life to come to England to find out why she left me."

Rachel drummed her fingers on the table beside her. "Have you told Ariana that you didn't ransom her?"

Jeremy laughed bitterly. "No, I haven't. We keep getting interrupted."

"Please, promise me that you won't try to speak with her again this evening. I don't want everything ruined if she should decide she doesn't want anything more to do with you."

"I won't leave London without her. . . ."

Rachel raised her hand. "Just listen to me. I am having tea with the Wellsley family tomorrow afternoon. I will talk with Ariana privately and explain the circumstances. If she tells me she wants to marry you instead of Brett, then I will talk with Denise and William. Now do I have your word that you will not attempt to talk with her again this evening?"

Jeremy had to laugh. "You're a tough old bird."

"Among other things," she said as she hugged him. "I want no more lies between us."

Jeremy looked sheepish. "Then there is one other thing I better tell you. . . ."

"Yes," she looked up at him through narrowed eyes.

"The Frenchman who's here as my guest — he's also a pirate."

"Why doesn't that surprise me?" Rachel said, looking heavenward.

For the rest of the evening Jeremy kept his distance from Ariana and Brett. It wouldn't have done him any good to try to talk to her anyway, since Brett wasn't letting her out of his sight. He did have the opportunity to talk with Lanie again, and she promised to plead his case with her sister.

"Jean Paul explained what happened," Lanie said. "I'm sure she will change her mind once she knows the truth. Then, if we can just convince Mother and Father. . . ."

"One thing at a time," Jeremy laughed. "I've given Rachel my word that I won't try to talk to her again this evening, but if you will, tell her that I intend to have this matter settled by this time tomorrow."

"I will tell her," she said, glancing up at Jean Paul, who was staring at her like a schoolboy in love. "I can't believe you are both pirates."

"Shh," Jeremy warned. "Let's not have a hanging party right here."

"I'm sorry. I doubt anyone would believe it," she laughed. "You are both so . . . so handsome," she said, then looked away, embarrassed. "You must forgive me. I'm afraid I'm a bit nervous this evening."

"As we all are," Jean Paul laughed. "Now I know what it feels like to be a guppie in a pond of sharks."

Jeremy saw Ariana dancing with his cousin. "Damn, I hate this," he hissed. "I should be talking with her right now and getting this matter straightened out."

"Be patient, mon ami," Jean Paul encouraged. "I'm sure everything will work itself out.

Jeremy glanced across the room and met Ariana's eyes. God, he'd missed her. It took all the willpower he had not to storm across the room and carry her away. Fate had played a very strange trick on him, he thought bitterly.

It had given him his heritage and a title, but in exchange, it had bound him with respectability and honor.

Ariana was tense and irritable when they returned home. After saying good night to her parents, she went to the kitchen to get a glass of milk. Lanie followed her, suggesting that they stay up and talk for a while.

"I don't want to talk about him, if that's what you mean to do," she snapped at her sister. "I saw you talking and smiling at him. Well, let me warn you, little sister, I'll be the first to admit he has a charm about him, but he's as deadly as a snake, and that goes for Jean Paul too."

"Jeremy says he did not ransom you," Lanie persisted, "and I believe him."

"Of course he'd say that. Do you think he'd want Rachel to know what he really is? He's a pirate, Lanie. He kills people so he can live like a king."

"You said you loved him, Ariana, and I don't believe that's changed. I saw the way you looked at him tonight."

"I don't wish to discuss this," Ariana said, storming past her sister. "You wouldn't understand."

When Ariana reached her room, she found a ribbon-tied box on her bed. Brett must have found a way to get it there, she thought. Perhaps she had misjudged him if he could be so thoughtful. She unwrapped the small box.

She lifted a beautiful gold heart on a delicate gold chain and held it to the light. It was exquisite, she thought with a long sigh. She picked up the note inside. *Happy Birthday, English,* it read.

Ariana dropped the necklace and note as if it had burned her. *"No, damn you, I will not let you hurt me again."* She began to cry.

Circumstances rule men; men do not rule circumstances.

Herodotus

Chapter Nineteen

Jeremy paced, waiting for Rachel to come back from her afternoon with the Wellsley family. This was stupid, he told himself. He should never have agreed to let his grandmother do his talking. He had learned years ago if he wanted something done right he had to do it himself.

He heard the front door open and then Simmons' voice greeting the duchess.

"Did you get everything straightened out?" Jeremy asked as he met her at the door.

Rachel removed her cape and handed it to

Simmons. "I'll have tea in the library. I hope you've kept the fire blazing," she said, rubbing her hands together. "I'm chilled to the bone. I do believe it is going to snow."

"Your fire is blazing, and tea is ready," Simmons said. "I will bring it right in."

Patience, Jeremy told himself. His grandmother was an old woman, and she wasn't about to be rushed. Rachel sat in the chair closest to the fire while Simmons poured her tea. Jeremy leaned against the mantelpiece, waiting.

"Do pour yourself a drink, dear. I know you don't care for tea."

"I don't care for anything right now, Grandmother. Just tell me what happened when you talked to English."

"Why do you persist in calling her English? She has such a beautiful name."

"It's just habit," he answered, trying to remain patient. "Please, Grandmother. . . ."

"I'm afraid I have distressing news, my dear."

Jeremy straightened up. "What did she say?" he asked.

"She says she still intends to marry Brett."

"You explained to her that I did not ransom her?" Jeremy asked, trying to stay calm.

"I told her, my dear. She said it didn't matter . . . that she was never sure of your love, and she will not be put through the heartache

414

of never knowing when you'll change your mind again."

"Damn it, I didn't change my mind," he shouted. "She left me; I didn't leave her. I knew I should have talked to her myself. Well, by God, it isn't too late. . . ."

"Jeremy, calm down and listen to me," his grandmother insisted. "I don't think Denise and William would ever have allowed Ariana to marry you, even if she had wanted to. You would have had to tell them the truth about who you are, and I don't think they would have been able to accept that. This is for the best, my dear; so please, for your sake and Ariana's, consider the matter closed. Give me your word that you will abide by her decision."

"I'm sorry, Grandmother; I can't do that. I came a long way to find out why she left me, and now that I know, I'm not leaving England without her. There's no way in hell I'm going to let her marry Brett. No, Grandmother, I'm sorry; the matter is far from closed!"

Rachel stared in stunned silence as he stormed past her out of the room. She shook her head. "I would have been surprised if you had said anything else, my dear boy." She took a sip of her tea and smiled. "How very like your father you are."

415

When Jeremy reached Wellsley Manor he met Jean Paul and Lanie as they returned from a walk in the park.

"I must see your sister," he demanded.

"I'm sorry, Jeremy. She and Brett are attending a music social this evening. I don't expect her to return for hours."

"Damn," he said, running his hand through his hair in frustration. "I've already wasted so much time," he said. He considered going to the social, but he knew he'd probably be thwarted again.

Seeing his consternation, Lanie placed a hand on his arm. "I tried to talk with her last night and this morning, Jeremy, but she refuses to discuss the matter with me."

"The whole mater has gotten out of hand. All I need to do is talk with her and I can straighten everything out." Jeremy suddenly noticed the woman only a few feet away. "Is she with you?" he asked.

"She's our chaperone," Jean Paul laughed. "Things are done a little differently here, mon ami."

"That's an understatement," Jeremy agreed. "I'll let you be on your way, but first, Lanie, tell me which room is your sister's?"

"Oh my, I can't do that," Lanie exclaimed.

"Lanie, I love your sister, and she loves me. Do you want to be responsible for her being

416

trapped in a loveless marriage with Brett?"

"No," she sighed. "I know she loves you, Jeremy, but she's afraid."

"Afraid of what?" Jeremy demanded.

"Of the unknown, I imagine," Lanie answered. "She knows what she's getting into with Brett. She'll live in London as the mistress of Rockglen, and be close to her family. She has no idea where she'd be living with you."

"That's exactly why I must talk to her. I have to make her see that I can take care of her and give her a good life. Please, Lanie, give me a chance at least to plead my case."

Lanie glanced at the servant. "Ariana's room is on the corner on the second floor. You can see it from here. What do you plan to do, Jeremy?"

"I'm going to wait for her in there. That way she won't be able to avoid me any longer."

"Oh, Jeremy, if Father should discover you, I'm afraid it will all be over for you and Ariana."

"That's a chance I'll have to take. Do the servants attend her when she retires?"

"Lately Ariana has insisted on her privacy."

"Good. I have Mattie wrapped around my little finger, but I haven't met any of the other servants."

"Mattie?" Lanie asked in disbelief. "How did you meet Mattie?"

417

"Yesterday I convinced her to place a birthday present on Ariana's bed. I thought for a while my charm was going to fail me, but she finally agreed."

Lanie laughed. "You've more charm than you'll ever know, if you charmed that one."

Ariana sat silently in the carriage next to Brett as they traveled back to Wellsley Manor. The evening had been long and boring, and she had a splitting headache. She wondered how she was ever going to manage to get through all the events that were planned before the wedding . . . particularly with Jeremy on the scene for most of them. Perhaps he'd leave and go back to New Providence, now that he knew she wasn't falling for any more of his scheming. She couldn't imagine why he bothered to come to London or lie about what he'd done. None if it made any sense.

"I don't believe you enjoyed yourself this evening," Brett commented.

"I found it a bit long, but it was very nice," she said. "I'm just very tired."

"We do seem to be caught up in a whirlwind, don't we? Between your family and my grandmother, I'm afraid we're in for a lot of long evenings. Tell me what do you think of my cousin," he said, catching her off guard.

"Your cousin?" she asked, feeling her heart race at the mere mention of his name. "I suppose he is nice. I only spoke with him for a few moments in the library."

"I don't believe his story for a minute," he said tersely.

"Oh," Ariana said, feeling a lump in her throat. What story was he talking about, she wondered.

"No, I think this is a very elaborate plan to get Rachel's money."

Ariana breathed a sigh of relief. "Everyone says he is the spitting imagine of his father. . . ."

"I know, but that could just be a coincidence. I mean, he has gray eyes and black hair. So what?"

"My heart goes out to Rachel if he is lying," Ariana confessed. "She looked so much better last night then she has for a while. Don't you agree?"

Brett squeezed Ariana's hand. "That's because she is excited about us, my love. Rachel is always at her best when she is controlling everyone's lives."

"That isn't a very kind thing to say," she snapped.

"No — but it's true."

"How does she control your life? It seems to me you've always done whatever you wanted," she said irritably.

"She controls my life in many ways, Ariana. She expects me to live off the pittance she supplies monthly. I'm tired of having to ask her for everything I need. Once we are married, that will all end."

Ariana fell silent. So that was it, she thought grimly. Rachel had apparently made some kind of deal with Brett to keep him interested in her.

"Here we are," he said as the carriage stopped before her house. "May I have a good night kiss before we get to the door?"

This was what she had dreaded, but she knew there wasn't any sense arguing about it. Since he considered her a fallen woman, he apparently didn't feel it was necessary to follow the proper social behavior any longer.

She leaned toward him and closed her eyes. "Nothing chaste like that, my dear. I don't want a sisterly kiss. I want you to kiss me like you kissed your pirate."

He pulled her in his arms and roughly captured her mouth. Ariana felt repelled by his kiss, but she knew there wasn't any sense fighting him.

"I certainly hope you have more spirit once we are married, Ariana. I'd hate to have to get my pleasure away from home," he said cruelly.

"Goodnight, Brett," she said, climbing from

the carriage without his assistance. "You needn't see me to the door."

Thomas, the butler, met her at the door and took her wrap. "Are you all right, m'lady?"

"Yes, I'm just tired, Thomas," she sighed. "The evening lasted much later than I expected. Has everyone gone to bed?"

"Yes, m'lady. Would you like me to get one of the maids to assist you?"

"No, I'll be fine, thank you. All I want to do is get into my own bed."

"Very good, m'lady. The lamp is on the table at the foot of the stairs. I will say good night."

Ariana picked up the lamp and slowly climbed the stairs. She felt as if she had the weight of the world on her shoulders. Why had nothing turned out the way she wanted? The man she loved was devious and scheming, and the man she was going to marry was selfish and repulsive. God, what had she done to deserve such a fate, she wondered.

Ariana opened the door of her room, lit only by the glow of the fire. She set the lamp on the table beside her bed, then let out a long sigh as she rubbed her temples.

"Is your conscience bothering you, English?"

She spun around and found Jeremy sitting in her chair, his long legs stretched out in front

421

of him. "My God, are you out of your mind?"

"Nearly," he answered. "I was beginning to think you were going to spend the night with my cousin, and if that were the case, I'd have had to kill him."

Ariana was finding it difficult to breathe. That he could have such an affect on her after what he'd done filled her with anger. "You'd better leave before someone finds you here," she said as she removed her gloves. "I wouldn't want to see you killed."

"That's comforting," he said sarcastically. "I'll leave when we have this matter settled between us."

"You don't have to explain anything to me, Jeremy," she said coldly. "I understand greed and animal lust."

"Did my cousin teach you about them?" he asked. "I understand he excels at both."

Ariana's eyes flashed angrily. "I will not discuss Brett with you." She turned her back to him.

"If you choose to marry him, I predict you'll spend your life making excuses for him," he said in a clipped voice. "Is that what you want?"

"You gave up any right to be concerned about me when you ransomed me to my father," she said between gritted teeth.

He was out of the chair and in front of her

before she realized his intention. "You don't understand a damned thing I've been telling you. I did not ransom you. I was devastated when I returned to New Providence and found you gone. I thought you had deserted me."

"So you decided to come to London and pretend to be the cousin of my fiancé so you could explain to me that you didn't ransom me?" she said in disgust. "Do you really think I'm so stupid that I'd believe such a story?"

He took a deep breath. "I know it sounds farfetched, but it's true, English. When Kennedy returned and said he'd been shanghaied, I began to realize something was very strange."

"Kennedy shanghaied?" Ariana asked in disbelief.

"That's right. He said while you were resting that morning after watching us leave the harbor, someone hit him over the head, and the next thing he knew he was on a ship."

She was speechless.

"Well, with a little bit of ingenuity that only Kennedy could have accomplished, he made it back to New Providence. That was when I started to be suspicious about the circumstances surrounding your departure."

"I searched for Kennedy that morning after that wretched little man was there," she said, vividly remembering the devastation she had felt that morning.

423

"What man?" Jeremy asked.

"I don't remember his name," she said, moving away from him to stare out the window. "All I remember is that he told me you and the Sea Witch had sailed together that morning."

Jeremy moved to stand behind her. "And you believed that of me after I told you how much I loved you?"

"You don't understand." She turned around to face him. "Everything started falling into place. Kennedy was gone, there was this man's story, and then Father arrived, telling me that he had paid you a ransom for my release . . . and your note, Jeremy," she said in anguish. "You said that no matter what happened, your time with me had been the best you'd ever had. What was I supposed to assume but that this was your farewell message? My God, can you honestly say you wouldn't have thought the same thing?"

"English, English," he said, gently wiping a tear from her cheek. "I never meant for you to think that. I meant that if anything should happen to me . . . if I shouldn't make it back, that my time with you had been the most important time in my life. And I still mean that, love."

Ariana didn't say anything. Again she moved away from him. "I don't know what to think anymore."

"Hasn't it occurred to you that someone could have been lying to both of us?"

"Tia wasn't on the island," she said bitterly. "That was the first thing I checked."

"I'm not sure of that," he said. "Perhaps she wanted us to think she had left the island. Dobson wasn't smart enough to pull this off by himself."

"Dobson?" Ariana spun around. "That was the name of the man who came to Devil's Reach that morning."

"I'm not surprised. My guess is that Tia and Saint-Gilles were behind the whole thing. Dobson was just a pawn in their devious scheme."

"They would go to such lengths to separate us?"

"That, and to get the ransom money your father paid for your release. I'm sure Tia never thought I'd come after you."

"You thought I had deserted you, yet still you came after me?" she asked, beginning to believe they had been cruelly tricked.

"I had enough faith in our love to have doubts about your leaving from the beginning, but it wasn't until Kennedy returned that I knew I had to find out for myself why you left me—and all the while I prayed that you hadn't left of your own accord."

Ariana stared into his eyes for a long time. Her anger had drained away, leaving confusion

425

and desolation in its place. Again she moved away from him and stared out the window. "You must know this changes nothing," she said softly.

"How can you say that?" he asked, bewildered.

"I am relieved to know that you didn't betray me, but I have to think of my family, and Rachel and Brett. I cannot just tear everyone's life apart for my selfishness."

"They would want you to be happy, English. At least I know Rachel would. I'll explain everything to Brett. I can't say I like the young man, but perhaps I can make him understand."

"I don't know. . . ."

He took her by the shoulders and turned her around to face him. "It was always intended that you be my bride." He smiled tenderly at her. "I am the first grandson of Rachel Leighton, and you are the first daughter of Lord Wellsley."

She smiled at him through her tears. "You make it sound possible, but I know it won't be easy, Jeremy."

"Nothing worth having is easily won, love. Now, will you please kiss me and tell me you're happy to see me. The past few days have been hell."

Ariana threw her arms around his neck. "Oh

426

Jeremy, is this nightmare really about to be over?"

"It will be for me, once you tell me you still love me." His voice was soft, tentative.

"I never stopped loving you, Jeremy, even when I thought you had betrayed me."

"That's what I needed to hear," he said, lifting her chin to tenderly kiss her. "I have been going out of my mind, English," he whispered against her mouth. The kiss deepened, becoming more passionate. She pressed her body against his, feeling the familiar ache of desire.

When he ended the kiss she stared at him, touching his nose, his jaw, then his scarred cheekbone. "How did you get this?" she asked softly.

"It is my victory scar," he smiled, kissing the palm of her hand. "I killed Salizar."

Ariana's eyes widened. "Oh Jeremy, I forgot the reason you really left New Providence."

"I have had other things on my mind, too," he said, pulling her closer. "You are too thin and too pale." He ran his hand down her back and over her hips. "I must do something about that."

"Well, that's bloody marvelous," she exclaimed, pretending to be insulted. "I would have thought that you'd be telling me how beautiful I am to you."

427

"You are," he kissed the tip of her nose, "but you don't belong here."

"No, I don't," she agreed softly. "I belong wherever you are." Suddenly she shook her head. "Oh, Jeremy, I hope we can accomplish that without hurting a lot of people. My family has been so good to me."

"I promise to do my best," he said, placing kisses along her neck.

Ariana pressed her hand against his chest, feeling his heart beating as rapidly as hers. She drew him toward her bed, but he hesitated. He whispered her name, brushing her eyelids with his lips. "Oh God, I've missed you, English. I could swear I heard your name on the soft sea breeze that caressed my face. When I'd look into the depths of the sea, I could see your green eyes staring back at me, laughing and teasing."

"I know, darling. When I found the gold heart on my bed, it opened a whole wellspring of memories for me, particularly our last night together on the island. I couldn't sleep all night for the turmoil of wanting you and knowing you were so near."

"We must put an end to this soon, English."

"Stay with me tonight," she pleaded.

"I cannot, love," he said in anguish. "I couldn't face your father in the morning if I had bedded his daughter under his own roof

428

the night before."

"Is this the pirate, Jeremy Corbett of New Providence?" she laughed softly.

"This is Jeremy Corbett who never wants to be the reason for you ever to be ashamed again." He kissed her nose, then her lips. "I love you, English, and I'll be back in the morning to claim you for my own." He opened the heavy drape and stepped out on the ledge.

"My God, is that how you got in?" she exclaimed. "Oh Jeremy, do be careful."

"I will, love. Until tomorrow." He threw her a kiss.

Ariana held her breath as she watched him climb down the vine-covered wall. Once he reached the ground, he quickly disappeared into the darkness.

"Until tomorrow," she whispered into the night.

The prince of darkness is a gentleman.

Shakespeare

Chapter Twenty

Brett had decided to stop and have a brandy with his drinking companions before going home. The hour was late as his carriage approached Rockglen, and he was surprised to see the lights still on. What was Rachel doing up at this hour, he wondered.

Silently he entered. He could hear Rachel's voice coming from the library. He laid his cape over a chair and crept down the hall.

"Please be happy for me, Grandmother," Jeremy said. "You told my yourself that you had betrothed your *first* grandson to Lord

Wellsley's first daughter," he reminded. "And I am your first grandson."

Rachel shook her head. "I have little doubt that you convinced Ariana of your love, dear, but what about her parents? What if they absolutely refuse to give their permission?"

"Then I will take her with me anyway, but with you backing me, I'm sure I can convince Lord Wellsley that I am suitable for his daughter."

Brett couldn't believe what he was hearing. So that was it: his cousin wanted Ariana. His grandmother's next statement left him stunned.

"I want them to know the truth about everything, even that you are the *Black Moriah*."

"Agreed," Jeremy smiled. "I will tell them that after I explain to them how much I love their daughter."

Brett leaned against the doorjamb, unable to believe what he heard. The bastard was the pirate who had held Ariana on New Providence—and who had robbed her of her virginity. He stumbled backward toward the front door, blind rage gripping him. The bastard wasn't going to get away with it. The Leighton title and fortune would never fall into the hands of this despicable pirate, he swore.

"Did your solicitor draw up the papers I

requested?" Jeremy asked.

"Yes, but I think you are a fool to waive your rights to the Leighton fortune," she snapped, "and I will absolutely not listen to this nonsense about giving up the title. No matter where you go, your title will help you. For God's sake, Jeremy, think of your children."

"If it will make you happy, Grandmother. I know Brett won't be happy about it, and I can't say that I blame him."

"Brett isn't interested in anything but money, I'm sorry to say."

"Perhaps I should offer him some type of retribution," Jeremy suggested. "Whether he knows it or not, he will be doing me a great service if he releases Ariana from her commitment without causing any problems."

"I suppose it is worth a try," the Duchess agreed, wishing her other grandson weren't so greedy. "I'm afraid you will have to wait until morning, though. He hasn't returned home yet."

The Earl of Orford, First Lord of the Admiralty, was a gambling friend of Brett's, and the person who Brett decided would be most interested in the whereabouts of a notorious pirate. He made his way to the house on

Romney Street, oblivious to the cold. The house was dark, but he beat upon the door until one of the servants woke and answered it.

"I must see the Earl immediately," Brett demanded. "Tell him it's Lord Brett Leighton."

Brett wandered into one of the dark rooms and proceeded to light a lamp. "What is it that couldn't wait until morning?" the Earl asked from the doorway.

"I thought you'd be interested to know that the pirate Black Moriah is staying at Rockglen."

"Come, Lord Leighton, surely you jest. Have you been drinking all evening?"

"It's the truth, m'lord . . . he's posing as my cousin. I overheard him tonight admit that he was the notorious pirate. I even know where his ship is anchored."

"The Black Moriah, you say: that would be quite a feather in our caps. I imagine Spain would be very generous if we turned him over to them."

"I'd rather see him hang from the gibbets here," Brett insisted.

"To be honest with you, Lord Leighton, he would probably get off scotfree if he went to trial at Old Bailey. The Black Moriah has always been very careful to avoid English ships, but he has made the seas a living hell

436

for the Spanish."

"He's a pirate," Brett said in disbelief. "What difference does it make whose ships he robs?"

"Calm down, my friend. I am sure we can do him in, and I assume that's what you are mainly interested in."

Ariana woke the next morning feeling nauseated. She was overtired, she told herself as she climbed from her bed. As soon as things settled down she would start to feel better.

She dressed with care, knowing that she would see Jeremy in just a few hours. She glanced in the mirror, not really seeing herself as she thought about Jeremy facing Brett. By now Jeremy should have talked to Brett and his grandmother, she thought excitedly. She took several deep breaths, trying to calm her queasy stomach. God, she would be glad when this was over!

There was a soft knock at her door and Ariana's heart skipped a beat. It was too early for Jeremy to be there. . . . Lanie hesitantly stuck her head in the door and smiled.

"Good morning," Ariana greeted her. "Have you been down for breakfast yet?"

"No," Lanie smiled. "I was just checking to see if you were ready to go down."

437

"Indeed I am, she smiled, taking her sister's hand.

"You are looking very pleased with yourself this morning," Lanie commented.

"I will tell you a secret, little sister—I think everything is going to work out for me and Jeremy," she whispered. "He is suppose to come here today and talk with Mother and Father."

"Oh, Ari, I'm so happy for you." Lanie hugged her sister. "I just knew everything would work out."

"Good morning, darlings," Denise greeted. "I am so pleased to see you both up bright and early this morning. We have so many things that need to be taken care of."

"Please, Mother, can't we have just one day without talk about this wedding?" Ariana pleaded.

"Well, I suppose so, dear." Her mother looked surprised. "Are you feeling all right? You look a bit pale."

"To be honest, my nerves are drawn so taut I feel I may snap."

"Then by all means, rest today," her mother said as she stood up. "There are things I can take care of without you."

"You will be around the house today?" Ariana asked, fearing her mother intended to leave.

438

"Of course, dear. I'll be here all afternoon," she said, kissing her daughter on the top of the head. "Enjoy your breakfast, my dears."

Ariana stared down at the plate of eggs Mattie had set before her, and her stomach did a flip. She quickly pushed the plate away and sipped at her tea, willing herself not to be sick, but it wasn't going to work. Suddenly she pushed away from the table and ran toward the pantry, barely grabbing a receptacle in time.

"Oh my God," she moaned.

"Ariana, are you all right?" Lanie asked, pushing her sister's hair away from her face.

Ariana glanced around at her surroundings and began to laugh. "I knew I couldn't make it back to my room. . . ."

"Is it what I think?" Lanie asked.

Ariana shook her head yes. "It seems Jeremy and I resolved our problems none too soon."

"Does he know yet?"

"No, I wasn't even sure myself until a few minutes ago. I've been trying to convince myself that I was just tired. I suppose I should look at the bright side: I don't think Mother and Father would refuse to let me marry Jeremy now."

* * *

"I don't believe he ever returned home last night, m'lady," Simmons said of her grandson Brett. "At least I haven't seen him."

"Damn!" Jeremy swore. "I wanted a chance to talk with him before I spoke with Lord Wellsley. I don't like springing this on him after the fact."

"Go ahead and talk with them," Rachel suggested. "If Brett returns while you're gone, I'll explain everything to him. As I said, he didn't want to be forced into this marriage in the first place. I'm sure he'll step aside once he realizes that you are waiving your rights to the Leighton fortune."

"I hope you are right, Grandmother. I wouldn't want to end up in a duel with my own cousin." Jeremy kissed his grandmother on the cheek. "Wish me luck."

"I still think you should let me go with you."

"I'm grateful, but I'd rather try doing this on my own first."

Rachel hugged her grandson. "Your father would be proud of you, Jeremy Leighton."

"Thank you, Grandmother. That means a great deal to me. I hope Lord Wellsley will take into consideration who my ancestors were, instead of what I have been."

"He's a fair man. I'm sure he will understand."

440

Jeremy stepped outside into the cold, windy London weather. He pulled his coat around him, wondering why anyone would want to live in such a climate. He glanced down the street looking for Rachel's carriage, which Simmons had summoned. If his mind hadn't been occupied with what he was going to say to Lord Wellsley, he would have noticed that the carriage pulling up in front of him didn't belong to his grandmother.

He opened the door and was shocked to see a gun pointed at him. Two men sat in opposite seats, the one holding the gun in a heavy dark overcoat, the other dressed in very fine, expensive clothing. "Get in," the latter said. "I've been waiting for you."

"Who are you?" Jeremy asked, pushing the gun barrel away with his finger as he climbed into the carriage.

"Timothy Barrens, First Lord of the Admiralty," the man smiled politely. "And I've been told that you are none other than the infamous Black Moriah."

"That's preposterous." Jeremy tried to bluff his way out of this mess. "Where did you get such an idea? I'm Lord Jeremy Leighton, the Fifth Duke of Rockglen."

"Yes, I know all about that," Barrens

laughed.

Ariana lay on her bed, a damp cloth on her forehead. It was nearly dark and still Jeremy hadn't come. Her door swung to; she didn't bother opening her eyes, knowing it was Lanie checking on her again.

"Mattie made you some chicken broth," her sister whispered.

"Thank her for me," Ariana said, "but I really don't think I can eat anything."

"You must keep up your strength."

Ariana suddenly sat up and threw the cloth across the room. "Don't give me that rubbish, Lanie; I'm not in the mood for it. Don't you realize he has deserted me a second time? What is wrong with this man? Did he just come here to be sure I still cared before he hurt me again?"

"Ari, don't do this to yourself. There has to be some reason Jeremy didn't come."

"Oh, I'm sure there is, Lanie," she said sarcastically. "He's probably on his way back to New Providence."

"No, Jean Paul would have said something. . . ."

Ariana stared at her sister. "You haven't become involved with him?"

Lanie looked down at her hands. "I haven't

known him long enough to become involved, Ari, but I am very attracted to him, and he is to me."

"Well you may as well forget him," Ariana hissed. "You'll probably never see him again."

Seeing the look on Lanie's face, Ariana softened. "I tried to warn you, dear: they are pirates. They care nothing for anyone else's feelings."

"I don't believe Jeremy has left you, Ari. I saw the look on his face yesterday when he wanted to see you, and it wasn't the face of a man playing games. Besides, you don't know what has happened. It's quite possible Rachel has been taken ill."

"Yes, there is that possibility — but why wouldn't he send a message?"

"Why don't we just wait and see if we hear something from either of them before you crucify them?" Lanie suggested.

"You are right, of course," Ariana admitted reluctantly. "But if he doesn't come, I've decided I must leave here."

"My God, what are you talking about? You're pregnant, Ari. Where would you go?"

"I don't know, but I couldn't stay here and bring shame on Mother and Father. Perhaps I'd buy passage on a ship going to the Colonies. All I know is that I can't marry Brett."

"What would you do in the colonies?" Lanie asked in disbelief.

"I'd say my husband had been killed," Ariana said stubbornly. "I have money enough to make a start."

"This is nonsense," Lanie said angrily, "pure and simple nonsense. The man is a few hours late and already you are talking about fleeing England for some godforsaken country. I do believe you are losing your mind, Ariana."

"Perhaps you are right," Ariana sighed as she rubbed her temples. She knew her sister didn't understand, but she had to make plans. She wasn't responsible just for herself now; she had a child that she had to take care of, and she would not let it be raised a bastard in London.

Lanie left Ariana alone, more concerned than she admitted that Jeremy hadn't shown up. She slowly descended the stairs, trying to think of a way to find out if their ship was still in the harbor. She knew where it was anchored, but did she dare go to that part of the city alone? Suddenly she heard the sound of carriage wheels rumbling on the cobblestone drive. She dashed for the door, hoping it would be Jeremy.

"Thank God," she exclaimed, seeing Jean Paul standing on the stoop. "Ariana was sure you and Jeremy had left London."

"You mean he isn't here?"

"No, he hasn't been here all day. He was suppose to come and talk with Mother and Father."

"Damn, I was afraid of that," Jean Paul swore. "Englishmen have been swarming all over the ship this evening. I knew something had to be wrong."

"Have you been to Rockglen yet?"

"No, but I've been watching the house for his return. He told me he was coming here today, and I didn't want to intervene until he had the situation straightened out."

"Let me get my wrap," Lanie said. "I'm going to Rockglen with you."

"Shouldn't I talk to Ariana first?" Jean Paul asked.

"No, not until we know something. She has enough on her mind right now."

Simmons answered the door of the great house. Lanie was just asking to speak to the Duchess when she heard her voice calling.

"Simmons, is that Jeremy?"

"No, m'lady, it's Lady Elaine Wellsley, and Lord Leighton's friend, Captain Moreau."

"Come in, come in!" Rachel exclaimed. "My dear Lanie, I'm surprised to see you out this time of night alone with this gentleman."

"Under the circumstances, I'm sure my parents will understand," Lanie assured. "Has Jeremy been here this afternoon, m'lady?"

"No, my dear. I haven't seen him since this morning, when he left to go to your house. I've been on pins and needles wondering if he was able to work things out with your parents," she commented.

"He never made it there, Lady Leighton," Jean Paul offered. "I have reason to believe there has been some foul play. Late this afternoon, English seamen swarmed over Jeremy's ship looking for something."

"Oh my," the Duchess exclaimed, "you don't think someone recognized him?"

"I don't see how they could. Jeremy has never plundered a British ship."

"Is your carriage outside?"

"Yes, m'lady," Lanie answered. "I have mother's carriage."

"Simmons, my cape and gloves, please. We are going to pay a visit to Lord Bellamont. If Jeremy has run afoul of the law, he should know something about it."

Rachel had feared for Jeremy's life, but finding that he was alive and in Newgate Prison didn't ease her fears at all. The three rode silently back to Rockglen after meeting with Lord Bellamont. He informed them that

Jeremy had been picked up outside her house that morning on suspicion of being the infamous pirate Black Moriah.

Rachel's threats didn't faze the man as he eyed Jean Paul suspiciously. "I will not allow this!" The Duchess slammed her cane on the floor. "I still have some power in this city. Jeremy Leighton is my grandson, the Fifth Duke of Rockglen."

"I know all about your long-lost grandson just recently arriving on the scene," Lord Bellamont sneered. "I suggest you take this up with someone else."

"I certainly will," the Duchess stormed past him. "I'll take it up with God Almighty if I have to."

The three rode silently as the carriage headed toward Wellsley Manor.

"What are we going to do?" Lanie broke the silence.

"We are going to get Jeremy out of that hellhole," Jean Paul said with determination.

"Is that possible?" she asked.

"We'll soon find out," he answered. "I have to round up the crew immediately.

"Not so fast, Jean Paul," the Duchess finally spoke. "We're going to get my grandson out, but we're going to do it with the least

447

amount of danger."

"That sounds reasonable," Jean Paul agreed.

"I have found that money can buy just about anything, and I'm going to see if it will buy my grandson's freedom."

"Tell me what you want me to do," Jean Paul offered.

"I have an acquaintance who has done me some favors in the past, and he is well acquainted with Newgate and its guards. I'll send a message tonight and ask him to meet with us first thing in the morning."

"What about your other grandson?" Jean Paul asked. "Can he be trusted?"

"Brett? Of course. I'm sure once I tell him the story he'll want to help."

"Does he know about Jeremy and Ariana yet?" Lanie asked.

"I assume not," Rachel sighed. "Lord Bellamont said Jeremy had been picked up this morning outside my house."

"Who could have tipped them off?" Jean Paul wondered aloud.

"I have no idea," Rachel answered. "What upsets me the most is that Jeremy's identity will be known now. Even if we get him out of Newgate, he'll have to leave England immediately."

"I'm sorry, Rachel," Lanie said, patting her hand. "I know that must make you very sad, after finally finding him. Perhaps you could visit Jeremy and Ariana with me," she said, glancing at Jean Paul.

"I can see that you have other reasons for visiting them," Rachel chuckled. "Thank you for the invitation, my dear. I may just take you up on your offer."

The carriage stopped in front of Wellsley Manor and Jean Paul got out to assist Lanie.

"I suppose there is no better time to talk with your mother and father than now," Rachel said, accepting Jean Paul's hand. "They have to be told what is going on sooner or later."

After ringing the bell for several minutes, the butler answered the door and looked shocked to see Lanie with the Duchess and Mr. Moreau. "I'm sorry, m'lady, but the family has already retired."

"Then wake them, my good man," the Duchess ordered, "and have one of your servants prepare tea and crumpets. "It's going to be a long night."

"Yes, m'lady," he hurried to do her bidding, knowing that the Duchess wouldn't be out at this time of night unless something important was happening.

"Lanie, I suggest you wake your sister."

"That isn't necessary," Ariana said from the top of the stairs. "I'm already awake."

Lanie rushed up the stairs and hugged her sister. "You were wrong, Ari. Jeremy didn't leave London."

Her hand went to her throat. "He's all right, isn't he?"

"He's been arrested and thrown in Newgate."

"Oh my God!" Ariana gasped, clutching the bannister for support. "When did this happen?"

"Apparently this morning. We have been to see Lord Bellamont and he admitted that they had arrested Jeremy."

"But how did you get involved in this already?" Ariana asked, realizing that Lanie had just returned home at this late hour with the Duchess and Jean Paul.

"Earlier this evening Jean Paul came looking for Jeremy," Lanie explained as they went downstairs. "He told me that English sailors were searching Jeremy's ship. When he said he was going to see the Duchess, I insisted on going along. Since then we've covered half of London."

By this time Lord and Lady Wellsley were descending the stairs. "My word, Rachel, what brings you to Wellsley Manor at this hour?"

"Please, sit down," the Duchess instructed,

taking charge. "I have asked your servants to prepare tea. I didn't think you would mind. Jean Paul, why don't you pour Lord Wellsley and yourself a drink? As a matter of fact, pour me one, too."

Ariana sat stiffly on the settee, still in shock from learning Jeremy was a prisoner. It was a moment before she realized Rachel was speaking to her. "I'm sorry. What were you saying?"

"Do you wish me to explain?" the Duchess asked, patting her shoulder.

"No, I suppose I should be the one," Ariana said as she stood up and faced her parents. "Jeremy Leighton, Rachel's grandson, is the pirate who I fell in love with."

You could have heard a pin drop. William and Denise stared at Ariana as if they'd been struck dumb.

"First, let me say that I still love Jeremy, and if he can be freed from prison I will leave London with him. We were going to tell you this afternoon, but he never made it here."

"But what about Brett?" her mother finally found her voice.

"I will take care of Brett," Rachel insisted. "By all rights, Jeremy has always been the one betrothed to Ariana. He is my first grandson."

"Rachel, aren't you forgetting the fact that this grandson is a notorious pirate?" William

Wellsley protested.

"By no means, William. But there are extenuating circumstances. Jeremy was saved from a burning ship by pirates. He had no control over the way he was raised. No matter what has happened in the past, he is still a Leighton."

"I don't know," William said in shock.

"Oh, William, what are we going to do? We'll be disgraced!" Denise sobbed.

"Denise Wellsley, stop acting like a blubbering idiot," Rachel scolded. "I can remember begging William's family to let him marry you, and they fought it tooth and nail. Never would they accept a Frenchie in the family, they swore, but knowing how much you and William were in love, they finally agreed. Should I point out that the two of you have done just fine?"

"This isn't the same, Rachel," Denise dabbed at her eyes.

"No, it isn't. There is more involved here than politics. We haven't the time to wage a battle over this," she said sternly. "I plan to put the wheels in motion tomorrow to have Jeremy escape. Once he does so, he will have to flee London immediately. What I want is for you to give your blessing for Ariana to go with him."

"Please don't try to stop me, Father. I love

452

Jeremy, and I'm carrying his child."

"Oh my God!" Denise sobbed.

"I'm sorry, mother." Ariana knelt in front of her. "I love you and Father very much, but I love Jeremy too. He never ransomed me. It was all a scheme by other pirates on the island."

"Are you certain about that, Ariana?" her father asked, not wanting to see his daughter hurt again.

"Father, do you remember the name of the Frenchman you said you gave the money to?"

"Yes, let me see — I believe it was Moreau. . . ." He looked at the man standing next to his youngest daughter. "My God, I knew the name was familiar, but not the face. It was Jean Paul Moreau, but it wasn't this man."

"Exactly, Father. This is the real Jean Paul Moreau. The man you gave the money to was named François Saint-Gilles. He and a woman who was in love with Jeremy tricked us all. When Jeremy realized it, he decided to come to England for me. That was when the people who raised him told him about his real identity."

"This is all so hard to believe," William Wellsley exclaimed.

"And Father, there is something else, if it makes you feel any better. Jeremy and I had already talked about marriage."

William sat next to his wife, a comforting arm around her shoulders. He smiled at Rachel. "My dear Duchess, I assume you already have a plan in mind to free the young man who is going to marry my daughter."

Men should be what they seem.

Shakespeare

Chapter Twenty-one

Newgate Prison was the principal jail of the City of London, and in the year 1713 it was already more than 500 years old. It was a disgusting place by any standards, so overcrowded that prisoners slept two or three to a bed, and so infested that lice crunched underfoot. The stench of urine and prison damp were so overpowering that visitors often brought bunches of flowers to bury their noses in. Before being taken into court, prisoners were washed down with vinegar so as not to offend the judge.

Unbelievably the prison was run as a private business; prisoners were made to pay rent for their cells and jailers exacted exorbitant fees for everything. Unbeknownst to Jeremy, this fact would be what would save him from the dark, cold, cavernous hole in which he found himself confined. He shivered as he heard one jailer tell another that he wasn't going to hang in London, but was going to be traded to Spain for gold. That would never happen, he thought determinedly. He would end his own life before facing the Spanish.

He must be getting use to the smell, he thought, a fact that concerned him as he paced a small area. Lice crunched beneath his feet like seashells, and occasionally someone would try to grab his heavy cape—the only thing that kept him from freezing. He wondered if anyone had missed him yet. Surely Ariana would be concerned that he hadn't shown up to talk with her parents—or would she assume that he had deserted her again? No, please not this time, love, he prayed silently. Surely his grandmother would realize something had happened. But that might not be for a while, he realized. You'll just have to make the best of this, old fellow, he told himself. Perhaps it will make you think twice before you ever go back to pirating.

Rachel Leighton looked like she was holding court. William Wellsley, Jean Paul, Brett, and several questionable-looking characters sat in her library discussing how to go about getting Jeremy out of Newgate.

"It should be a sum of gold that no one can refuse," Brett suggested.

"I've already taken care of that," Rachel smiled at her grandson. She had been pleased that he'd understood the situation between Ariana and Jeremy and had quickly volunteered to come to his cousin's aid.

"I know just the gent to offer it to," Palmer, Rachel's connection, commented.

"I suggest I go along when the money is handed over," Brett volunteered. "We are dealing with an unsavory lot, and God knows what may happen before the gold is transferred to the guard."

"The Duchess' money is safe with me," Palmer said defensively.

"I'm sure it is, my good man, but we are talking about a large sum of money here. You could be hit over the head and robbed, and then where would we be?" Brett warned.

"There should be at least two of us," William Wellsley agreed. "I'd be willing to go along."

"It would be wiser if you stayed in the background, William," Brett quickly suggested. "Besides, someone should stay here with Grandmother."

"How long do you think we have before

they realize one of their prisoners has escaped?" Rachel asked Palmer.

"Not before morning, m'lady," he answered.

"Good. That will give us a little time," Rachel mused. "It is settled, then: Brett and Palmer will make contact with the guard and then wait for Jeremy to make his way out. Jean Paul, you will see that the ship is ready."

"I ordered the crew to change its anchorage as soon as the British soldiers had finished their search."

"Don't you think they may impound the ship?" Brett asked with a sniff of disdain.

"If they do, they'll only leave a skeleton crew aboard. We can handle that," Jean Paul assured.

"I would suggest you tell me where you've moved it. I don't want to be dragging my cousin around searching for his ship when half of London is looking for him."

"That won't be necessary, Brett," Rachel interrupted. I want Jeremy brought back here first."

"You can't be serious, Grandmother. Don't you realize that makes you an accomplice?"

"Of course it does, but who would dare come arrest an old Dowager Duchess?" she laughed. "Now everyone has a job to do. Brett, Simmons has the gold waiting for you and Palmer. Don't let anything go awry," she warned.

"Don't worry, Grandmother. I will take care of everything."

As Jean Paul watched Brett and Palmer leave, an uneasy feeling nagged at him. He knew the crew would have the ship standing by, so he decided to keep an eye on Jeremy's cousin instead. "If you have no further need of me, Lady Leighton, I would like to check on a few things."

"You tell my grandson that a hot bath and a change of clothes will be waiting for him when he gets here."

"M'lady, are you sure that's wise?" Jean Paul asked, afraid after going through all this that Jeremy would be captured again.

"Palmer has told me what Newgate is like, Jean Paul. I know Jeremy wouldn't want his happy reunion with Ariana to be ruined because he smelled so bad."

Jean Paul had to laugh.

Suddenly a frown creased her brow. "You don't think I'm placing Jeremy in any more danger, do you?" she asked.

Remembering that Jeremy might never see his Grandmother again, Jean Paul smiled. "Palmer said they wouldn't miss him until morning, so it should be all right. I'll have some of my men stand guard just in case."

"Jean Paul, I may not have a chance to talk to you later, so I want to thank you now for all your help. My grandson is very fortunate to have a friend like you."

"Thank you, m'lady," he said, bowing over her hand. "Now if you will excuse me. I have a matter to take care of."

"William, you have a few hours to say your farewells to Ariana. I suggest you go home and do that. I'll be fine here with Simmons" Rachel suggested with tears in her eyes. "Jean Paul said he would have one of the crew waiting at the dock to show you where the ship is anchored. If everything goes as planned, Jeremy should be there in two hours."

William kissed Rachel on the cheek. "Your grandson is a fine young man, Rachel. I'm proud to be able to call him my son-in-law."

"Thank you," she said, wiping away a tear. "If only I had had more time with him. . . ."

When Jean Paul caught up to Brett and Palmer, they were arguing outside the gate of the prison. "What's the matter here?" he asked, his suspicions well founded.

"What are you doing here, Moreau?" Brett asked angrily. "You were supposed to see that the ship was ready to sail."

"It's ready," Jean Paul said. "I thought it would be better if there were three of us here. There's always safety in numbers, you know."

"Numbers?" Palmer laughed bitterly. "The young lord here was just insisting he do this by himself. I told him his grandmother was counting on me to get her other grandson out of Newgate, but he wouldn't listen."

"Now why would you want to do this by yourself, Lord Leighton?" Jean Paul asked suspiciously. "I had understood Palmer was the one who knew the guard who would help."

"That's bloody right," Palmer agreed. "He may not even go along with us, if he doesn't know who he's dealing with."

"I just thought the fewer involved the better," Brett replied cooly.

"Let's stick to the original plan, gentlemen. Palmer, where will you come out with Jeremy?" Jean Paul asked.

"There's a tunnel in the back where garbage is hauled out to the rear of the prison. That would probably be the safest."

"Good, then I'll meet you there. Do you have a gun with you?" he asked.

"We're not fools, Moreau. Just let us handle this," Brett said in disgust. "Who the hell needs a Frenchman hanging around giving orders, anyway?" he said as he wandered off toward the gate.

"Keep a close eye on him, Palmer," Jean Paul warned.

"Right you are, guv'nor." The little man

hurried off after Brett.

Jeremy sat on the floor, his back against the cold, damp wall. This would be his second night in this hellhole, he thought in despair. Hadn't anyone thought to look for him, he wondered. Then a frightening notion hit him: maybe they knew where he was but couldn't do anything about it. He could hear the turn-keys overhead playing cards. Then suddenly a guard with a torch caught his attention. Even in the daylight there was very little light in the prison, so the torch light seemed extremely bright to him. He shook his head, wondering at himself. Wasn't it strange how the smallest things could be of interest in a place like this?

"Leighton, where are you?" the guard shouted. "The captain wants to see you, so you better bloody well get off your ass and come with me."

Jeremy hesitated, wondering if he wouldn't be better off pretending not to hear the guard. What could they possibly want to see him about at this hour?

"Where the hell are you, Leighton?" the guard shouted, kicking one of the sleeping prisoners.

"I'm here," Jeremy said, standing up. "What does he want?"

"How the hell should I know? They don't

464

tell me nothing around here," the guard said, prodding Jeremy forward.

The captain of the guard was a short, stocky man with a greedy gleam in his eye. While Jeremy stood there, he circled him, poking him with a stick. "You got a mighty rich grandmother, m'lord," he said sarcastically. Hope sprang into Jeremy's eyes. "The Duchess is willing to set me up for life if I just turn my back and let you leave here with your cousin."

The prospect of leaving there with his cousin wasn't too appealing, but then, beggars couldn't be choosers, he told himself. Besides, there was always the possibility he had misjudged him. "Where is my cousin?" Jeremy asked.

"Just don't get impatient, m'lord. You'd better hear me out before you go out on the street thinking you're a free man. I'm telling you for your own good, you'd bloody well better get out of England before morning, because once the Admiralty realizes their precious Black Moriah has escaped, there'll be hell to pay."

"I find your suggestion has merit," Jeremy agreed. "It may not even take me that long to say my farewells."

"There's something else," the captain of the

guard pointed a finger at Jeremy's face. "Don't you ever mention to nobody how you got out of Newgate."

"You have my word. If that is all, shouldn't I be on my way?" Jeremy asked impatiently.

"I ain't going out there with you," he advised. "When you leave here, take a sharp right down the long corridor. When you come to the food crates, go left into a tunnel. That will bring you out in the back."

"Right, then left," Jeremy repeated.

"Your cousin should be waiting somewhere between here and there for you."

That is what I'm afraid of, Jeremy thought silently.

There were no torches in the corridor, and Jeremy had to feel his way along the damp wall. He couldn't see the food crates the captain of the guard had mentioned, but he could smell garbage and filth. He moved to the far side of the corridor and froze in his tracks as a blast of icy air hit him in the face. This has to be the tunnel, he thought silently, feeling his way along the cold, wet bricks.

"Palmer, go back and tell the Frenchman to join us," Brett whispered. "I'm sure he'll want to be here when his friend comes through the tunnel."

"I'd rather wait," Palmer said.

"Do as I say," Brett hissed.

"That won't be necessary," Jeremy said a few feet in front of them, "I'm already here. How nice to see you, my dear cousin—or should I say hear you. And who is this loyal friend whose voice I don't recognize?"

Brett could barely speak, he was so angry. He had planned to stab his cousin, knowing that in the darkness no one would discover his body. Now he was going to have to kill the two of them, he decided. "We've time for introductions later," he advised. "Move in front of me," he whispered to Jeremy. "Palmer will lead the way."

"If it's all the same with you, cousin, I'll follow you."

"What the hell is the matter with you? I've risked my life and reputation to get you out of here."

"I appreciate that, but I must admit, I wonder why."

"Come on, you three," Jean Paul urged in a loud whisper from the end of the tunnel. "I can hear you all the way out here."

"After you," Jeremy said to his cousin in the darkness.

"I wish you were coming with us, Lanie," Ariana sighed as she folded a dress and placed it in the chest. "I will miss you so much."

"I'm going to come visit as soon as you're settled, and this time you must keep in contact with us," Lanie exclaimed. "We'll all be anxious to know that you are well."

"I will," Ariana promised. "Mother and Father have been very understanding through this, and I know it's been hard on them."

"I hope they will do as well if *I* should decide to marry a pirate," Lanie laughed.

"What do you mean?" her sister asked, her eyes wide with surprise.

"Jean Paul asked me to come with him," she said shyly, "but I thought Mother and Father would need me right now. I hope to join you before your baby is born, though, Ari."

"Oh, Lanie, I can't tell you how happy that makes me," Ariana exclaimed.

"You were right about one thing," Lanie mused. "They do make the men in London seem like dandies. It must have something to do with the sun and ocean air."

Ariana laughed. "Oh, it's not that at all. It's because they're not soft like the men in London. Jeremy and Jean Paul both work very hard."

"I knew that," Lanie laughed. "I don't envy you being on a ship while you're with child, Ari."

"I can't think of any place I'd rather be," Ariana assured her sister. "I'll probably never suffer another bout of sickness with this pregnancy once I can breath the fresh salt air."

"How did you get into this family?" Lanie laughed. "You're the only one who doesn't get seasick."

Ariana stopped packing as she remembered a conversation aboard the *Black Moriah*. "I am a born sailor," she said softly.

Rachel hugged her grandson, oblivious to the odor that waifted from his clothes. "I was so worried about you."

Jeremy held her at arm's length. "I knew you wouldn't fail me, Grandmother. I appreciate what you and Brett did for me."

"It was what any family would do," Rachel smiled lovingly at him.

"I must talk to English and convince her to leave England with me tonight," he said.

"You've got to get out of those clothes and into a bath," his grandmother laughed. "My whole house is beginning to reek."

"I don't think there's enough water in London to get the stink off me," Jeremy replied. "But Grandmother, I really must talk to Ariana. Can you send a message to her?"

Rachel patted her grandson on the cheek. "Everything is already taken care of, Jeremy. Ariana will be sailing with you when you leave

London."

"No one is forcing her to go with me?" he asked.

"Hardly, my dear. Ariana made this decision on her own."

Jeremy said his farewell to his grandmother, promising to write to her, then he looked for his cousin to thank him for his help and understanding, but Brett was nowhere in sight.

"Jeremy, we must be on our way," Jean Paul insisted.

"Have you seen Brett?"

"Not since we returned to Rockglen," he answered nervously. "I wanted to thank him for his help getting me out of Newgate."

"If we don't get the hell out of here, that may only be a short reprieve," Jean Paul warned.

The docks were shrouded in fog, turning the blackness into an eerie spectre. The only sound was the water lapping at the wooden dock.

"They must have already gone aboard," Jean Paul whispered. "I'll go find the long-boat. Stay here in case they come."

Jeremy leaned against a crate, thinking how fortunate he was to have such good friends.

"So, I finally find you alone, *cousin,*" a voice broke the night's silence. "I couldn't let you leave without telling you what I thought of you," Brett said.

Jeremy straightened up from the crates and stared at his cousin, who moved into view with a gun in his hand. "What the hell do you think you're doing?"

"You didn't really think I was going to let you just walk away with everything, did you?"

"I'm taking nothing but Ariana," Jeremy growled. "I have no use for the title or the Leighton fortune."

"How considerate of you. But you see, I've decided I want everything, including Ariana. When they find you murdered on the docks, they will assume some drunken sailor robbed and killed you. I'll give Ariana my support and sympathy, and in a few months I'll marry her."

He raised the gun and aimed it at Jeremy's heart. A shot rang out over the silent water-front—but it was Brett who slowly sank to his knees. Jeremy turned to stare in disbelief at the smoking gun in Ariana's trembling hand.

"How could you, Brett?" she asked in a choked voice.

Brett held a hand to his bloody shoulder, staring incredulously at Ariana. "He was taking everything from me, Ariana, can't you see

471

that? I had to kill him."

Jeremy slowly walked toward English and took the gun from her. "I can almost understand why he tried to kill me, English. If someone tried to take you from me, I'd have done the same thing."

"How can you say that, Jeremy?" she asked. "He was going to shoot you in cold blood."

"Greed makes people do a lot of strange things, English," he replied, putting an arm around her trembling shoulders. "So does love."

"What the hell happened here?" Jean Paul asked as he and William Wellsley appeared on the scene.

"My cousin tried to kill me, but English saved my life," Jeremy explained.

"My God, I let her come over here alone, thinking you two would want a few minutes— If I'd had any idea, William exclaimed."

"It's all right, sir. As you can see, she does pretty well at taking care of herself," he said, hugging her, "and I understand I have you to thank for that."

"Get on your feet," Jean Paul grabbed Brett by his coat. "What do you want me to do with him?" he asked.

"Nothing, Jean Paul," Jeremy said.

"I'll turn him over to the authorities," Ariana's father volunteered.

"No, I don't want you to do anything," he

said as he stood by Brett. "I want you to go back to Rockglen and never mention that any of this ever happened," he told his cousin. "I will contact William, and if I ever hear that you are anything but a loving, considerate grandson, I'll come back here and slit your throat myself," he warned. "Is that understood, *cousin?*"

"I understand," Brett said, tears in his eyes. "I'm grateful for your understanding."

"Jeremy, I hear people coming. The shot must have drawn their attention," William warned.

"Let's get the hell out of here," Jean Paul said. "The boat is over here."

Jeremy grabbed Ariana by the hand and pulled her along. "Wait," she cried, running back to kiss her father. "I'll write to you soon," she promised. "I love you and Mother very much."

As they watched the shoreline of England disappear, Jeremy held Ariana in front of him, his arms clasped around her waist. "We will have them come visit as soon as we're settled," he promised. "I will always be grateful for the way they helped me."

"So will I," she whispered. She thought about the journey they were about to take. It was an uncertain future, but a future she knew would be filled with their love. He had said it was a new beginning for them, and she knew they would have a good life. Jeremy wouldn't let it be anything else, she smiled as she cuddled closer into his arms.

"Do you think it was wise to let Brett go unpunished?" she asked.

"He has been punished enough, love. He lost the most precious thing in the world."

"I am so glad you feel that way," she said, leaning her head back against him. "What are we going to do, Jeremy? Will we go back to New Providence?"

"No, love. New Providence and the Black Moriah are a thing of the past. We are going to start a new life in the Carolinas," he said, excitement in his voice. "We won't be alone, though, English. Mary, Avery, and Jean Paul will be there to help us, if that's all right with you."

"It sounds wonderful," she laughed, turning to embrace him, "and I think Lanie will join us soon."

"Wonderful. Jean Paul will be glad to hear that. We'll have to take new identities, English. Will you mind that very much?"

"The only identity I want is as your wife and the mother of your children. But may I suggest that you not wait too long to choose a name for us. . . ."

He lifted a dark brow. "Do you have something to tell me, English?"

"Yes, Jeremy—I am carrying your child. I realized it the day before yesterday."

Jeremy gave out a whoop that carried across the sea. "Avery, get out the Bible. There's going to be a wedding before the *Black Moriah* is put to rest." Giving Ariana a deep kiss on her waiting lips, Jeremy embraced her with the love of their yesterdays—and the promise of their tomorrows. . . .

EXHILARATING ROMANCE
From Zebra Books

GOLDEN PARADISE   (2007, $
by Constance O'Banyon
Desperate for money, the beautiful and innocent Valentina
rett finds work as a veiled dancer, "Jordanna," at San Franci
notorious Crystal Palace. There she falls in love with hands
wealthy Marquis Vincente—a man she knew she could never
as Valentina — but who Jordanna can't resist making her
and reveling in love's GOLDEN PARADISE.

MOONLIT SPLENDOR   (2008, $
by Wanda Owen
When the handsome stranger emerged from the shadows
pulled Charmaine Lamoureux into his strong embrace, she
she should scream, but instead she sighed with pleasure at h
ductive caresses. She would be wed against her will on the
row — but tonight she would succumb to this passic
MOONLIT SPLENDOR.

TEXAS TRIUMPH   (2009, $
by Victoria Thompson
Nothing is more important to the determined Rachel McKi
than the Circle M — and if it meant marrying her forema
scare off rustlers, she would do it. Yet the gorgeous rancher
a secret thrill that the towering Cole Elliot is to be her man —
despite her plan that they be business partners, all she truly
sires is a glorious consummation of their vows.

DESERT HEART   (2010, $
by Bobbi Smith
Rancher Rand McAllister was furious when he became the gu
ian of a scrawny girl from Arizona's mining country. But whe
finds that the pig-tailed brat is really a ripe voluptuous beauty
resentment turns to intense interest! Lorelei knew it would b
biggest mistake in her life to succumb to the virile cowboy —
she can't fight against giving him her body — or her
DESERT HEART.

*Available wherever paperbacks are sold, or order direct from
Publisher. Send cover price plus 50¢ per copy for mailing
handling to Zebra Books, Dept. 2348, 475 Park Avenue So
New York, N.Y. 10016. Residents of New York, New Jersey
Pennsylvania must include sales tax. DO NOT SEND CASH.*